Jealousy
Filled
Donuts

Books by Ginger Bolton

SURVIVAL OF THE FRITTERS

GOODBYE CRULLER WORLD

JEALOUSY FILLED DONUTS

Published by Kensington Publishing Corporation

Jealousy Filled Donuts

GINGER BOLTON

KENSINGTON BOOKS
www.kensingtonbooks.com

KENSINGTON BOOKS are published by

Kensington Publishing Corp.
119 West 40th Street
New York, NY 10018

All Kensington titles, imprints, and distributed lines are available at special quantity discounts for bulk purchases for sales promotion, premiums, fund-raising, educational, or institutional use.

Special book excerpts or customized printings can also be created to fit specific needs. For details, write or phone the office of the Kensington Sales Manager: Kensington Publishing Corp., 119 West 40th Street, New York, NY 10018. Attn. Sales Department. Phone: 1-800-221-2647.

Kensington and the K logo Reg. U.S. Pat. & TM Off.

ISBN-13: 978-1-4967-1192-2 (ebook)
ISBN-10: 1-4967-1192-0 (ebook)
Kensington Electronic Edition: September 2019

ISBN-13: 978-1-4967-1191-5
ISBN-10: 1-4967-1191-2
First Kensington Trade Paperback Edition: September 2019

10 9 8 7 6 5 4 3 2 1

Printed in the United States of America

Acknowledgments

Many thanks to my supportive friends, including Krista Davis, Daryl Wood Gerber, who also writes as Avery Aames, Laurie Cass, who also writes as Laura Alden, Kaye George, who also writes as Janet Cantrell, and Allison Brook, who also writes as Marilyn Levinson. And then there are the Deadly Dames: Melodie Campbell, Alison Bruce, Joan O'Callaghan, Cathy Astolfo, and Nancy O'Neill, who always have great suggestions. And jokes. And potluck lunch dishes.

Sgt. Michael Boothby, Toronto Police Service (Retired), again took time to read my manuscript and make helpful suggestions. If any of the police officers in *Jealousy Filled Donuts* don't behave, blame them, not Mike.

Thank you to the organizers and volunteers who make Malice Domestic conferences inspiring and give fans of this type of mystery a chance to enjoy one another's company.

I really appreciate the enthusiasm and help of my agent, John Talbot, and of my editor, John Scognamiglio. Thank you also to the rest of the Kensington team, especially Mary Ann Lasher, the cover artist, and Kristine Mills for the cover design. And many thanks to Michelle Addo for coordinating and organizing the Kensington CozyClub Mini-Convention in Forest Park, Illinois—another chance to get together with authors and readers. It was fun!

Thank you to my family and friends, especially the late Lorne Creor, who introduced me to the combination of cheddar cheese and maple syrup as a delicious dessert or snack.

Thank you to librarians and readers. What would we do without you? May you enjoy many warming mugs of coffee and yummy donuts.

Chapter 1

✺

Every morning, the aromas in the Deputy Donut kitchen were enticing, and the morning of July Fourth was no different. I smelled coffee, yeast dough, cinnamon, nutmeg, and the two types of jelly we'd just opened—raspberry and blueberry.

I was in the midst of an argument.

Well, sort of. Making a very stern face, I settled my Deputy Donut hat firmly on my rowdy curls. "It's perfectly fair, Tom," I informed my father-in-law. "I won the coin toss, and *I'm* driving our donut car in the parade this morning." Unfortunately, the hat did not quite give me the authority of a real police hat, maybe because of the fuzzy white donut glued in front where the badge should be.

Tom was also trying to look serious, a difficult task considering that his dark brown eyes were twinkling and his Deputy Donut hat was jammed crookedly on his salt-and-pepper hair. "Emily," he warned, "I'm the police chief."

"Retired," I reminded him. "And our donut car police cruiser is from 1950, way before you were a rookie cop."

"All the more reason for me to drive it. You're barely over thirty."

"And a half. When you were my age, you drove real police cars with real sirens and real flashing lights. It's only fair for me to drive our pretend cruiser this morning while you and Jocelyn keep making Fourth of July donuts."

Tom grinned at our new assistant. "Never expect to win an argument with Emily."

Jocelyn's dazzling smile included both of us. "With either of you."

The athletic nineteen-year-old was dressed like Tom and I were, in knee-length black shorts, white polo shirt, Deputy Donut apron, and donut-trimmed "police" hat. Like me, she had dark hair, but she pinned hers, which was long and straight, into a bun she wore low to accommodate the cap. Her eyes were almost black, not blue like mine.

Pasting on a fake glower, Tom shook his index finger at me. "Someday, *I'm* going to drive that car."

I frowned and wagged my finger right back at him. "How about next Fourth of July?"

Off to my side, something whirred and clicked.

Jocelyn glanced past me. Her smile disappeared, leaving her face blank and unreadable. She twirled on one toe and glided out of the kitchen and into our storeroom, out of sight of Tom and of me. And also out of sight of everyone in our dining room.

I turned toward the sounds I'd heard.

A man on the other side of our serving counter lowered a camera from his face. Like nearly everyone else besides Jocelyn, he was taller than I was, maybe about five ten, but his slight stoop made him appear shorter. He seemed too thin for his faded jeans, khaki photographer's vest, and formerly white T-shirt that must have been washed with the dark clothes. Everything about his face seemed droopy—skin, eyes, mouth. Wrinkles bracketed his mouth. He looked about forty but could have been thirty.

I asked him, "What would you like? In honor of the Fourth of July, our special coffee today is one of the few coffees grown in the U.S., Ka'u from Hawaii. Like all Hawaiian coffees, it's mellow and flavorful."

Still holding his camera near one shoulder, the man gave me a long, silent, and disapproving look. Without a word, he turned around and walked quickly but quietly out of the café.

That was odd.

Jocelyn's abrupt departure a few moments before was even odder. I traded concerned glances with Tom and then looked for her in the storeroom.

I found her poking at slotted spoons hanging from hooks. "Do you know that man?" I asked.

She didn't turn to face me. "No."

"He left."

"I was just checking on things." Her voice was small, like she didn't believe her own words.

"Is anything wrong?"

"No." Then, more forcefully, "*No.*" Without turning those dark eyes toward me, she retreated toward the bins of flour. "We have plenty of flour." She sounded more like her cheerful self, but she didn't fool me. Something about the man with the camera had alarmed her. Jocelyn was a world-class gymnast. She should have been used to photographers. Maybe she was, and maybe she was also sick of them. A semblance of her smile returned. "It's nearly nine. If you don't get out there, Tom might take the car and drive it in the parade." She skipped back into the kitchen.

Obviously, she didn't want me pestering her with questions. Pondering what had just happened or not happened, I chose a clean apron from the shelf and tied it on. Our logo, the black silhouette of a cat wearing a rakishly tilted Deputy Donut hat, was on the bib.

In the kitchen, Tom was frying donuts, and Jocelyn was mixing frosting. "See you later!" I called.

Greeting customers, I walked through the rear section of our dining area. Bright morning sunlight poured in through the front windows and gleamed on the red, white, and blue bunting that we'd draped around our pale peach walls. We'd also put red, white, and blue napkins on our glossy sliced tree trunk tabletops. The entire shop felt festive.

I closed myself into our office. My cat, who had been named Deputy Donut before we'd borrowed the name for our donut shop, was curled on the couch with her tail covering her nose. She stood up and stretched, showing off her ginger, cream, and black tabby stripes and the donut-like circles on her sides. She came to work with me every day, but health regulations didn't allow her in the kitchen or dining area, so she stayed in our office.

Tom and I had designed that room to be much more than an office.

Dep could scramble up carpeted pillars, ramps, and kitty-width staircases to get to and from tunnels and catwalks that Tom and I had built near the ceiling. All four sides of the office had large windows. When Dep wasn't dozing or cavorting around in her indoor gym, she could sit on wide windowsills and peer into the kitchen, the dining area, the parking lot behind our building, or the driveway leading to the parking lot.

Having thoroughly stretched, she leaped to the back of the couch and stared up into my eyes. "Meow!"

I kissed the orange-striped patch on her forehead. "I'm going out without you, but Tom and Jocelyn will cater to your every need. Meow at the window into the kitchen if you want attention." She didn't need the advice. I added, "I'll be back after the parade."

She jumped down, turned away from me, and settled into the couch's comfy cushions. I seemed to be garnering a lot of disapproval, first from that photographer and now from my cat, not that she ever approved of my going anywhere without her.

After making certain that the office door was locked from the outside, I went to the rear of the parking lot and backed our donut car out of the garage. The car was a meticulously restored four-door Ford. The name of the model was actually Fordor, and there'd been a two-door version which the Ford Motor Company had cutely named the Tudor. Our Fordor was painted like a police car, black with white doors and roof. We had stencilled the Deputy Donut logo on the front doors.

I loved the Ford's authentic details, like the large-circumference steering wheel with the gearshift on the steering column, the windows that had to be cranked open and closed, and the two-piece windshield, divided down the middle by a chrome strip. I was particularly fond of a feature that was definitely not vintage. We'd added a giant plastic donut, which lay flat on the car's roof. White plastic frosting with multicolored sprinkles imbedded in it dripped down the sides of the donut. The sprinkles were lights that could be programmed to dance, either to the music we broadcast through the megaphone-shaped speaker in front of the donut or to preset patterns. None of the lighting displays resembled the strobe lights on actual police cruisers, but they made people smile.

Following over a hundred years of Fallingbrook tradition, Fourth of July parade participants were supposed to assemble far from downtown, at Fallingbrook Falls. I didn't have time to drive out to County Road G and take the scenic route. I drove quickly south on Wisconsin Street and then turned onto a tree-lined country road.

I kept worrying about that photographer in Deputy Donut. Did he frighten Jocelyn or merely surprise and annoy her? I couldn't believe she was shy about having her picture taken. She was often featured in local papers.

Feeling responsible for the girl's safety and comfort when she was working at Deputy Donut, and wondering if Tom and I could gain her trust enough for her to tell us if she was upset, I pulled into the parking lot near the base of Fallingbrook Falls.

I couldn't actually see the falls, but I could hear them. I had climbed all of the trails around the falls many times, and I knew how beautiful the roaring sheet of water, the rocky cliffs, and the trees dewy with spray were.

Carrying clipboards and wearing fluorescent green safety

vests crisscrossed by orange and silver Xs, teens directed me to position my car out on the road facing town. My friend Misty Ossler was behind the wheel of a real police cruiser at the beginning of the lineup. A big red fire truck was second. I parked behind the fire truck, rolled my driver's window all the way down, and got out.

Breezes teased leaves in the trees shading the road. I leaned against the donut car's broad front fender and listened to the distant rush of water. Farther down the line of vehicles, people wearing kilts were trying out bagpipes.

No one had actually marched the entire route from Fallingbrook Falls to downtown Fallingbrook since about the time our donut car was made. These days, parade participants got in line at the falls, drove quickly to downtown Fallingbrook's outskirts, and then slowed to a normal parade speed. When I was a kid, some of the groups clambered out of their vehicles at that point and marched the rest of the way, but for the past ten or so years, the parade participants simply stayed in their vehicles or on their floats.

It was nearly time to start. Members of the bagpipe band and the Fallingbrook High Marching Band climbed aboard their floats. The high school kids had labeled theirs FALLINGBROOK HIGH FLOATING BAND.

I straightened my donut hat and smoothed my apron. Where were my passengers? They had to be among the people milling around on the road.

Fallingbrook always elected a court to reign over the Fallingbrook Fabulous Fourth Festivities—a queen, a king, a duchess, and a duke. We knew that celebrating Independence Day with a mini-monarchy was a little strange, but we always pointed out that our monarchy was democratically elected and reigned for only a year. The members of our local royalty were always just barely out of their teens. None of it made having a royal court less odd, but we proudly celebrated the holiday the way Fallingbrook always had, except for marching long distances on hot and sunny days.

This year's king and queen were supposed to ride in the rear seat of the Deputy Donut car.

A girl with a clipboard and a megaphone herded two men and a woman toward me, and I figured out which man must be this year's king. He was one of those tall, chisel-featured, dark-haired, dark-eyed men who, with those bagpipes squalling nearby, would not have looked out of place in a kilt and no shirt. Instead, he wore an open-necked white dress shirt tucked into tight jeans. He had loafers on his feet, and no socks. He looked a little sheepish about the jewel-encrusted gold crown that he could not quite hide behind one muscular thigh.

Beside him, a similarly young woman in a slinky white gown and a red, white, and blue striped faux-fur cape was hectoring him to put on the crown. She was probably about as short as I was, but her heels made her almost three inches taller. Most of her gleaming brown hair was pinned behind a sparkly red, white, and blue tiara. Tendrils of hair curled artfully around her ears and neck. Her nose and chin were both narrow considering the roundness of her face and her doelike brown eyes. "*I'll* crown you!" she told the king in a playfully threatening tone. The heels were bright red. The cape was short, barely bigger than a collar, but even in the shade, it looked like overkill on the rapidly warming day.

I opened the door behind the driver's seat, swept a curtsy, grabbed my hat before it could land on the pavement, and announced, "Your Majesties, your coach is ready."

The king shook his handsome head without disturbing one hair on it. "The queen's not here."

The woman in the red, white, and blue faux-fur capelet gave him a coy smile. "I'll be queen and ride in her place."

The second man, another handsome and very young twentysomething, glared at her. "No, you won't." He had to be this year's duke. The crown on his head was only silver.

The woman in the tiara dimpled up at him. "Chill. I was only teasing."

"And you're only the duchess." How had he been elected duke? Usually, personality helped win votes in the Fallingbrook Fabulous Fourth Festivities elections. To be fair, though, this man's looks went a long way toward making up for his lack of congeniality. He was not quite as tall as the king, but he was every bit as noticeable with his white-blond hair and amazing tan. His woolly black suit probably wasn't helping his mood.

"So?" the duchess demanded. "You're only the duke." Wearing faux fur around her neck probably wasn't helping her mood, either.

The king tapped that bejeweled gold crown against his leg, shifted from foot to foot as if fuzzy caterpillars were checking out his bare ankles, and kept glancing toward town.

We were supposed to pull out at nine thirty. Nine thirty came and went. Nine thirty-five. Beyond the parking lot, the falls continued their subdued roaring.

Closer, bagpipes, trumpets, and tubas continued their *un*subdued warm-ups.

Nine forty. The queen did not arrive.

Chapter 2

The duchess inched a phone out of her evening bag. "I'll call her. She's my best friend."

The duke rolled his eyes and tapped the screen of his phone.

The king glared at the duke.

Neither the duchess nor the duke got an answer.

Tucking her phone away, the duchess turned to me. "You should go find her and bring her back. She works at Freeze."

Freeze was my favorite ice cream shop. It was a little surprising that no one there had told me that a fellow employee had been elected this year's queen. Even stranger, Jocelyn had worked at Freeze until we hired her only a week before the Fourth, and even though Jocelyn must have heard me mention that the king and queen were riding in my car, she hadn't said that the queen was one of her ex-coworkers.

The duke scowled at the duchess. "She's only fifteen minutes late."

The duchess squinched her mouth to about the size of a raisin. "Just trying to be helpful. And it's more like twenty minutes."

The girl with the megaphone turned a pair of puppy-like and hopeful liquid brown eyes on me. "Would you, please? I . . . don't have my license yet." She blushed. She couldn't have been much over sixteen, if that.

"Sure." I gave her my phone number. "Call if she shows up?"

I pulled out of line. Waving, I zoomed past the fire truck and the police cruiser. I drove as quickly as was safe all the way to downtown Fallingbrook and I parked beside Freeze. Inside, the shop smelled like especially good chocolate and vanilla.

Kelsey, a clerk I recognized from my frequent visits, was behind the counter. She was younger than I was, and quite pretty with her hazel eyes and a sprinkling of freckles across her cheeks. A strand of auburn hair escaped from underneath her frilled pink paper cap. She was barely taller than I was. With a welcoming smile, she asked what I'd like to buy.

"Everything, but I can't right now. I'm looking for . . . you, maybe? Are you today's queen of the Fabulous Fourth Festivities?"

"That's Taylor Wishbard, but she won't be in today. She has the day off. She's going to be in the parade this morning. Maybe you can catch her when the parade arrives at the village square. She gets to sit in the reviewing stand."

"She was supposed to be at the parade-marshaling grounds at nine thirty and ride in my car, but she wasn't there."

Kelsey glanced toward the closed kitchen door, and then looked back at me. "I thought that if she would ever be on time for anything, it would be this Fourth of July stuff. It's a big deal."

The middle-aged woman who owned Freeze and told everyone to call her Mama Freeze backed into the swinging door from the kitchen. She turned to face us. Like Kelsey, she wore a cute apron, pink and white striped with ruffles around the edges. She was carrying a cardboard barrel of ice cream. "What's a big deal?"

Kelsey gave her a bright smile. "Taylor being queen today."

Mama Freeze set the cardboard barrel on the counter. "Brrr! Yes, Taylor deserves this honor. She's gorgeous, for one thing, and she works so hard here. We're very proud of her, aren't we, Kelsey?"

"We sure *are!*"

My phone rang. "The queen's here," a girl said over the phone. "Can you come right back?"

I promised to be there as soon as I could, told Kelsey and Mama Freeze that Taylor had been located, and tore out of Freeze.

Concerned about further delaying the parade's start, I exceeded a few speed limits on my way back to the falls. I parked in the spot I'd left, behind the fire truck and in front of a long, low maroon and silver 1970s sedan. I got out of my car.

The girl with the clipboard and megaphone escorted a tall young woman in a curve-hugging white gown toward me. Queen Taylor could barely wobble in her very high white satin heels. Waves of blond hair cascaded over her bare shoulders. Dramatically, she placed a bling-studded gold crown on her head. Her crown, along with the shoes, made her almost as tall as the king. With a coy smile, she placed a hand lightly on his arm.

His handsome face remained impassive, and he didn't turn his head toward her. He still wasn't wearing his crown.

I again opened the door to the seat behind mine. I rolled down the window in that door and pushed the cute little side vent window open.

Looking panicked, the girl escorting Taylor lifted her megaphone to her lips. "Everyone, get into place!"

Taylor let go of the king, grabbed the girl's megaphone, and shouted into it, "Sorry I'm late, everyone! The hairdresser that my bestie, the *duchess,* recommended was an absolute disaster!" She separated the word into three separate syllables with pauses between them. "I had to go to a different salon!" One arm outstretched, she waved toward the crowd, the road, the woods across the road, and the waiting vehicles and floats. "Don't *ever* get your hair done at Felicia's," she blasted at full volume. "She was so jealous of my hair that she tried to make it as ugly as hers."

Felicia? When my parents were in the area, staying in the campground beyond the trees across the road from where I'd parked my car, Felicia was my mother's hairdresser.

Taylor shoved the megaphone toward the girl, who nearly dropped it.

Other teens with clipboards shooed the duke and duchess toward the 1970s sedan.

The girl with the megaphone pointed Taylor and her king toward my car.

Taylor balked. "I'm not riding in *that* thing."

That *thing? Our beautiful 1950 Ford?* I felt my eyes open wide.

Blushing, the teenager with the megaphone whispered, "It's all planned." The poor girl probably wasn't used to standing up to a queen.

Taylor grabbed the megaphone again and announced, "I'm not riding in a clown car with a ridiculous donut on top."

I felt my eyes open even wider, but I didn't mind taking some of the pressure off the flustered teen. I smiled and said quietly, "It's a police car."

Taylor spoke into the megaphone again. "This lady says it's a police car. I'm not riding in any police car. People will think I've been arrested."

The girl whose megaphone had again been co-opted didn't look any happier. My smile became a little strange, going from grin to grimace to grumpy.

And that was just marvelous—the photographer who had been in Deputy Donut earlier that morning had wedged himself between a couple of the teens in safety vests, and he was aiming his camera in my direction. His long lens was the kind that could pick out every single wrinkle deepening between my eyebrows.

My slighted donut car was about seventy years beyond being capable of serving as a police car, and I had it on good authority that it had never been one. I opened my mouth. And closed it.

"Besides," Taylor shouted into the megaphone, "I'd get sick in the back of an old car like that!"

I tried another smile, undoubtedly not a very believable one. "Would you like to ride in front with me?" The king could squeeze between us on the wide front seat.

Taylor stomped one of her white satin heels. "No, I would not."

The duke stepped forward. "Would you like to ride in the vintage car *we* were assigned?"

Taylor cast a disdainful look at the maroon and silver 1970s sedan. "Old cars stink. Just looking at it makes me queasy. Besides, it's not a convertible." She pointed toward the parking lot. "I was forced to leave my convertible way over there. Why don't *you* drive my convertible, Nicholas?" She simpered up at the duke and then tilted the side of her head toward the king. "And *he* and I will ride in it?" She flapped a hand toward her bestie, the duchess. "*She* can ride in the clown police car."

Queen Taylor was so over-the-top that I almost laughed. *What are friends for?*

Luckily, some of us did have kind and helpful friends. Misty had been quietly watching the drama. She went to the girl who was attempting to retrieve her megaphone from Taylor and asked, "How about if I drive this lady's convertible, and she and the king can ride in it?" She waved a hand toward the front of the line. "My partner will drive our cruiser." Misty was as tall as Taylor but, with her genuine smile, much more beautiful, even though she was about a decade older than the members of the royal court and was wearing a police uniform and no crown. Beneath her police hat, her long blond hair was tied in a neat ponytail.

Queen Taylor muttered ungraciously, "I suppose." She let go of the megaphone. This time, the teenager caught it, slung its strap over her shoulder, and quickly stepped back, out of Queen Taylor's reach.

The duchess clapped her hands. "Goody! Nicholas and I

can ride in the darling old-fashioned police car." She tugged at the duke's arm. "Come on!" She climbed into the back of my car, scooted across the wide bench seat, and sat behind the front passenger seat. She opened her window and called out, "It doesn't stink in here!"

Thank you for the faint praise, I thought, grinning.

Giving one of the clipboard-carrying boys her car keys, Taylor didn't react.

I slid behind the steering wheel. Duke Nicholas sat behind me.

The teenager with Taylor's keys raced to the parking lot, returned in a minuscule robin's-egg blue convertible, and tenderly parked it beside my car.

Misty, the queen, and the king tucked themselves into the tiny convertible. The teens unfurled banners with magnets attached to the corners. They stuck banners identifying the king and queen on both sides of the cute convertible and banners identifying the duke and duchess on both sides of my car. Our Deputy Donut logo would be hidden, but everyone in and around Fallingbrook had to know that the vintage Ford with the donut on top belonged to the donut shop a few blocks south of the village square.

Queen Taylor and the king perched on the top back of the convertible's rear seat. Because my car window was down and the convertible was beside me, I heard Misty's refusal to take her foot off the brake until the royal pair got down and buckled themselves in.

"We're too tall," Taylor complained.

Misty didn't budge.

Grumbling, Taylor eased down to the seat. She and her king had to sit nearly back-to-back with their knees squashed against where the rear doors would have been if there were any.

Misty relented. "At first, we'll be going too fast for you to ride safely up there. I'll stop before the actual beginning of the parade and let you climb up again and ride there while we creep along." It must have pained my police officer friend to make that suggestion. However, if anyone could drive carefully, fast or slow, it was Misty.

The girl with the megaphone waved at Misty's partner to start driving the real police cruiser toward town. The fire truck followed. Misty pulled Queen Taylor's convertible into line behind the fire truck. I put my car into first gear, let out the clutch, pressed the gas pedal, and stayed close behind the little convertible.

We were almost an hour behind schedule.

In the far corner of my car, the duchess let out a laugh with a cruel edge to it. "Taylor's such a diva!"

Nicholas snarled, "Shut up!"

The duchess crowed, "Look how much room we have in *this* car!"

I stared straight ahead and shifted into second.

Through my open window, I heard whirrs and clicks.

That photographer was loping along next to my car, aiming his camera toward the driver's side.

Chapter 3

The duchess leaned past Nicholas and waved at the photographer. Settling back into her seat, she nudged Nicholas. "Aw, c'mon, Nicholas. Taylor and I have been besties since kindergarten. We can say anything to each other."

He demanded, "And behind her back, too?"

"I've said it to her face. Calling each other divas is a term of endearment."

Nicholas snorted.

The duchess claimed, "We've been in a friendly rivalry all of our lives."

Nicholas objected. " 'Friendly' wasn't the word I heard."

"You heard wrong," the duchess insisted. "By competing with each other, both of us got better grades all through school, and everything. You know, awards and stuff. She probably won being queen by one vote. Or we tied and she got it because she's taller."

Nicholas made a noise that might have been clearing his throat.

Apparently, the duchess didn't notice that he seemed less than impressed. She went on, "Taylor won't always be an ice cream store clerk, and I won't always be waiting tables at Frisky Pomegranate."

Thinking that it was about time for someone in the car to be positive, I said, "I've heard it's good." It was a new pub across the street from the north side of the village square. "I'll have to try it someday." I shifted to third, the Ford's highest gear.

The duchess leaned forward. "You should! Like, come tomorrow afternoon. We have Happy Hour Fridays. We get raves. For the food *and* the service. I'm service. I'm good. Like Taylor. She and I are *going places.*"

"Yeah," Nicholas agreed, "like back to the middle of Fallingbrook." Speaking to the back of my head, he added, "This is a really cool car, ma'am."

I thanked him. *Ma'am?* Maybe to a twenty-year-old, a thirty-and-a-half-year-old was as antique as the car she was driving.

Misty's policeman partner set a fast pace in the lead car. He and the driver of the fire truck behind him turned on their strobes. Not to be outdone, I caused the "sprinkles" in the donut on top of my cruiser to flash and dance.

Actually, I *was* being outdone. The sprinkles would barely show up in the bright sunshine.

A small black car sped past us, heading toward town, also. I caught a glimpse of the driver. The photographer?

Behind me, the duchess asked Nicholas, "How long have you been dating Taylor, anyway?"

"How come you don't know? I thought you were best friends."

"We don't tell each other everything. It was very cute that she was elected queen and Ian was elected king back in May when they were still dating each other. So appropriate!"

The duke was Nicholas, the queen was Taylor, and now I knew that the king was Ian. I glanced into the rearview mirror and caught the duchess's eye. "What's *your* name?" I asked.

"Gabrielle." She drew out the *l*'s.

Nicholas imitated her.

She batted at his arm. "It's so sexy when you say it!"

Nicholas didn't answer.

In the convertible in front of us, Queen Taylor was using both hands to hold her crown in place.

Gabrielle laughed. "Taylor should have stuck with Felicia's styling. Felicia uses tons of hairspray. Look at Taylor's hair flying around. If she lets go of that crown, she'll lose it. Too bad she didn't win duchess instead of queen. My plastic tiara is heavier than the cardboard crowns you three have to wear. Prettier, too, and it has built-in combs that keep it in place."

"Wonderful." Nicholas's tone was distinctly sarcastic.

Gabrielle was undaunted. "If she didn't want her hair to be blown, she could have ridden in this car like she was supposed to. I bet it's worth more than hers. I bet that big car behind us is, too, even though it's old."

Despite having no passengers, the driver of the 1970s sedan gamely stayed behind us.

Nicholas heaved a very loud sigh.

Gabrielle accused, "You said you liked this car, Nicholas."

"I do, but there's nothing wrong with Taylor wanting to ride in her own convertible."

"So she can show off. Too bad her hair's a mess."

At the edge of downtown Fallingbrook, we all stopped. Misty let Queen Taylor and King Ian ride where they'd wanted to before.

Teen volunteers dragged the bunting-draped sawhorses barricading the road out of our way, and the parade began.

Queen Taylor waved and blew kisses at everyone while King Ian held one hand up, elbow bent. As if a robot had taken control of it, his hand turned slowly, toward the crowd, toward the front of the convertible, and back toward the people lining the sidewalks.

"What a cute couple," Gabrielle gushed. "Only, Ian needs to sit up straighter. He must be really depressed, if Taylor dumped him. Maybe he can win her back."

"Good luck with that," Nicholas scoffed.

Misty's partner started the siren in the lead police car. The fire truck's siren wailed. I turned on a siren recording and broadcast it over the loudspeaker in front of the donut on the roof.

If more flirting and bickering went on in the back seat, I didn't hear it.

Kids lining the route flapped small flags. Adults applauded. Gabrielle leaned out of her open window and yelled, "Happy Fourth of July!"

Beside the twin patios flanking Deputy Donut's front door, I gave the horn a soft toot. Our regular customers lifted their coffee mugs in a toast. Handing a plate of donuts to one of the knitters who met weekday mornings at Deputy Donut and called themselves the Knitpickers, Jocelyn looked up and gave us that dazzling smile.

A few blocks farther north, the village square had been transformed for the holiday. Red, white, and blue bunting was draped around trees and also around tables showcasing local delicacies and handcrafts. People wearing red, white, and blue strolled on the close-cropped and very green lawn. Everything seemed to sparkle.

The drivers ahead of me slowed and stopped. I turned off my siren, left the rooftop donut's sprinkles dancing, and parked behind Misty and her royal passengers. We were next to the reviewing stand, an open-fronted shed perched on a platform with stairs leading to it. The shed was painted white, inside and out, and decorated with more bunting.

Safety-vested teens swooped down on Taylor's convertible, removed the banners, and helped Taylor and Ian out. The teens guided the royal pair up the stairs and seated them in the red and gold jewel-encrusted thrones. Taylor wiggled her fingers at parade watchers and blew kisses. Ian looked stern and kingly. Certain that he was merely trying to hide the pain of being next to Taylor after their breakup, I felt sorry for him.

The teens removed the banners from my car and escorted Gabrielle and Nicholas to a pair of navy blue and silver jewel-encrusted thrones flanking Ian's and Taylor's thrones.

The teens seated Nicholas beside Taylor and Gabrielle beside Ian. Gabrielle gave Ian's elbow a playful jab. He ignored her.

We moved our vehicles forward again. The parade continued north for a few blocks. At the designated end of the parade route, I turned back toward Deputy Donut. Avoiding the parade still moving up Wisconsin Street was easy. I drove south through parking lots behind stores, parked the donut car near our loading dock, and went inside through the office.

Purring, Dep rubbed against my ankles. I told her, "You're the one who deserves a tiara."

She briskly licked one shoulder as if to show that, unlike Duchess Gabrielle, Dep was wearing real fur.

Jocelyn bounced inside from the front patios and poked her head into the office. "Emily! Come see what we made." She led me into the kitchen, to a stack of large, flat boxes, white with our logo printed on them in black. With a gleeful smile, she opened the top box. All of the donuts in it were frosted with white icing. Jocelyn had piped narrow red stripes on the raspberry jelly–filled donuts and had sprinkled dark blue sugar stars on the blueberry jelly–filled ones. She and Tom had arranged the donuts in a checkerboard pattern.

I smiled at Jocelyn. "They're perfect. You're really good at decorating them."

Her dark eyes gleamed. "I like doing it."

"As much as gymnastics?"

Dimples showed beside her delightfully mischievous grin. "Almost!"

I said, "You didn't tell me that one of your former coworkers was elected queen of today's festivities."

She stared at me for a second as if puzzled. "I thought *everyone* knew."

Screeching at full volume, the bagpipe band crept past on its float.

Jocelyn and I carefully loaded the boxes of donuts, assorted sizes of Deputy Donut paper bags, a red and white plaid tablecloth, and white platters with red stripes around their rims into the rear seat of the 1950 Ford. Tom would stay in the shop to make more donuts and wait on anyone who didn't attend the picnic.

I asked Jocelyn, "Would you like to drive?"

"I'd love to!"

She neatly piloted the car the quickest way around the parade to the far side of the square and then parked near the table assigned to us. The tail end of the parade was passing the reviewing stand.

The Fallingbrook Fabulous Fourth Committee had provided pretty blue-flowered vases containing vivid red geraniums and a small flag for every table on the square. We moved our centerpiece temporarily and spread our red and white plaid tablecloth over the table. Leaving most of the donuts in their boxes in the car so they'd stay fresh, we arranged a selection of donuts on the platters, and then we put the cheery geraniums back on the table along with the platters of donuts, a selection of paper bags, and our Deputy Donut napkins, fanned out to display the logos printed on them.

Other goodies, including hot dogs and potato chips, were being given away during this annual community picnic, but folks immediately crowded around our table. I let Jocelyn chat with everyone and give them donuts while I dove into the car for more.

The royal court made a walking tour of the square. Duchess Gabrielle asked for a donut decorated with star sprinkles. "Because I'm a star," she explained.

Queen Taylor gave her a look that could have turned those sugar stars into cinders. She pointed at the donut with the most stars on it and asked for that one. King Ian and Duke Nicholas, who had removed his black woolly jacket, ate their red-striped donuts right there, but Queen Taylor and Duchess Gabrielle said they wanted to enjoy theirs after they changed out of their white gowns. We'd run out of the smallest Deputy Donut paper bags and had to pack the women's star-studded donuts in bags big enough to hold about eight donuts, and then the court moved off to visit other subjects. Nicholas and Ian strolled. Taylor and Gabrielle minced, obviously having difficulty keeping their heels from sinking into the soft turf. Gabrielle reached for Nicholas's arm. He sidestepped away. Ian held his arms stiffly at his sides. I felt sorry for all of them. Finding a way through the maze of romance could be tough for twentysomethings.

A mom, a dad, and their four kids came to the table. The smallest boy, whose blond hair stuck out in adorable tufts, announced, "Today's my birthday!"

Jocelyn smiled down at him. "How old are you?"

He held one hand up, fingers and thumb spread out. "Five."

I asked him, "Want us to stack the donuts for you and your brother and sisters and mom and dad into a sort of birthday cake?"

"Yes!"

"Please," his mother said.

"Please," he echoed.

Jocelyn suggested, "We could make a skyrocket, since your birthday is the Fourth of July."

He beamed. "Okay!" He glanced at his mother. "*Please.*"

Three members of the family wanted red-striped donuts and the other three wanted donuts decorated with blue sugar stars. Jocelyn asked the birthday boy which kind of donut should be on top.

He didn't hesitate. "Stars!"

Jocelyn put a red-striped donut on a doily on the table and stacked the others on it, alternating blue stars with red stripes. Ordinarily, we would hold the donuts together with toothpicks or use frosting as a sort of paste, but we didn't have any toothpicks and the frosting on the donuts had dried too much to be sticky.

When we finished, the slightly unwieldy skyrocket needed one more thing. "Just a second," I said. Recently, I'd left a spare dark blue birthday candle in the donut car's glove compartment. I dug it out. The candle was only slightly curved after a few days in the occasionally hot car. I returned to the table and poked the candle into the top blueberry jelly–filled donut. It would serve both as a birthday candle and as a fake fuse for the fake skyrocket.

Carefully, I held the stack of six donuts while Jocelyn opened a Deputy Donut paper bag that was the same size as the ones we'd given Taylor and Gabrielle.

This time, I recognized the whirrs and clicks.

The photographer who'd been in Deputy Donut and at the marshaling grounds was now aiming his camera at Jocelyn, me, and the family with the four kids.

Jocelyn dropped the bag onto the table, turned her back on the photographer, and disappeared on the far side of the donut car.

Chapter 4

✣

In Jocelyn's absence, the kids' dad helped me slip the sky-rocket cake made of donuts into the bag. Crowing about having the best birthday cake ever, the birthday boy held his dad's hand and grasped the top of the bag in the other fist. The family wandered out onto the lawn. The kids pulled in different directions. The mother said something about hair.

The oldest boy asked, "Do we have to?"

The father boomed in a jolly voice, "After we're done here. Next stop, bouncy castles!" They headed toward a cluster of balloon-like structures at the north end of the square.

Jocelyn returned to my side. "I brought a bigger bag." It was huge.

I thanked her. "We managed." I eyed Jocelyn's too-pink face, but she turned away. I didn't think it was a coincidence that she had again made herself scarce at the exact moment that the photographer and his camera showed up or that she had again stayed away until after he left. More excited people arrived at our table, though, and I didn't ask.

I decided to keep a protective eye on her.

The picnic wound down around one, just as we gave away the last of our donuts. For the rest of the afternoon, games, skits, mini-concerts, and other fun activities would entertain kids and adults. We relinquished our table to a troupe of face-painting clowns. Jocelyn drove us back to Deputy Donut and backed the car perfectly into its garage.

Cheerful and appreciative customers kept us busy until we closed as usual at four thirty. After we finished tidying, I shooed Tom and Jocelyn out. "I'm going to stay and make another batch of Fourth of July donuts to share with friends at the fireworks."

Jocelyn offered, "Want me to help?"

"No, thanks. I'm doing this for myself, not for promotion. And you meet with your gymnastics coach every evening, don't you?"

"Not tonight. It's a holiday. I'm going to the fireworks." She looked about to execute a cartwheel right there in the Deputy Donut kitchen. Instead, she pirouetted. Although she now concentrated on gymnastics, she'd been taking both gymnastics and ballet since she was a toddler. I wasn't sure when she slept.

Tom told her, "We sometimes take leftovers home. Usually, we leave them for the Jolly Cops Cleaning Crew to deliver to the food bank. Emily always pays for the donuts she makes here for herself."

"He only lets me pay half the retail price," I complained teasingly.

He countered, "You're doing the work."

I said, "I'm too cheap to pay either of you to help, and I'm also too lazy to make them at home. Everything's all set up here."

"Not quite," Jocelyn confessed. "I used all of the blue sugar stars for the donuts we took to the picnic. I didn't let Tom have any of them for the customers here, not even before the picnic."

Tom joked, "We hired a tyrant."

"You obviously needed one," Jocelyn retorted.

I pointed toward our storeroom. "I'll find something else fun for decorations."

Tom left in his SUV. Jocelyn hopped onto her blue one-speed coaster-brake bike and pedaled away.

Peering through the window between the kitchen and the office, I explained to Dep that the two of us would stay a while longer. She opened one eye and closed it.

I mixed a small batch of yeast dough. While it rose, I rejoined Dep in the office and started catching up on paperwork.

Dep yawned, stretched, and then dashed to her catwalk. She tore around up there doing her own chores, which seemed to consist of flinging toys down at me and the computer. Jocelyn wasn't the only tyrant at Deputy Donut.

I put Dep's toys away in her basket.

Back in the kitchen, I rolled out the dough, being careful not to smash it completely. With a plain circle cookie cutter, I cut out twelve circles. I let the donuts rise until they doubled in size and then lowered them into the hot oil. When their undersides were golden, I gently turned them over and cooked them until they were golden on the other side, too, and then I slid them onto racks to cool while I sorted through our supply of sprinkles for something I could use in place of the blue stars. I found some tiny light blue spheres.

I jabbed a skewer into the sides of the cooled donuts and worked it around to form cavities in the donuts' centers. With a pastry syringe, I injected blueberry jelly into six of the donuts and raspberry jelly into the other six. I frosted all of the donuts with vanilla frosting and put the minuscule blue balls on the blueberry jelly–filled donuts. I piped red stripes on the raspberry jelly–filled donuts. The frosting could harden while I took Dep home for dinner.

In the office, my persistent and hardworking cat had not quite removed all of the toys from her basket. She stood almost still while I fastened her halter around her and snapped on the leash. Although it was after seven, the sun was high and the evening was pleasantly warm, making the six-block walk to our neighborhood of Victorian homes even more en-joyable than ever.

I knew I was biased, but I thought that my yellow brick cottage was just about the cutest house around. A wooden porch trimmed in white gingerbread spanned the front, and there were stained-glass panels above the door and the living room window. The Stars and Stripes fluttered from a pole jutting from the porch roof. The front porch was like an invitation to sit with friends or a book. I had put red, white, and blue cushions on the white wicker armchairs, and a ruby glass vase of red, white, and blue flowers on the table between the chairs.

The front door opened directly into the living room. I released Dep. When my late husband and I had bought the house, we'd stripped the wide pine-plank floors to reveal their golden luster. Alec and I had painted most of the interior walls white. The sofa, armchair, and wing chair in the living room were upholstered in dark red and deep blue to go with the stained-glass windows. The Oriental-style rug was red, cobalt, navy, and ivory.

Dep scampered up the stairs. I followed. In my Wedgwood blue and white bedroom, I changed out of my Deputy Donut uniform and into blue pants, a red and white striped blouse, and red sneakers. I put on the backpack that contained my phone, wallet, and keys, picked up a red cardigan in case it would be chilly later, and headed down the stairs. Dep reached the bottom before I did.

I went through the living room and dining room to the kitchen. Although Alec and I had tried to preserve most of the home's Victorian details, we had created an efficient and beautiful kitchen where we could indulge our foodie hobbies. We'd installed pine cabinets that went with the house's woodwork, but we'd added granite countertops, a terra-cotta tile floor, and stainless-steel appliances.

I fed Dep and gave her fresh water. Expecting to snack at

the fireworks with my friends, I slathered Icelandic-style yogurt on celery sticks for a satisfying mini-supper.

By eight thirty, the sun was low. I left Dep at home, walked back to Deputy Donut, and packed the donuts I'd made after work into an oversized paper bag. I carefully set the bag, complete with its cute cat-in-a-fake-police-hat logo, on the bench front seat of our pretend squad car. For fun, I turned on the donut's sprinkle lights and let them dance all the way to the fairgrounds.

The parking lot at the top of the hill was nearly full. I found a space near the back. Wearing my backpack and carrying the bag of donuts, I wended my way toward the big red fire truck on the other side of the lot. As I approached, I could see the tops of an ambulance and then a police cruiser on either side of the fire truck. My first-responder friends had arrived early and parked in the spaces reserved for them.

The four friends were sitting together on a brown and green plaid blanket in front of their vehicles. Samantha Andersen was on the left end of the row. She was small considering the work that EMTs did, but she was capable. She and I always claimed, especially to our tall friend Misty, that we were small but mighty. Samantha was in her EMT uniform. In honor of the holiday, she had streaked her short dark brown curls in red, white, and blue. She turned around, grinned at me, and called, "Emily!"

Beside her, Misty's patrol partner, Hooligan Houlihan, leaped to his feet. "Hey, Emily." The freckle-faced, auburn-haired policeman shook my hand.

I gave him the bag of donuts.

He made a show of unrolling the top of the bag and inhaling deeply. "Mmmm. All for me?"

I laughed. "You might share."

Samantha reached playfully for the bag. "He will!"

Hooligan grinned down at her. I thought he blushed, but maybe the rosy post-sunset glow was tinting his face. Also wearing her police uniform, Misty gave me a hug, and so did the man who had been sitting beside her, our fire chief. Tall and blond, Scott Ritsorf looked handsomer than ever in his dress uniform, shiny brass buttons and all. The four of them made room for me beside Scott.

Samantha, Misty, and I had been best friends since junior high. We'd known who Scott was back in high school, but at the time we hadn't paid much attention to the lanky, studious teen. I'd met Alec, a police officer in Fallingbrook, when I was a 911 dispatcher. Naturally, Alec had known the fire chief, and I had become friends with Scott, also. Misty really liked Scott, but Scott always gave everyone around him equal attention.

And he did it again, making certain that I was included in the teasing and bantering as we passed donuts, peanuts, chips, popcorn, and soft drinks to each other. The slope below us filled with other people sitting on blankets.

Dusk gave way to darkness, and the first rockets soared into the sky. Saplings and bushes dotted the hill, but they weren't tall enough to obstruct our view. I leaned back, watched, and enjoyed simply being near my friends.

I'd been matchmaking when I'd suggested, several weeks before, that we should sit together at the fireworks. It would have been nice if the others weren't on duty, but all four of them were in their uniforms and prepared for crowd control, illnesses, and accidents. I knew they could be called away at any minute, leaving me alone on someone's plaid blanket.

Before Hooligan joined the Fallingbrook Police Department the previous October, I'd earmarked Brent Fyne, Alec's former partner on the police force, for Samantha. She'd never seemed particularly interested in Brent, though, especially after she met Hooligan. Both Samantha and Misty liked to tease me that Brent was right for me.

They were wrong.

Brent had been Alec's best friend. Brent was a good detective and a good man. I liked him, but I had no desire to risk the friendship that he and I had rebuilt after my grief-filled three years of avoiding him because I hadn't wanted to think about the night that Alec was killed.

That night, I had switched shifts with a new 911 dispatcher so I could spend the evening with friends who were visiting from out of town.

Brent and Alec had been shot.

Brent had been merely grazed, but Alec's injuries had been critical.

I would always wonder if, with my experience, I could have acted faster than the new dispatcher and could have arranged help for Alec in time to save his life. Brent claimed that I couldn't have. He had radioed for help immediately, and his call had mobilized an ambulance even while a distraught onlooker was stammering through her emergency call to my untried colleague.

Brent's assurances had assuaged my guilt a little, but I didn't think I would ever completely get over it. I knew I would never recover from the grief of losing Alec.

I had another reason for not being interested in Brent except as a good and supportive friend—even if I wanted to date again after five years of widowhood, I would not choose a man doing the job that had led to Alec's death.

Alec's life had been like these fireworks, brilliant, awe-inspiring, and over much too soon.

My hand tightened on the emptied donut bag. Sparkling patterns burst above us, the crowd oohed, and pungent smoke drifted. Maybe I thought the same thing every year, but this seemed to be Fallingbrook's most extravagant fireworks display ever.

However, people began leaving before the show was over. Some were carrying small children up the hill toward the cars. Others probably wanted to drive out of the parking lot before the inevitable traffic jam began. Maybe some folks were leaving because they were cold. I was. I'd left my sweater in the donut car. I shrugged my backpack on. That didn't help.

I was really, really cold.

I whispered to Scott that I'd be right back, and then I ran up the hill and across the parking lot to the donut car. The sweater warmed me immediately. I put my backpack on over it and started toward my friends and their blanket. Between dodging pedestrians walking in the opposite direction and vehicles leaving the parking lot, I could catch only glimpses of the fireworks above me. It didn't help that headlights glared into my eyes and smoke from spent fireworks hung just above the pavement.

Looking like he hated fireworks, King Ian strode toward the rear of the lot. Duchess Gabrielle was close behind him, throwing admiring looks at his back. If he knew she was there, he wasn't acknowledging it. I almost didn't recognize Kelsey. At Freeze, her hair was always pinned up underneath her frilly cap. I hadn't guessed it was longer than shoulder-length. Several Deputy Donut customers greeted me. Jocelyn didn't notice me, probably because she was holding hands with a broad-shouldered boy who looked about her age. Closer to Scott's fire truck, I caught a glimpse of Felicia, my mother's hairdresser, the woman Queen Taylor had complained about over the megaphone. Mama Freeze was beside her, but I couldn't tell if the two middle-aged women were together or just happened to be walking next to each other.

I plunked myself down on the blanket next to Scott, grabbed the empty donut bag I'd left behind, and stared upward. Multicolored chrysanthemum-shaped starbursts filled the sky. People cheered.

The crowd plodding uphill beside me thinned for a moment.

Beyond a scraggly shrub just down the hill, something glittered. Sparks were shooting from the top of a strangely bulging cylinder.

I dropped the empty paper bag, leaped to my feet, and ran to the side of the shrub.

Jamming my hand over my mouth, I froze.

The lumpy cylinder looked like the stack of donuts that Jocelyn and I had given to the five-year-old boy for his sky-rocket cake, but the partially melted birthday candle that I'd stuck into the top donut could not have been spewing flames like this one was.

It wasn't a birthday candle resembling a fuse. It was an actual fuse.

The bulging cylinder had to be a firework.

It was only about a foot behind a tall blonde sitting on a blanket. Worse, the firework was leaning downward and aimed directly at the woman's back. A platinum-haired man had wrapped his arm around the woman, from her shoulder to her hip.

I shouted at the couple, "Run!"

Chapter 5

The endangered couple in front of me must not have heard my shouted warning. They didn't move.

With a loud bang, the oddly bulky firework right behind the woman's back exploded. I couldn't help closing my eyes.

Small, hard particles peppered my face. People near me yelped.

My eyes flew open. The thick liquid oozing down my stinging cheek couldn't be blood. It was no warmer than the night air.

Dense smoke surrounded me, along with the acrid odors of gunpowder and scorched wool. Some of the people who had been near the firework ran up the hill toward the cars. Others backed away. Farther from us, most of the crowd continued watching the sky. They probably didn't realize that one of the explosions had come from up the hill near the parking lot.

The smoke thinned slightly, and I recognized the man who had been closest to the leaning firework. He was Nicholas, the duke of this year's festivities. The slim blonde who had been sitting next to him had folded forward like a limp doll, with her head downhill and her right arm and leg flung outward. Nicholas was on his knees, leaning over her. With his right hand, he awkwardly draped the edge of their blanket over her, but he was holding his left hand close to his chest. His face contorted in a scream I couldn't hear.

"Samantha!" I yelled. "Scott! Misty! Hooligan!" My four friends were already heading toward the stricken couple.

Samantha's EMT partner, who must have been in the ambulance behind us, ran down the hill. He and Samantha knelt beside the woman while Misty and Hooligan talked to Nicholas. Scott stomped through the grass as if searching for embers.

Apparently, he didn't find any. Positioning himself between the injured pair and me, he placed his hands lightly on my shoulders. The brass buttons on his dress uniform jacket glimmered in the dim evening. "Sit down, Emily. You're bleeding."

Misty must have heard him. She glanced at me, stood, and ran—three whole strides for her—to us.

I licked my lips. "I'm not bleeding. I think it's blueberry jelly."

Scott looked really concerned, probably because I wasn't making a lot of sense.

Misty shined a flashlight at the side of my face. "I think it is, too." She reached forward, fingered my curls, and pulled. "What's this?" Her light showed a small dark blue object pinched between her thumb and forefinger.

At the risk of sounding even less coherent than I had a few seconds before, I answered, "It's a . . . a sprinkle. A sugar star."

Scott tilted his head and raised one eyebrow in a skeptical way.

I added, "It came from a blueberry jelly–filled donut." The statement didn't seem to help my case, but that wasn't important. I demanded, "Did you two see what happened?" Panic and shock squeezed my chest.

Scott tightened his hands on my shoulders. "No. Did something misfire?"

I asked, "Misty, did you see?"

"I didn't see any big chunks of fire falling from the sky."

I gazed up into the concerned eyes of these two friends. "It didn't fall. I saw it before it exploded. A firework was on the ground directly behind the woman's back." I asked Misty, "Is she Taylor? The queen whose car you drove in the parade this morning?"

Misty's face was solemn and her answer curt. "Yes."

My words tripped over each other. "Someone must have planted that firework there, in the grass behind her."

Scott let go of my shoulders. "Stay here, Emily." He sprinted to his fire truck, switched on a powerful floodlight, and aimed it at the group surrounding the injured pair.

As the senior police officer present, Misty was in charge. I led her around the puny bush to a blackened and partially split tube sticking out of a torn jelly-filled donut. The donut still had vestiges of red stripes on a background of white icing. "See how that tube is leaning downhill?"

Misty nodded.

I explained, "I didn't get a good look at any of it." I described the five-year-old's birthday cake made of donuts. "But just now, I wasn't seeing a birthday candle. The flames were too big. It had to be a fuse. And then the thing exploded." I brushed a straying curl, weighed down by blueberry jelly, no doubt, away from my eye. "Someone must have inserted a firework into a stack of jelly-filled donuts, crept behind this bush, aimed the thing at Taylor, and lit it."

Frowning, Misty made a call on her radio.

I asked loudly enough for everyone nearby to hear, "Did anyone see someone behind this bush or notice the firework before it went off?"

Nicholas rasped out an abrupt "No."

Samantha and Hooligan said they'd been looking up.

Samantha's EMT partner pressed a stethoscope against Taylor's neck. "I was sleeping." The blanket that Nicholas had managed to partially pull over Taylor looked singed.

Misty asked police dispatch for backup officers, including

the night's on-duty detective. She signed off and told me that she had been looking at the sky and not at the people around us. She shined her flashlight down at the remains of the firework behind Nicholas and Taylor.

I picked up a morsel of donut. It was harder and dryer than the donuts I'd brought to the fireworks that evening, the ones that my friends and I had devoured. Toeing at the grass, I uncovered a cigarette lighter, a transparent dark red one that I'd almost missed seeing despite Scott's gigantic flood-light. The shrub's small twigs were casting surprisingly large shadows. Knowing I shouldn't touch the lighter, I pointed it out to Misty.

Nicholas was still hunched protectively over his left arm. He could easily hear us, so I didn't point out that the lighter was very close to where I'd seen his hand when I realized that the bulky cylinder was concealing a lit firework.

Leaving the lighter in place, Misty wrote in her notebook. I could tell from the way her pen moved that she was drawing a diagram.

Samantha fastened a sling around Nicholas's left arm.

Misty beckoned me farther up the hill, away from the shrub that had mostly shielded the firework from view. "The man will be okay, but Taylor is seriously injured." Her face became hard with suppressed anger. "Judging by her condition, that skyrocket was homemade. It must have contained strong explosives, and I found a marble that might have shot from it. Stick around, okay, Emily, to give us a complete statement?"

"Okay."

Misty rejoined the group around Taylor and Nicholas. Samantha's partner dashed up the hill toward the ambulance.

I stayed where I was. Crossing my arms in an attempt to warm myself, I thought about who might have deliberately harmed Taylor, and why. Earlier that day, Taylor had insulted both Felicia and her supposed best friend, Duchess Gabrielle. And in the minutes before the donut skyrocket exploded, I'd seen both Felicia and Gabrielle leaving the area, along with throngs of other people, including Taylor's former boyfriend, Ian.

Samantha's partner ran down the hill carrying a rigid stretcher that I knew from my days at 911 was called a Stokes basket. Protecting Taylor's neck with a collar, he and Samantha carefully transferred her from the grassy hill to the stretcher.

Misty told Hooligan to keep people away from what was now a crime scene.

Scott, Samantha, her partner, and I grabbed handles on the sides of the Stokes basket. Samantha directed our lifting. Although Taylor was tall, she was slim, and with four of us sharing her weight, she didn't seem heavy. Misty put one arm around Nicholas's waist. Nicholas leaned on her, and the two of them walked slowly beside us.

We loaded Taylor, still in the Stokes basket, into the ambulance. Scott and Misty helped Nicholas into a seat near Taylor. Samantha's partner climbed in back with them.

An opening between the front seats of the ambulance would allow the EMT to leave his patients to confer with Samantha after she got in and started driving.

That lighter, so close to where I'd seen Nicholas's hand . . .

Could Nicholas have deliberately lit the firework to harm Taylor? He could have decided that they should sit in front of a bush that would partially hide them. Could he have believed he could aim a homemade firework at the woman beside him without being hurt after he lit it?

Chapter 6

I grabbed Samantha's wrist and murmured, "Don't let the injured man be alone with the injured woman, not even for a second."

Samantha's eyes opened wide. "My partner will keep close track of both of them." Samantha mouthed something to her partner. He met my gaze and nodded. Samantha shut the ambulance's back doors and then swung herself into the driver's seat. The ambulance roared off, its siren wailing and its lights flashing.

Scott frowned down at me. "Are you okay, Emily?"

I summoned up a strong and confident voice. "I'm fine. Nothing hit me besides flying donut pieces."

"I can take you to the hospital."

"In the fire truck?"

"Sure." His grin was a little strained. "Or in your vintage cruiser, which, by the way, I've never driven." He was a darling for trying to distract me.

I tried an answering grin, which was probably as strained as his. "I'll let you, someday, even though I know you'll never let me drive your fire truck."

"Become a firefighter and that's one of the things you'll learn to do."

"Thanks, but I prefer a life of boiling things in oil."

His deep sigh was patently phony. "Do me a favor and keep

the temperature of your oil below the flash point. Meanwhile, do you want a ride to the hospital in the fire truck?"

"It's tempting, but there's no need. I'll be fine after I wash my face." Even though my sweater had no hood, I knew I shouldn't feel as cold as I did.

"You're shivering," he said. "Wait here." He strode to the plaid blanket we'd been sitting on and grabbed it and the empty donut bag. He peered into the bag, shrugged, and handed it to me. Then he shook the blanket and wrapped it around me, backpack and all.

Even though I'd been hit by a hail of donut bits and my cheek still stung, I was physically fine. Emotionally, I didn't know. Taylor had been annoying, but no one should have to suffer like that.

Still frowning, Misty came down the hill with a roll of yellow crime scene tape. She gave it to Hooligan and then joined Scott and me. She grabbed my wrist. I managed to hang on to both the blanket and the paper bag.

Up the hill to my right, a light flashed.

Another explosion?

Flinching, I started turning my head toward where the flash had been.

There was another flash, probably from a camera or a phone, but I wasn't sure, and I didn't get a chance to focus on whatever it was. Misty demanded, "Look at me, Emily." Dutifully, I faced her. Misty must have been certain that the flash did not pose any danger.

Peering into my eyes and checking my pulse, she apparently convinced herself that I truly was unharmed, if a little twitchy. She went off to talk to other potential witnesses. I peered into the darkness but couldn't see anyone near where the flashes had originated.

Standing side by side, Scott and I watched Misty talk to people while Hooligan wound yellow police tape around bushes in a large circle enclosing the area where Nicholas and Taylor had been sitting.

I was still hanging on to the empty donut bag as if I expected it to fill itself with fresh donuts. I wadded it up and crammed it into a pocket. Holding the blanket around myself with both hands, I tried not to shiver.

An unmarked police car pulled into the spot where the ambulance had been. Detective Brent Fyne got out of the cruiser. Misty started up the hill toward him.

As always, Brent looked good. He was dressed for work in nice slacks, a white shirt, a tie, and a summer blazer that probably hid a shoulder holster. He wasn't quite as tall as Scott, who was lanky but wiry and fit. Brent was more solidly built and very obviously muscular.

Talking in low voices, Brent and Misty walked down the hill toward Scott and me.

My shoulders started to relax. Brent's calm capability had a way of making a pain-filled crime scene less chaotic and more bearable.

He often kept his thoughts from showing. This time, his expression was grim.

"I can tell from your face, Brent," I said. "The woman didn't make it."

Beside me, Scott inhaled swiftly.

Brent shook his head. "No, she didn't."

"I didn't think she would," Scott admitted to Brent, something he hadn't said to me. I wasn't as fragile as Scott occasionally acted. "Her back was punctured, right behind her heart."

Misty said, "I'm guessing that the projectile was a marble. There was at least one more nearby."

Scott turned to me and spoke softly. "She was unconscious when we reached her. She couldn't have felt much."

I managed to speak through tightened lips. "That's good to hear. But her boyfriend, the guy with the injured arm, is going to miss her." *Unless he purposely harmed her.* "And she must have other family and friends."

Studying my jelly-streaked face, Brent asked if I was injured. After I assured him quite firmly that I wasn't, he reached into his blazer's inner pocket and took out his notebook. "Misty, can you take Scott's statement while I take Emily's?"

She nodded and touched the sleeve of Scott's jacket.

Scott glanced at my face again as if to assure himself that I was okay, and then he and Misty moved out of earshot.

Brent wrote down my statement, including the names of everyone I'd seen when I'd gone to the donut car and returned with my sweater.

"Who is Jocelyn?" he asked.

"Tom and I hired an assistant." Brent and I had been getting together for impromptu dinners at my place every so often for nearly two years, but we hadn't seen each other during the past couple of weeks. I had mentioned that Tom and I wanted to hire a third person to work at the donut shop, but I hadn't told Brent that we'd actually done it. I added, "I'm sure that Jocelyn doesn't have a mean bone in her body." I thought about it for a second. "Actually, I'm not sure she has any bones. She's a gymnast."

"Oho. The famous Jocelyn."

"She and Taylor both worked at Freeze until we hired Jocelyn. I can't imagine Jocelyn planting that thing, but almost anyone could have. There were thousands of people here, and crowds of them were leaving. I don't know how fast or slow that firework's fuse was, so I don't know if it was lit before I went to get my sweater, while I was gone, or after I came back."

I described everything that had happened and told him about giving the birthday boy and his family a stack of donuts with a candle in the top. "I don't know who they were." I explained that the only donuts that Jocelyn had decorated with blue sugar stars had been given out at the picnic. "Taylor and her best friend, the duchess, each received one." My cheek had stopped stinging. I wiped my hand across it and ended up with more jelly on my hand. "This looked *per-*

sonal. That thing was only about a foot from Taylor. It was aimed directly at her back."

"What are you saying?" he asked.

"I think she was targeted. This was deliberate, malicious, and preplanned."

I didn't have to add the word *murder*. Brent must have gotten the gist. Lips compressed, he wrote in his notebook. Then he asked again, "Are you positive you're not injured? It's hard to tell by looking at you."

"I'm sure."

He turned away and faced the taped-off crime scene. "Good." He said it so quietly that I almost missed it. He asked more loudly, "Can you give me a tour without going past the tape?"

"Yes." I showed him where fragments of donut might be lying in the grass and pointed out what was left of the donut skyrocket. He stepped over the tape and set an orange crime scene marker on the ground beside the blackened tube and the portion of raspberry jelly–filled donut surrounding its base. I showed Brent where I'd sat to watch the fireworks and where crowds had been hurrying up the hill on both sides of Taylor and Nicholas. Brent put one marker next to the red disposable lighter and two more where Taylor and Nicholas had been sitting.

A police photographer arrived. Brent talked to him and then returned to me. "You can go, Em. Call me if you think of anything else. If you discover you've been injured, get help, okay?"

I pulled the blanket more tightly around myself. "Okay."

After a long, assessing look into my eyes, he returned to the police photographer.

Scott was still hovering nearby. I asked him, "Whose blanket am I wearing?" Although the blanket had warmed me enough that I didn't actually feel cold, I had to make an effort to control my trembling. "I don't think you or Samantha carry plaid ones like this in your fire truck or ambulance." I removed it from my shoulders and folded it.

"Hooligan's." Hooligan was still guarding the crime scene. I reassured Scott that I'd be fine, told him good night, trudged up the hill, and plunked the blanket on the hood of Misty and Hooligan's cruiser where they'd see it.

The crumpled donut bag was still in my pocket. I wiped my sticky hands on the bag—kind of late, considering that I'd been handling Hooligan's blanket—and then dumped the bag in a trash can near the cruiser. Tired and also saddened by Taylor's death, I walked toward my car. My shoulders slumped and my head was down, but at the moment, I couldn't care about good posture.

I unlocked the donut car's front door.

A bright light flashed. Another lethal firework?

Jerking my head up, I turned toward where the light had been. My pulse raced. I managed not to gasp, even after my eyes adjusted and I recognized the photographer who had seemed to frighten Jocelyn twice that day.

He lowered his camera from his face.

"I saw you," he accused. "I saw you light the firework that injured those people."

Chapter 7

✺

I was alone on the dark side of the parking lot with this wild-eyed and accusing photographer. I could scream, but my friends across the parking lot were too far away to hear.

Grasping the car door handle and standing as tall as I could, I snapped, "That's impossible. You couldn't have seen me light the firework because I didn't do it." *Calm down, Emily. Showing your anger won't help and could put you in danger.*

Smirking, the photographer placed a hand on the long lens of his camera.

I pointed toward the fire truck and its floodlight. "Police officers are over there. Go tell them what you think you saw."

"What I *know* I saw."

"And if you have photos showing someone lighting that firework, give them to the police." Despite my earlier warning to myself, I was still sounding angry.

"Are you sure you want me to?"

I swung the car door open. "Of course. I did not light that thing, and I'd like to know who did."

"You're bluffing." His voice was as oily and insinuating as the way he kept suddenly showing up where I didn't expect him. "This morning, that woman insulted your car, and tonight, you got your revenge."

"That's ridiculous." I flung myself into the driver's seat, slammed the door, and sped away.

My anger at the photographer and his false accusations did not distract me from the sadness of Taylor's senseless death, a death that appeared to have been deliberate murder. Who would have, who *could* have, done such an evil thing? And why?

That photographer who kept popping up . . .

I was tempted to drive home and park the 1950 donut-topped Ford in the driveway for the night so I wouldn't have to walk home alone from the garage behind Deputy Donut.

I couldn't let fear rule my life.

I parked the cruiser in its garage and then I walked quickly through the brightly lit streets of downtown Fallingbrook. My own neighborhood was almost as well illuminated, but I couldn't help expecting murderous strangers and threatening photographers to push through hedges or race out from between houses.

Finally, I was on my own block. With relief, I ran up the porch steps and locked myself into my sweet little cottage. Dep greeted me with heartfelt meows. I cuddled her all the way upstairs.

I almost didn't recognize myself in the bathroom mirror. Even after I washed the blueberry jelly off my cheek, I looked exhausted and scared. The spot on my cheek that a sugar star must have hit was only a tiny bit pink. It no longer stung, and I didn't think there would be a bruise.

When I was in bed, Dep tucked herself behind my knees and purred until I was able to stop picturing the night's events and fall into a troubled sleep.

For a few seconds after the alarm went off in the morning, I didn't think about Taylor and Nicholas, but then the memories surfaced, sickeningly and all at once. I had to channel those memories into something productive, or they might overwhelm me.

Taylor's complaints about others had been excessive, but had they been enough to make someone want to harm her?

She had insulted my mother's hairdresser. Could Felicia be a killer? My mother liked everybody, and my father was the same. *Everyone has their good qualities,* they'd often counseled me when I was a kid and upset about someone's behavior. *Let's focus on those.*

Had my mother focused too hard on Felicia's good qualities and failed to notice that the woman had a dangerous side?

Taylor and her bestie, Duchess Gabrielle, seemed to have shared a love-hate relationship. Gabrielle had obviously thrived on it. Would she have wanted to end it?

According to Gabrielle, Taylor had recently dumped Ian, the king. He had obviously been attempting to conceal his emotions before, during, and after the parade. I'd believed he'd been hiding his pain, but maybe the emotion he'd been tamping down had been rage. Had he decided that if he couldn't have Taylor, no one could?

And then there was Nicholas. Could he have tired of Taylor and decided to end their relationship in a drastic way?

By claiming that he'd seen me light the firework, that sneaky photographer was admitting that he'd been there when it was lit. Had *he* lit it? Jocelyn seemed afraid of him, and now I was, too.

Early dawn light filtered through windows, and Dep began scuffling with my slippers on the floor beside the bed. Before she could bat them out into the hall and down the stairs, I thrust my feet into them and picked her up. Crooning, I carried her to the kitchen. She wriggled to be put down. I obeyed. Still groggy, I fed her and made a red bell pepper omelet for myself. The sun rose as we ate.

I showered, dressed, and checked my face in the mirror. I no longer looked horror-struck, and my cheek looked fine.

No bruises. I ran downstairs, snapped Dep's halter and leash on her, and took her outside. The morning was warm and scented with honeysuckle and roses rambling over white picket fences and trellises. Dep's friskiness lifted my spirits. By the time we arrived in her playground, also known as our Deputy Donut office, I was almost smiling. I settled my kitty into her room and then headed into the kitchen.

Yeast dough was rising, sending out that warm and delicious aroma. I quickly told Tom what had happened at the fireworks without mentioning how close I'd been to the explosion. About five years had passed since Alec's death, but both Tom and my mother-in-law, Cindy, continued to treat me like a beloved daughter, and I never wanted to worry them.

Jocelyn came in through the storeroom. As usual, she must have parked her bike just outside the door next to the loading dock. She was wearing her Deputy Donut uniform, apron, and hat.

And a too-bright expression on her face. "Did your friends like the donuts?" she asked.

"They gobbled them up. I saw you at the fireworks with a hunky guy."

"Oh! When we were leaving, I noticed the donut car, but I didn't see you. Sorry! I would have said hello. My boyfriend was here for a few days, but we had to leave the fireworks early. His parents took him back to Madison last night. He's lifeguarding down there this summer."

"Did you meet him in high school?"

"No. At summer games. He's a swimmer." She smiled proudly. "He wins a lot."

"Like you do."

"More than that. He's *really* good." She turned away and scooped coffee beans into the grinder. "I . . . I heard that something terrible happened. To Taylor." She paused. Because her back was to me, I couldn't see her face. "I hope it's not true. She died?"

I wasn't sure how much the police were telling. "A firework hit her," I said.

"You always hear warnings that fireworks can kill, but I thought they were just, you know, adults exaggerating. That's terrible. Poor Taylor. I knew her at Freeze, but I knew her in high school, too. She's a couple of years older than I am."

Which meant, as I'd guessed, that Taylor's life had been cut short at only about twenty-one. Wanting more information from Jocelyn, I made a clumsy segue. "You know a lot of people. Do you know the family who were at the picnic, the family with the little boy who was turning five?"

She turned to face us again. Her eyes were pink rimmed while the rest of her face was pale. "Why? Did something happen to him or his family?"

"No, but the detective I talked to last night, Brent Fyne, will probably ask you for names of people we gave donuts to at the picnic."

"I know a few, but . . ." Her voice trailed off. "Do detectives always ask such weird questions?"

Tom chimed in. "Yep!"

"Did you, when you were a detective?"

"I hope so." He flattened dough with his enormous marble rolling pin.

Jocelyn answered my question. "I don't know that family. I went off to look for a bigger bag, and I didn't pay them much attention. Just that little boy. He was cute, wasn't he?"

"Yes, and I didn't catch even his first name." Although I wasn't a detective, I had another weird question. "Do you know that guy who was taking pictures in here and then later at the picnic?"

"I know who you mean, but I don't know him." She turned toward the coffee grinder again.

"I saw him after the fireworks."

"Maybe he's a reporter?" Jocelyn started the grinder. No one spoke while it rumbled.

Tom and I exchanged glances.

He lifted one shoulder as if to say he didn't know who the man was, either. He gave his head a quick shake, glanced at Jocelyn's back, looked at me again, and thinned his lips. I thought he meant that we shouldn't interfere with the police investigation, or that my questions were making Jocelyn clam up, or both. After his years as a Fallingbrook police officer, detective, and police chief, Tom was more expert at investigating and interrogating than I was. I followed his unspoken advice, at least for the moment.

I cut out donuts and Tom fried them while Jocelyn started the first pots of coffee and then filled our cute creamers and sugar bowls. Like our mugs and plates, they were off-white ironstone with our Deputy Donut logo printed in black on them.

Except for the police officers, our customers wanted to talk about what they called the accident at the fireworks the night before. The cops avoided the subject even when people asked. "We can't talk about police investigations," one said, softening his words with a smile.

At a table beside a front window, the Knitpickers chatted and knit. At the next table, the retired men teased the Knitpickers about sitting inside on a warm and sunny day. "What?" one of the men asked in joshing tones. "You sit outside on the patio only on the days when there's a parade going by?"

"What about you guys?" Cheryl, a white-haired knitter who never seemed to quite finish her projects, retorted. "Why aren't *you* out on the patio on a day like this?"

One of the men winked at me. "We don't want to wear Emily out."

I poured him a mug of the day's specialty coffee, the so-called "Monsooned Voyage" Malabar from India, made from beans that had been soaked for a long time to replicate the complex flavor of beans shipped across oceans for months during damp conditions. Although it sounded potentially disgusting, it was delicious. I told the man, "The more running around I do, the more donuts I can eat."

"That does it!" Cheryl exclaimed. "From now on, we're going to the counter and carrying our own food and beverages so we can eat more of your delicious donuts, Emily."

Virginia didn't look up from the soft yellow baby sweater she was knitting. "*I'm* not. Emily doesn't want us spilling hot coffee down people's necks."

The Knitpickers and the retired men laughed. A Knitpicker accused, "You just don't want to miss a second of knitting time."

Virginia deadpanned, "Guilty as charged."

Cheryl pulled a newspaper out of her tote and studied the front page. "Hey, Emily! You're in the *Fallingbrook News*."

Chapter 8

Cheryl ran a finger rapidly down the first column and then raised her head. Her usually cheerful face showed pain. "The police are saying that the death of that Fabulous Fourth Festivities queen, Taylor Wishbard, is *suspicious*."

"Like it wasn't an accident, after all?" a Knitpicker asked.

Cheryl's answer was surprisingly clipped. "Yes."

I peered over her shoulder. The photo beside the headline showed Taylor sitting on her throne, high in the parade's reviewing stand. Wearing her crown and a huge smile, she was waving. Everyone else was cropped out of the photo.

Cheryl pointed at a photo near the bottom of the article. "Isn't this you, Emily? I recognize your curls." Horror still lurked behind her kind blue eyes, but she gave me a tight-lipped attempt at a smile. "Even though they're mostly hidden by your funny hat when you're in here."

Guessing that she wanted to lighten the mood, I complained with great drama, "It's *not* a funny hat. But yes, that's me."

The picture was taken from my right and slightly behind me. It showed Misty looking very stern and holding my left wrist as if restraining me. This must have been the first picture the photographer took of me after the ambulance left with Taylor and Nicholas. I'd been looking at Misty, and only part of my right cheek, the one that wasn't stained with jelly, showed. With my right hand, I was holding the edges of the plaid blanket close to my throat while also clutching the empty donut bag.

Cheryl touched the picture of Misty's face. "Doesn't that police officer come in here a lot?"

"Yes. She was checking my pulse because she thought I might also have been hurt. I wasn't."

The other Knitpickers clucked. "I should hope not," one said.

Cheryl's forehead wrinkled as if something worried her. "Why would they put that picture in the article, and not one of, say, a police car or an ambulance? It almost looks like she's arresting you."

Whoever took that picture probably meant it to look that way. I guessed, "They never publish pictures of badly injured people, but maybe they wanted to show a first responder and a bystander."

Cheryl looked slightly happier. "It doesn't say who you are, Emily, and only people who know you would recognize you."

Virginia gestured with a bamboo knitting needle, knitting and all, to indicate the entire donut shop. "Lots of people know Emily." She started another row.

I checked the credit with the photo. The photographer's name was Philip Landsdowner.

Returning to serving customers and helping Tom and Jocelyn make and decorate donuts, I wondered if Philip Landsdowner was the photographer who had taken pictures in Deputy Donut, at the parade-marshaling grounds, and at the picnic.

As usual, the Knitpickers and the retired men departed around noon. I joined Jocelyn at their tables to pick up mugs and plates. Cheryl had left the newspaper behind.

Jocelyn bent over it and then straightened and let her gaze meet mine. "That policewoman is your friend, right?" she asked. "And she wasn't arresting you?"

I smiled at the obvious concern in the nineteen-year-old's

voice. "Yes, that's Misty, and no, she wasn't arresting me. She was worried that I might have been hurt."

"Were you close to Taylor when she was . . . hurt?"

"A little," I admitted.

"Did you see what happened?"

"Not really." I pointed at the photographer's name below the picture of Misty and me. "Could Philip Landsdowner be the photographer who was in here yesterday morning? I saw that same man at the fairgrounds about an hour after Taylor was rushed to the hospital. He was carrying a camera."

Jocelyn flushed. "I don't know. Lots of people were taking pictures at the fireworks, some with cameras and some with phones." She picked up her tray and carried it to the kitchen.

Had Philip Landsdowner been following Jocelyn around yesterday? It seemed just as likely that he could have been following me. Or both of us. Maybe he had simply been going from place to place, wherever he thought there might be interesting pictures for the *Fallingbrook News*. I took the newspaper into the office and put it on the desk.

Blinking sleepily, Dep sat up and watched me.

"It's a newspaper," I told her, "not a bed."

She yawned.

Misty and Hooligan didn't come in for their breaks, and neither did Scott, which wasn't surprising. They'd all been working late shifts the night before. Still, I would have liked their company after the experiences we'd shared.

During a lull in the afternoon, I went into the office. Dep was sleeping on the newspaper. She didn't open an eye even when I phoned the number for the *Fallingbrook News* and asked if Philip Landsdowner was in the office.

The receptionist said, "We don't have anyone by that name working here."

In a way, that was the answer I wanted—I hadn't been sure what I was going to say if he actually came on the line. However, calling the newspaper had not given me the name of the man who had appeared near me several times and had claimed he'd seen me light that firework. I thanked the receptionist and ended the call.

I probably should have phoned Brent the night before and told him about the photographer's accusation. By now, the photographer could have told investigators about it.

However, if I didn't also tell Brent, he might wonder why I hadn't. His personal line went to message. I asked him to call me.

Although I wasn't certain she was asleep, Dep was still using the newspaper as a bed. Maybe she thought that if she didn't open her eyes, I wouldn't see her. Grinning at her transparent tactics, I went back out to the dining room.

After we closed Deputy Donut for the day, Tom, Jocelyn, and I packed our Fourth of July decorations away. We decided we didn't need supplies except for blue star sprinkles, and they could wait until we ordered other trimmings. We tidied the shop. The Jolly Cops Cleaning Crew would come in during the night and do the heavy cleaning, including removing the cooking oil we'd used during the day and scrubbing the deep fryers. Tom and Jocelyn left.

I tried to corral Dep. I rattled her halter and leash, but she must have decided it was a good time to play hard-to-get. The pupils of her eyes huge, she stared down at me from her catwalk.

Maybe she guessed that I wasn't sure I felt like going home yet. Brent hadn't returned my call. Dep could always cheer me, but without other humans around, I might dwell on the shock of Taylor's murder.

It was Friday. Gabrielle had told me I should go to Frisky Pomegranate for their Friday Happy Hour.

That probably wasn't the best place, especially if Gabrielle was working there that evening, to be distracted from thinking about Taylor. Worse, a pub happy hour sounded a little too much like a singles event, something guaranteed to make me want to run away screaming.

However, if that photographer was trying to convince readers of the *Fallingbrook News,* and possibly the police, too, that I had lit the firework that killed Taylor, spending some time around Taylor's best friend might be useful.

"I'll be back for you later, Dep," I told my wide-eyed cat.

She didn't stir from her perch even when I opened the back door.

Feeling almost guilty for trying out a new pub, I bypassed the Fireplug, where I often hung out with friends, and walked north on Wisconsin Street to the village square. The reviewing stand looked empty and desolate now that the cheerful red, white, and blue bunting and the four jewel-encrusted thrones had been removed.

Frisky Pomegranate was across from where the bouncy castles and other inflatables had been. I took the kitty-corner flagstone pathway through the square. Windows spanned the front of Frisky Pomegranate below an awning that spelled out the pub's name and featured a pomegranate with arms, legs, and a toothy grin. The pomegranate appeared to be dancing.

The sunny patio in front of the pub was crowded with tables topped by jaunty pomegranate-red umbrellas. People sitting at the tables were laughing, drinking, and talking. I saw couples, groups of friends, and possibly a few singles, too.

Singles. Without conscious effort, I slowed down.

What could Gabrielle tell me that the police or I didn't already know? Maybe grief had kept her at home, and looking for her would be a waste of time.

It turned out that I wasn't going to be able to use that excuse to avoid Friday Happy Hour at Frisky Pomegranate. Wearing a short-skirted ruby-red uniform and balancing a tray of drinks, Gabrielle came out of the pub onto the patio. I didn't know if she'd seen me, but if she had, I was committed. Crossing the street, I hoped that no one would think I was on the prowl for eligible men.

The patio was surrounded by a shoulder-high railing with boxes of flowers hanging from it facing the sidewalk. I stepped into the enclosure and halted. The tables appeared to be full.

Gabrielle breezed past. She didn't seem to recognize me, maybe because I wasn't wearing my Deputy Donut hat. "There are seats inside at the bar," she told me.

A woman at a table beside me said, "Here, we're just leaving."

She and the other three women at her table gathered their bags and stood. I sat down and scooted the chair closer to the table.

Gabrielle brought me a small bowl of salty mixed nuts. "Happy Hour is almost over. Drinks will be full price in five minutes, so order as much as you're going to want now." The corners of her mouth twitched upward in something resembling a smile. Her eyeliner was smudged, and wisps had escaped from her pinned-up hair.

Frisky Pomegranate offered my favorite craft brewery's light beer on draft. I asked for a mug of it.

"Is that all?" Gabrielle's question was tinged with disbelief.

"I can't stay long." Dep, when she finally came down from her just-below-the-ceiling playground, would agree.

While Gabrielle was inside drawing my beer, I wondered how to go about asking questions about the day before.

Gabrielle solved the problem. With a clunk, she set the frosty mug in front of me and said, "Hey, I just realized where I saw you before. You drove Nicholas and me in the parade in that adorable old police car."

"Yes. How are you doing?"

"Fine. Yesterday was fab. I'm keeping my tiara forever."

"Did you enjoy the fireworks?"

"They were okay. I left before they were over so I could avoid the crowds. Did you see me there?" Those big brown eyes looked completely guileless. Someone at the next table called to her, and she turned away. "Gotta go," she called over her shoulder, "and get their drink orders in before I have to charge them full price. Enjoy!"

I finished my beer and nuts in record time. Unless she was pretending, Gabrielle did not know about Taylor's death.

I didn't want to be the one to tell her, and I wasn't sure how to go about asking if she knew of anyone who might have wanted to kill Taylor. I tucked a nice tip underneath the nut bowl and left.

"Coward," I muttered to myself as I cut across the green.

My phone rang.

It was Brent. "Sorry for taking so long to return your call, Em. Can I come talk to you this evening?" He sounded tired. Defeated, maybe.

Chapter 9

❧

Had Brent learned new and disturbing details about Taylor's death? Maybe the investigation wasn't going well and he hadn't slept much. Or eaten, probably, either.

"Sure," I answered. "Come for dinner?"

He hesitated. "I have to ask you some questions."

I bit my lip. Brent seldom came across as formal, at least with me.

Something was wrong.

Maybe that oily photographer had told Brent or other investigators that he'd seen me light the firework's fuse. "I'll try to answer. We both have to eat. Hamburgers will be quick. Dep and I should be home in about ten minutes."

"That would be great." To my relief, warmth crept back into his voice. He seemed to thrive on helping people whose lives were impacted by crime, but being close to others' tragedies had to take a toll.

We disconnected. As I walked, I stared toward the two large buildings across the road from the south end of the square. The modern one with large garage doors was the fire department. Beside it, a magnificent limestone-trimmed yellow brick Victorian building housed the police station.

Had Brent seen me from the police station, either a few moments before he called or earlier, when I was on my way to Frisky Pomegranate?

Maybe I shouldn't be surprised that he had questions for me.

Dep was waiting just inside the back door of our office in Deputy Donut. "You didn't want to be left behind, after all?" I asked her.

She yawned.

I went out to our display counter next to the kitchen. We still had a few orange marmalade–filled donuts. I put them into a bag, gathered Dep, armed the alarms, and locked up.

Carrying the bag in one hand and holding the end of Dep's leash in the other, I walked. Dep pranced and pounced.

We arrived at our cottage before Brent did. In the kitchen, I fed Dep and then formed six thick but not *too* thick patties from lean ground beef. I put a dollop of beautifully blue-veined Roquefort cheese on three of the patties, placed the remaining three patties on top of the first three patties, and squeezed the edges of all three double-thick patties together. "It's almost like one method of filling donuts," I informed Dep. She didn't pause her wrestling match with a catnip-stuffed fake-fur donut. I washed and dried my hands just in time to answer the door.

Despite the possible seriousness of his visit, Brent's smile was friendly. "Hey, Em. Thanks for letting me invite myself over." He was wearing black chinos, a black polo shirt, and a black blazer. He looked dangerous. In a good way.

Often when he wasn't on duty, we shared a quick hug.

If he was here to ask questions, he was on duty. . . .

I avoided the awkward moment by skirting around him and closing the front door. "It's better than being questioned at the station." I tried to make it clear that my serious tone was phony.

"I was going to do that if you didn't invite me to dinner," he teased.

I droned in a dramatically ominous voice suitable for a TV announcer reading the day's worst news stories, "Extortion and corruption in our local police force." I cocked my head toward the back of the house and said in my normal voice, "Come on back to the kitchen."

"Where's Dep?" Brent was one of my cat's very favorite people, and only one thing would keep her from rushing to him the moment he arrived.

"She has a catnip toy."

She was lying on her back on the kitchen floor and holding the fuzzy donut with both front paws. Her face was somewhere behind the donut.

"Hey, Dep," Brent said.

Dep let go of the donut and stretched out invitingly on one side. Still in her catnip-fueled world, she didn't look at us.

Brent got down on one knee beside her. She flipped up onto her feet and batted the fuzzy donut into the sunroom. Her tail up and all four feet skidding in more directions than seemed possible, she bounced across the kitchen and into the sunroom after the toy.

Laughing, Brent stood. "How can I help with dinner?"

"Light the grill, please."

I watched him walk through the sunroom. It was one of Dep's favorite rooms. With windows on three sides and deep windowsills, it had inspired Tom's and my design of the office at Deputy Donut. A comfy couch against the wall separating the sunroom from the kitchen, a rocking chair, a coffee table, and bookshelves underneath some of those windowsills made the room a perfect place to relax. Because the windows looked out into my paradise of a yard, the view was fabulous. Dep thought so, too.

Brent opened the back door. Dep actually left her catnip donut and went outside with him. I didn't worry. My yard was surrounded by a high wall constructed of smooth bricks. When she was a tiny kitten, Dep had learned not to try to climb the wall or trees and shrubs. After falling a couple of times while trying to run forward down trees, she'd gotten stuck—or so she thought—clinging partway down a trunk. She had meowed piteously until Alec fetched a ladder and rescued her. After that, she had not attempted to scale walls, trees, or bushes with flimsy branches that sagged almost to the ground when she put her insubstantial weight on them.

I took the plate of burgers and buns outside to the patio.

Standing beside the grill, Brent was watching Dep. My funny feline was hunkered down, staring into a shaded cave between drooping forsythia branches in the back of the yard. She undoubtedly thought she was a lion, at the very least.

Brent turned and faced me. A smile lit those gray eyes, and I was struck again with how caring he was. *Like Alec had been.* Quickly brushing that thought aside, I made an inane comment about needing to fetch the rest of our dinner and then asked him, "Is eating outside okay?"

"It's fine."

Still slightly off balance because of unthinkingly comparing Brent to Alec, I copied Tom's usual joke about Brent's last name. "Fine, *Fyne.*"

Brent shook a long-handled spatula at me. "Watch it, Westhill." He was smiling but watchful.

Suspecting that he could detect from my expression that a sudden memory of Alec had jolted me, I fled into the kitchen. I loaded a tray with two place mats, two glasses of freshly squeezed lemonade, and a plate of lettuce leaves and slices of tomatoes, dill pickles, and onions. I took the tray outside. Brent appeared to be concentrating on the yummy aromas coming from the grill.

My final trip to the kitchen was for plates, napkins, cutlery, mustard, ketchup, relish, and a bowl of carrot and celery sticks. By the time I arranged everything on the table, the burgers were cooked and the buns were toasted.

We sat down. As usual, Brent had grilled the meat perfectly. After a few delicious bites, I reminded him that he'd said he wanted me to answer questions.

He glanced toward the brick wall surrounding the yard and said quietly, "When we're inside."

Chapter 10

❧

Later, after Brent had accepted my offer of coffee and we were sitting at the granite-topped island in my kitchen where we often ate when he was my only visitor—the table in the dining room might make a meal feel too much like a date—he polished off a donut and then took out his notebook. "Em, I don't suspect you of anything—"

"Phew."

Smiling back at me, he asked, "Can you tell me why you threw out a bag from Deputy Donut after I talked to you last night?"

"I'd brought donuts in it, but they were gone, and that paper bag was jammed inside my pocket while you were talking to me after the fireworks." Realizing how it sounded, I quickly added, "The donuts around that firework did not come from that bag. But I did wipe my hand on that bag after it got jelly on it from one of the donuts that exploded, so I apologize to anyone who handled that bag. It was probably sticky."

Without looking at me, Brent wrote in his notebook.

Explaining why I'd taken donuts with me that evening could be slightly embarrassing. Brent knew that Misty, Samantha, Scott, and Hooligan had all been at the fireworks, but it was possible that no one had told him that we'd arranged beforehand to sit together and share snacks.

Brent was also a friend, and I hadn't included him. I'd had what seemed to me a perfectly good reason. Brent and I were not, no matter what Misty and Samantha might dream up, a couple. During the almost two years since Brent and I had begun to discover that we could be friends again, I had never invited Brent anywhere except to come play with Dep—when Dep wasn't occupied with a catnip toy—and have a quick dinner, usually followed by donuts. He never stayed long. And he never invited me anywhere, either. He took his turn feeding us, bringing takeout, steaks, or even a meal he'd cooked in his own home. I hadn't been inside Brent's house since before Alec's death, back in the days when we used to get together with Brent and whatever woman he was dating at the moment. Maybe Brent was as determined as I was to keep his and my relationship casual.

But that didn't mean he couldn't feel left out when I got together with people he knew, and I had certainly not set out to exclude him.

He paged back and forth in his notebook as if he thought I hadn't quite told him the whole story and he was waiting for me to blurt out more. Many of the people he questioned probably found his silence intimidating. So they talked.

And I did, too. I confessed, "I took donuts to the fireworks to share with Misty, Scott, Samantha, and Hooligan. I was doing a little matchmaking."

Brent looked up at me then, and something like surprise crossed his features before the detective stone-faced expression took over again. "Matchmaking?"

"I think it's working with Samantha and Hooligan. And Misty really likes Scott, so that's half of that battle." I gave him a thumbs-up.

A slight softening appeared momentarily in the stony face. "You're trying to throw Scott and *Misty* together?"

"They'd be perfect for each other, don't you think?"

His eyes inscrutable, he studied my face until the backs of my ears heated and I decided it was time to stare at my oversized fridge, which, cool as it might be, did not help me control the heat creeping around my scalp and flushing my face.

A couple of times, including the night before, emotionally fraught life-or-death emergencies had thrown Scott and me into temporary closeness, and then Brent had arrived to investigate. He had to have noticed that Scott and I were being more than usually attentive to each other. Scott and I were good friends, and we'd mostly been concerned about each other's safety.

Scott was a firefighter. Worrying about other people was part of his training. It was also part of his personality, which was probably why he'd gone into that dangerous profession in the first place. And Misty was the same. They cared.

Had Brent thought I was romantically interested in Scott? Brent had to know that I didn't want to date. I was sure that Scott understood that. Brent and Scott were kind men who looked out for other people, which sometimes included me. I hoped I reciprocated.

"I . . ." Brent began. He stared toward the fridge as if wondering what I'd found so interesting about it only moments before. "I hadn't thought about whether or not Scott and Misty might be perfect for each other."

An idea teased at the side of my brain. Until about a year and a half ago, Brent had dated a series of different women, all of them tall like Misty. I hadn't heard of him dating anyone recently. Had he been biding his time, hoping that Misty would return his interest? Maybe I'd just dashed his hopes.

I couldn't tell myself that it was none of my business. If I wanted to matchmake—and, apparently, I did—I had to believe that the romantic notions of my friends *were* my business.

Thinking about Brent's original question, I frowned. "How do you know I was the one who threw out the bag?" When I'd left him and started toward my car, Brent had been talking to the police photographer and, as far as I knew, had not been facing me. Had the police photographer watched me walk away and throw out the bag?

Brent gave me another of his assessing, policeman-like looks, the kind that often meant he wasn't going to respond to my questions. This time, though, he did, with very few words and a lack of facial expression. "You were seen."

If Brent had seen me toss the bag in the trash can, he would have said, *I saw you,* not, *You were seen.* I asked, "Who saw me?"

Brent continued examining my face but didn't answer.

I ran a finger along the smooth granite countertop. "I think I know, and it goes with what I called you about. Shortly after I threw out that bag, a photographer who had been taking pictures of the festivities all day claimed he saw me light the firework. He couldn't have, because I didn't. I told him to go find police officers at the scene and tell you his accusations, and I also said he should give you pictures of me lighting it, of *whoever* he saw lighting it."

Maybe I was being too adamant. I thought I saw Brent's lips twitch. I asked less forcefully, "Did he give you photos?"

"Only a description."

"That figures."

Brent didn't acknowledge my comment. Instead, he paged back in his notebook. "I saw you last night, but can you refresh my memory? What were you wearing?"

"Navy blue pants, a red and white striped blouse, a red cardigan, and red sneakers. By the time you arrived, I had a green and brown plaid blanket wrapped around my shoulders. I took that off only moments before I threw out the bag. The blanket was Hooligan's, so I left it on the cruiser that he and Misty were using." *And I hope it wasn't terribly sticky. . . .*

"Navy blue pants?" Brent repeated. "Jeans?"

"No. Just plain, regular pants. Like khakis, but not khaki."

"Did you carry a bag?"

"Only my usual backpack. And when I arrived at the fairgrounds, I was carrying that paper bag of a dozen donuts, in my hand, not in my backpack."

"Would they have fit?"

"Not without crushing them. A half dozen would have, though. Plus a birthday candle. But I wasn't the one who brought the birthday boy's stack of donuts to the fireworks."

In past years, Brent had interrogated me about other cases. I should have been used to the way he looked and acted when he was on duty, but this time his constant examination of my face was disconcerting. To give myself something to look at besides his questioning expression, I eased off my stool and topped up his coffee without asking if he wanted more. "Yesterday was Independence Day, and many people were dressed more or less alike in blue pants or jeans and red and white tops. I'm short. So is Jocelyn, not that she would ever hurt anyone. Gabrielle, the woman who was the duchess for yesterday's festivities, is, too. Last night, all three of us were wearing blue pants and red tops. We all have dark hair. Both of them had pinned their hair up, and their long hair could have looked short in the dark. I'm the only one with lots of curls, though." Disordered ones, most of the time.

His gaze rested on those disordered curls, and I thought I caught another glimpse of warmth in those enigmatic gray eyes. "Were you wearing anything on your head last night, Em?"

"No."

"Before I got there?"

"No."

"Not a hood?"

"No, but as the evening became chilly, I wished I'd brought a hoodie. I didn't notice if Jocelyn's and Gabrielle's tops had hoods. If they did, the hoods were not covering their hair, at least when they were walking toward the cars shortly before the end of the fireworks."

Brent glanced at my hair again as if to confirm that it really was very dark brown, and then he wrote in his notebook.

On the floor, Dep pursued a jingly ball that kept mysteriously rolling away from her.

I asked, "Did the photographer say I was wearing blue jeans and a hood? That the person he saw lighting the skyrocket was wearing them?"

"We're not sure what he saw. We're not sure he's sure."

"I'm sure he's *not* sure. But I can think of a reason for him to pretend he is."

Brent's stare into my eyes was almost painfully intense. "What is it?"

This time, I managed not to look away. "He's protecting the person who lit the firework, maybe a short friend in jeans and a red hoodie. Or maybe he's making up stories to protect himself, which I find much more likely than that he saw anyone else light it."

Brent asked softly, "Are you angry?"

Dep meowed and jumped up onto my lap.

"Of course I'm angry." Stroking Dep was calming me, however. "Not at you. That photographer came out of nowhere. The first thing yesterday morning, he was taking pictures inside Deputy Donut, and then he kept showing up, and this will sound self-centered, but he often aimed his camera at me. I have no idea why a complete stranger would have singled me out that way. And someone, I don't know if it's the same photographer, took a picture that's on the front page of today's *Fallingbrook News*. It shows Misty in uniform, and she's holding my wrist. She was checking my pulse, but from her serious expression, anyone looking at the picture might think she was arresting me. And I had a feeling that the picture was published to *encourage* people to think that."

"I haven't seen that paper, but I understand why a picture like that could worry you."

"Thanks. I have the paper at work."

"Can you save it for me in case I don't find a copy?"

"Okay." Holding Dep against my heart, I told Brent about

Jocelyn making herself scarce whenever the photographer appeared. "She seemed frightened of him when he first showed
up yesterday morning."

Brent had started closing his notebook. He opened it.
"Any idea why?"

"She wouldn't say. She claimed that she didn't know him
and didn't know his name. I'm guessing he's the photographer credited in the article in today's *Fallingbrook News,*
Philip Landsdowner."

"That's the man who claims he saw you throw out the
bag." Brent pocketed his notebook, gulped down his coffee,
and stood. "I'm sorry. I'd like to talk longer . . ." He paused,
glanced toward my mop of curls again, and added quickly,
"About your impressions of this Landsdowner, but I'll have
to go back to the office to hear what other investigators have
learned, and tell them what you've told me." Dep jumped
down to the floor.

I walked Brent to the front door. Mewing, Dep came
along.

Beside the closed door, Brent placed both hands on my
shoulders. He stared into my eyes for a burning second until
I had to look past him at the blank door. "Be careful, Em,"
he said quietly. "Especially around Landsdowner if he shows
up again." His hands dropped to my upper arms. He held
them with a firm grip.

Staring down at Dep doing figure eights around our ankles, I nodded. "Okay," I said in case he didn't see the nod.

"And call if you need help. Any time of the night or day,
okay?"

"Okay. Or if I think of or learn anything else."

"You know the drill."

The slight smile in his voice encouraged me to risk looking
up at him again. "Yes."

He unnerved me with another quick detective-like assess-
ment, and then he gave my arms a quick squeeze and let go.

Suddenly all business, he turned and reached for the door knob. "Lock up."

He nearly always said that. I agreed. He left. I locked the door.

"Meow," Dep said.

I picked her up and carried her to the kitchen. Mechanically, I tidied up.

Something in Brent's and my relationship had gone off kilter, and I wasn't sure what I thought about the change. He was always observant, but several times that night he'd spent longer moments than usual studying my face.

The subtle shift had begun shortly after I'd mentioned that I was trying to throw Scott and Misty together. I'd toyed with the idea that Brent was interested in Misty, but I wasn't certain that was it.

Had Brent believed that I was actually considering dating Scott, and when he found out that I wasn't, had he wondered if I wanted to date him? *Brent?*

And did I?

I closed the dishwasher with more force than I meant to. "It was your imagination," I informed Dep. "There were no sparks flying between Brent and me, not when he asked me about matchmaking, not when he stared at me for longer than usual, not when I stared back, and not right before he left, when, if he'd hugged me, I would have hugged him back, maybe more warmly than ever before." Why was my face heating when there was no one with me besides Dep?

"Meow," she said.

"Now that he knows I'm not interested in dating Scott, why would he think I might want to date anyone?"

"Mew."

"I don't, you know. I might never want to."

Dep licked a shoulder.

I explained, "Since Brent and I reestablished our friendship, we've been casually affectionate with each other, just like we were when Alec was still around and we were all good friends. That's all it was tonight. Nothing has changed. I'm just tired and overwrought."

Dep stopped smoothing her fur. Leaving the tip of her tongue sticking out, she gave me a goofy, wide-pupiled stare for a second, and then she licked her shoulder again, faster.

I added, "Besides, if we're going to think about Brent, we should ponder what we might know or could learn that would help him figure out who intentionally harmed Taylor."

"Meow."

"Because it certainly was not me."

Dep mewed again and stood up with her front paws just barely touching my shins. I picked her up, carried her to the wing chair in the living room, and opened the book I'd left beside the chair. She purred on my lap. Both of us probably stopped thinking about Brent.

Probably.

I definitely stopped thinking about him and his investigation later, after I finally fell asleep.

Chapter 11

The Knitpickers did not usually get together in Deputy Donut on weekends, so I was surprised the next morning, Saturday, when Cheryl and Virginia came in. Catching my eye, Virginia laid a folded newspaper on the table.

Before I could open my mouth to ask what I could get them, Virginia told me, "You're all over the newspaper today, Emily."

I couldn't help sighing.

I didn't want to look at the paper, but Virginia stabbed her finger down onto it. "You're famous!"

Great. "For making delicious donuts, I hope."

She glanced at me out of the corner of her eye. "That's partly it."

She unfolded the newspaper to show me the Saturday feature, a pictorial essay that filled the paper's center two pages. The headline was FALLINGBROOK'S FABULOUS FOURTH FESTIVITIES. Cheryl inched her chair closer to Virginia's.

I quickly skipped to the bottom of the page. Philip Landsdowner was credited for all of the photos.

"You're not in *every* photo, Emily," Cheryl told me.

I grinned at her. "You don't have to apologize."

Smiling back, she flapped her hand at me. "Oh, *you!*"

The photo in the top left corner was taken in Deputy Donut before the parade. It showed Tom and me pretending to glare while pointing at each other. Our fingers were blurred, making it obvious that we were shaking them.

Cheryl quipped, "That's the first time I ever saw Chief Westhill actually threaten you, Emily."

"We were only teasing each other."

Cheryl's white curls bobbed when she laughed. "We figured. But you look about to punch him in the nose."

"Never." I bent forward for a better look. "Something's wrong with that picture." Seconds after it was taken, Jocelyn had fled to the storeroom, but when Tom and I were shaking our fingers at each other and heard those first clicks and whirrs, Jocelyn had been close to Tom and me.

Jocelyn was not in the picture.

I knew the layout of our shop perfectly, knew how it looked from every angle, but I still had to go check. I took Cheryl's and Virginia's orders and told them I'd be right back.

Careful not to plow into customers, tables, or chairs, I hurried to the serving counter and paused for a second where Philip Landsdowner had been when he took the picture.

No wonder it had looked wrong. Landsdowner—or someone—had cut Jocelyn out of the center of the picture and had also cut out the espresso machine behind her. Then the person who had edited the picture had pasted a section of blank wall in the space where Jocelyn and the espresso machine had been.

I returned to Cheryl and Virginia. Pouring the day's special coffee, an almost chocolaty full-bodied medium roast from Sumatra, into their mugs, I told them that the photographer had removed the espresso machine from the picture. I didn't think it was necessary to tell them that he had also removed Jocelyn.

"Artistic license," Virginia concluded. "With your espresso machine in the photo, the background would have been too busy. A plain background shows you and Tom better."

"And the way you two were about to trade punches." Cheryl wasn't letting that thought go, but she was smiling.

"Sure," I joked. I returned to the serving counter for the donuts that Cheryl and Virginia had consented to try, raised maple ones filled with medium Wisconsin cheddar.

As I gave them their plates, Virginia pointed at the next photo in the feature. "Where was that one taken?"

"At the parade-marshaling grounds out near the falls."

"Isn't that the woman who was crowned queen?" Cheryl asked. "The poor dear, may she rest in peace. What was she doing with a megaphone?"

I put Taylor in a better light than she'd put herself. "She was apologizing for being late."

"She looks like she's complaining about your donut car. Look at that scowl on her face. And you're scowling as much as she was." Imitating me in the picture, Cheryl made an angry face and folded her arms.

"I was perplexed. Until that moment, I'd never met anyone who didn't want to ride in, and preferably drive, our donut car."

"Well . . ." Virginia pointed at another picture. "In this one, you're driving your donut car, Emily, and you're still frowning."

"That's my *serious* expression. Driving is serious."

Cheryl nudged the paper with the blunt end of her purple aluminum knitting needle. "No wonder you thought you had to scowl like that. Who's that in the seat behind you, and why is he snarling?"

"That's Nicholas, Thursday's duke. The duchess, Gabrielle, was in the other rear seat, and Nicholas didn't seem to like what she was saying." None of the three of us in that car looked particularly happy. Outsiders glancing at the photos might conclude that the Fallingbrook Fabulous Fourth Festivities had begun with everyone grumping at everyone else.

Cheryl bit into her donut. "Yum, try your donut, Virginia. I wasn't sure about mixing cheese with maple, but that surprising little bite of cheese inside is buttery and delicious."

Virginia took a small bite, and then another. "This might

be my new favorite. You could even add some crispy bits of bacon."

"That sounds good." I glanced toward Tom and Jocelyn, decorating donuts and chatting to each other at the work-table in the kitchen. "We'll have to try it."

Cheryl aimed a knitting needle at another photo. It showed Queen Taylor and King Ian riding on top of the back seat of Taylor's convertible. Ian was frowning or squinting in the bright sunshine. Waving at flag-bearing parade watchers, Taylor was smiling. "It's quite plain why that poor dear queen didn't want to ride in your donut car," Cheryl concluded. "No offense to your car, but it's not a convertible. Royalty needs to see and be seen."

Luckily, *I* wasn't being seen in all of the pictures. Besides the one of Taylor and Ian in Taylor's convertible, there was a photo of the high school band on their float, one of serious-faced bagpipers with their cheeks puffed out, and two pic-tures of cute kids sitting on curbs, their eyes huge as they watched the parade.

Other photos showed the picnic. Cheryl homed in on one of me in front of the table where Jocelyn and I had handed out donuts. I was wearing disposable food handlers' gloves and holding a stack of jelly-filled donuts in both hands. "Carrying donuts is apparently as serious as driving," Cheryl joked. "Look at that frown!"

I argued, "I wasn't frowning."

"You're not smiling."

I informed her with my best fake haughty expression, "I was concentrating on not dropping any donuts."

Virginia tilted her head and stared hard at the photo. "Where was that taken?"

I saw why she wondered. This picture had also been strangely edited. "At the table we were assigned for the picnic." I pointed toward Deputy Donut's northern wall. "It was on the east side of the village square."

She asked, "How did the police station get behind you?"
Cheryl retorted, "Someone picked it up and moved it."

"Not physically," I said, "but the photographer must have
cut the actual background out of that picture, too. It should
be grass and bunting-wrapped trees, with bouncy castles beyond them, not the police station."

Virginia pushed her glasses up her nose. "So, this time, the
photographer inserted a background that was almost as busy
as the original, maybe busier. He must have had a reason, but
I can't understand it. I wouldn't call it artistic license. *Non*-
artistic license would be more like it. The only thing I can
think of is that the photographer or the newspaper wanted to
make it clear that the picnic was in Fallingbrook. Our his-
toric police building is famous all around here."

When I'd been holding that stack of donuts, Jocelyn had
been beside me. Once again, she'd been completely removed
from a photo and replaced by a backdrop that didn't belong
there. Both times, only seconds after the pictures were taken
she had abruptly removed herself from the vicinity of Philip
Landsdowner and his camera.

Virginia pointed at a picture of a man blowing up long,
skinny balloons and twisting them into animals, flowers, and
tiaras. "Look. Here's the police station where it belongs. You
can tell from the angle of the sunlight and the shadows on the
porch that the police station was copied from this picture
and inserted in the one of you and your stack of donuts."

I pointed at the credit at the bottom of the page and asked
if either of the women knew Philip Landsdowner.

Neither of them remembered having heard of him. "Except
he took the pictures that were in yesterday's newspaper," Virginia said.

Photos of the fireworks were on the bottom half of the article's right page.

I didn't tell Cheryl and Virginia that Queen Taylor, before
she was injured, was the blonde behind the scraggly bush in

one photo. Duke Nicholas's arm was around her, where I'd seen it after the fatal skyrocket was lit and before it exploded. I didn't think the stack of donuts was in this photo. It was possible, but not likely, that it was eclipsed by the gnarled trunk of the shrub. The picture had probably been taken early during the fireworks display. No one was walking uphill toward their cars.

Cheryl pointed at the photo. "Look, Emily, here you are again! That photographer must like you!"

Or not. I didn't say it.

Just uphill from Taylor and to her left, I was sitting with my backpack beside me and the empty paper bag on my outstretched legs. My hands were behind me, bracing me, and my face was tilted up toward blazing starbursts in the sky. I hadn't yet gone to the car to fetch my sweater.

"Don't tell me you went to the fireworks by yourself!" Cheryl's kind face crinkled with something resembling pain.

"I didn't." It did look like I was alone on one end of the plaid blanket, however. "My friends were to my left." Maybe I was worrying too much, but I wondered if Landsdowner had zoomed in and cropped the picture to show that I was seated relatively close to Nicholas and Taylor on that crowded hill. Although my expression couldn't be seen in this picture, other photos in the pictorial essay could be seen as evidence that I'd been in a bad mood most of the day. Maybe Landsdowner wanted to imply that, at the end of the evening, my supposed bad mood had erupted into a horrific act.

Cheryl said, "Look at this last picture. Her face doesn't show, but isn't that your friend, the police officer who comes in here, the one you said was checking your pulse in yesterday's picture?"

"Yes, that's Misty." She was holding my wrist.

"This picture is a lot like yesterday's. In both of them, your friend looks like she's arresting you, but in this one, more of your face shows. And you look angry?" Cheryl's tone rose, making that last comment a question.

This had to be the second picture that Landsdowner had taken while Misty was checking my pulse. I had turned toward where the first flash had been, but Misty had regained my attention and I hadn't seen the photographer. However, most of the right side of my face was in this photo, enough for Cheryl to understand my expression. I confessed, "I knew that the queen and her boyfriend had been injured. I was upset."

"Understandable," Virginia said. "You could have been shocked, too."

"Or scared," Cheryl contributed.

I admitted that I was probably feeling all of those emotions and maybe a few more, besides.

Their faces solemn about the death of the young beauty queen, Cheryl and Virginia nodded.

More customers came in, and I had to excuse myself. Cheryl and Virginia finished their donuts and coffee, waved at the three of us in the kitchen, and went outside into the brilliant July sunshine. Again, Cheryl left her newspaper behind. I put it on the desk in the office with the one from the day before. Dep sat up straight on the couch and eyed the papers.

"Go ahead and sleep on the growing pile of newspapers if you want to, Dep."

"Mew."

"You're welcome." I eased out of the office.

Wondering if Brent had found a copy of yesterday's paper and if I should tell him about the pictorial feature in today's, I shut the office door and went back to the dining area.

Customers kept Tom, Jocelyn, and me racing around all afternoon. After we tidied for the day, Jocelyn left on her bike.

I showed Tom the pictures in the two newspapers where Jocelyn had been replaced by backgrounds that didn't belong there.

Tom asked, "Does Jocelyn know the photographer who was in here?"

"She says not."

"I wonder." Tom waved goodbye and headed outside.

My phone rang. It was Brent. He asked, "Can you come to my office?" He sounded impersonal, the way he often did when he was with colleagues. "We have questions for you."

Chapter 12

❦

We? Brent's office?

I'd been in the lobby of the police station several times since Alec's death, but the last time I'd been inside Brent's actual office was when Alec and Brent shared it. "Sure." I sounded anything but sure.

I wasn't worried about questions that Brent—and who knew how many other police officers—wanted to ask me. I was afraid that if I went into Alec's former office, memories would bubble up and I might become weepy.

Brent asked, "Where are you? Want me to pick you up?"

"I'm at work. I'll walk. I still have to lock up here. I should be there in about ten minutes." *That might give me time to partition off my rawest grief and keep it contained. . . .*

I disconnected the call and apologized to Dep. "I shouldn't be long." I tried to sound upbeat. "Unless someone decides to arrest me."

Dep scooted up a kitty-width stairway and peered down at me from a catwalk.

"You're right," I told her. "There's no reason for anyone to arrest me." But usually, if Brent wanted to ask me questions about one of his cases, he visited Dep and me at Deputy Donut or, more often, at home. Why the formality this time? And who did he mean by *we?*

I went out to the back stoop and locked the office door. It

was a lovely, warm evening. The summer solstice had been less than three weeks before, and at a quarter to six in the evening, the sun was high. Chin up, I strode down the alley to Wisconsin Street. *I can go into the office where I used to see Alec. I can.*

As I had the night before on my way to Frisky Pomegranate's Happy Hour, I turned left and started north toward the village square. Chatting with one another, turning to peer into windows, cheerful pedestrians meandered along sidewalks.

I can do this. . . .

In front of Deputy Donut, two women I'd never seen before were strolling toward me. As we passed, one of them said to the other, "I hear they make the best donuts in Wisconsin."

The women were already behind me. I smiled, anyway. I was wearing my summer uniform of white polo shirt and knee-length black shorts, but there was no logo on my shirt and I'd left my hat and apron in Deputy Donut, so unless someone recognized the shirt and shorts, they wouldn't know I worked in Deputy Donut. *The best donuts in Wisconsin.* I'd have to tell Tom. Brent might get a kick out of hearing it, too, if we were merely going to meet at my place, where he could play with Dep.

I can be inside Alec's former office without melting into a puddle of grief.

I crossed Wisconsin Street, passed the Fireplug Pub, and turned right on the road bordering the south end of the village square. The square was now a beautifully calm green space with sunlight slanting between the leaves of tall trees onto neatly clipped lawns bordered by colorful flower beds. The reviewing stand had been removed. I remembered Queen Taylor sitting up there, wearing her cardboard crown and smiling and waving at her fans.

That poignant memory reminded me that I wasn't the only

person in and around Fallingbrook mourning the loss of a loved one. Taylor's friends and family had to be in shock from her sudden death.

I would never stop missing Alec, but I had become accustomed to some of the pain. Still, I couldn't help slowing. I was in front of the fire department and almost at the police station. I forced myself to keep going. *I can do this.*

I could.

Brent was ahead, waiting for me up a flight of stairs on the police department's wide stone-floored veranda. Setting my feet carefully on the worn, century-old limestone steps, I climbed toward him. *When Alec wasn't using one of the back entrances, he climbed these very steps, fit the soles of his boots and shoes into these very indentations.*

Brent looked detective-like in a navy blue suit, a white shirt, and a blue tie with small green figures on it. "Hey, Em." We shook hands. Maybe the tie wasn't as detective-like as I'd originally thought. The small green figures were turtles. Some of my apprehension evaporated, and I couldn't help grinning.

Brent opened a massive oak door and let me precede him inside. In the lobby, he cupped my elbow in one gentle hand. "I said my office, but we're actually going to a meeting room."

"Thank you." The soaring ceiling made me feel small, and my voice came out barely above a whisper. Trying to keep my sandals from clacking on the terrazzo floor, I thought of something that might be worse than having to enter Alec's old office. "Are we going to an interview room?"

"Not one that we take hardened criminals to."

"Oh." I paused. "Good." Another pause. "I guess."

He squeezed my elbow. "Don't worry."

He guided me down a hallway that was painted the same institutional pale yellow as the lobby and floored with the same yellow, green, and gray terrazzo. The hallway ceiling had been lowered and paneled with acoustical tiles, but it was still high. All of the doors were honey-colored oak with pebbled and frosted glass windows in their upper halves.

Brent opened one of the doors. Dropping his hand from my elbow and touching my back gently, he again let me go in first.

The room was carpeted in serviceable gray and furnished almost like a living room. Couches and chairs were uphol-stered in tweedy grays and yellow faux leather. The side and coffee tables were low. A kitchenette, with a sink, a pint-sized fridge, and a coffeemaker, was in one corner. The cabinets were painted dull gold to match the walls. Gray and gold mugs were upside down on a yellow gingham tea towel on the gray laminate counter. The room's only window looked out over the parking lot behind the building. I recognized some of northern Wisconsin's waterfalls in photos hanging on the walls.

I suspected that there was at least one hidden camera, but I didn't have time to search for it. A man I'd never seen be-fore had been almost hidden in a gray wing chair with its back to the door. He stood, turned around, and greeted us.

His brown suit, careful grooming, and the way one pant leg hiked up slightly as if distorted by an ankle holster marked him as a detective. He wasn't as tall as Brent, but he was wiry, with dark, intelligent eyes and brown hair touched by gray at the temples. Brent introduced him as Agent Rex Clobar from the Wisconsin Division of Criminal Investiga-tion.

Detective Clobar shook my hand. "Call me Rex," he said.

Without Brent's steadying hand at my elbow or his light touch at my back, I felt slightly wobbly. *Buck up, Emily,* I told myself.

Rex gestured toward a sheeny yellow couch on the other side of a coffee table from him. "Have a seat. Would you like a coffee?"

I eased onto the couch. "No, thanks." The air-conditioning

in the building must have been set to keep police officers in bulletproof vests and detectives in suits comfortable. The faux leather felt clammy against the backs of my knees and calves, and I missed the long pants we wore at Deputy Donut on cooler days.

Brent sat on the opposite end of my couch and waited for the other detective to speak. When the DCI helped the Fallingbrook Police Department with an investigation, Fallingbrook police officers, including detectives, reported to the DCI detective. Although I knew that the DCI could call on more resources more quickly than local police forces could, the system never made complete sense to me. Brent had solved a couple of earlier Fallingbrook murders despite interference from a rather inept DCI detective. Once again, an investigation was probably losing a couple of days while Brent and his team reviewed the crime with the DCI detective and showed him the evidence they'd already collected.

Trying to look interested and cooperative, I took a deep breath.

Rex removed a folder from the coffee table. "I believe that Brent has already told you that, at the Fallingbrook Fairgrounds, you were seen throwing out a bag from your donut shop."

I was sure that goose bumps were popping out all over my body. "Yes, he did."

"Can you describe that bag?" His expression matched his stern chin.

"It was white paper, slightly sticky after I wiped blueberry jelly on it, and about ten by twelve inches." Squinting, I reconsidered. "Probably larger than that. It was big enough to hold a dozen jelly-filled donuts without squashing them. The logo for our café, Deputy Donut, was printed on it."

Rex smiled. People, especially police people, tended to smile when they heard the name of our donut shop.

I offered, "I can show you bags exactly like it at our shop if you want to come over."

"That won't be necessary," Rex said, probably because in-vestigators had picked up everything from the trash cans at that parking lot and he had seen the actual bag I'd thrown out. He added, "Can you tell me exactly where you put the bag you just described?"

"I put it in the first trash can I came to, near where Brent parked his unmarked car that night, close to the northeast corner of the lot."

Brent nodded.

Rex asked, "And you drove to the fireworks that night. Can you describe your vehicle?"

I did and then added, "You can come over to Deputy Donut and have a look at it."

"That won't be necessary, either. Can you describe where you parked that car that night?"

Still trying not to shiver, I inched forward on the cold couch. "It was closer to the northwest corner of that same lot, a few spaces south of the actual corner."

Rex shot a quick glance at Brent.

"That's where I saw it when I drove into the parking lot," Brent confirmed. "She left before I finished at the scene that night."

Rex took a photo out of the folder and held it for me to see. It showed a wrinkled, flattened white paper bag on a black table. "Do you recognize this?"

"It's a bag from Deputy Donut."

"Do you remember where you tossed this bag out?"

Confused, I shook my head. "I don't remember throwing one like that out recently. The one I threw out in the parking lot at the fairgrounds was larger."

"How can you be sure?" Rex asked. "It had been wadded up. We straightened it for this photo, but the creases in it probably make it look smaller than its original size."

"Our logo is the same size on all of the bags. I can tell by the proportion of the logo to the bag that the bag is one of the ones we use for a maximum of eight jelly-filled donuts.

Besides, the bag I threw out at the fairgrounds must have at least some blueberry jelly on it, and if there's any jelly on that bag, it's on the other side."

"Maybe I can jog your memory." Rex spoke with an encouraging good-cop voice, but the kindness didn't reach his rather piercing eyes. In this situation, he would probably expect Brent to play the good cop. "You were seen throwing *this* bag"—he tapped the photo of the small bag—"into a trash can beside your car."

Chapter 13

Mystified, I could barely speak. "That's impossible," I finally managed. "I didn't take that size of bag to the fairgrounds. I couldn't have thrown it out there."

Rex suggested, "Maybe you saw it lying on the ground and didn't want one of your bags littering, so you picked it up and threw it out and didn't really notice what you were doing? That evening must have been stressful. You might have forgotten some of the things you did."

I was not about to allow him to cajole me into making false confessions. "I didn't even *see* a bag like that at the fireworks display. If someone threw out one of those smaller bags, it wasn't me."

Rex didn't seem convinced. He pulled another photo from his folder. "Can you tell me what's in this picture?"

"Besides a section of a ruler?"

"Yes."

"It looks like one of the blue sugar stars that we put on some of the donuts we gave away at the picnic. And are those donut crumbs beside it?"

"Seems so," he answered.

"And those thin red strips would be pieces of the red icing stripes that began the day on our raspberry jelly–filled donuts."

Rex informed me, "The star, the crumbs, and the red icing

were found inside the bag that you said you did not possess on Thursday evening at the fireworks."

"I didn't," I repeated. I leaned forward. "I'm guessing that the person who brought that bag to the fireworks also brought jelly-filled donuts and inserted the homemade skyrocket into them before lighting it."

Rex asked in a dangerously mild tone, "What makes you think that the firework was inside a stack of jelly-filled donuts?"

"It was obvious. For one thing, when the homemade skyrocket went off, it shot a sugar star into my hair and blueberry jelly onto my face."

"You were close," Rex stated.

I touched my cheek where something had bounced off and stung it. "Yes."

"For argument's sake," Rex pointed out, "the sugar star and blueberry jelly could have transferred to you when you were handling the donuts earlier that evening."

"That didn't happen." I wasn't sure how I could prove it, but I explained, "I'm almost certain that other people in the vicinity were hit by flying donut parts. I saw pieces of donut in the grass around the split and blackened remains of the skyrocket. And I suspected that a stack of donuts had hidden that tube because I saw the remains of a jelly-filled donut, one with white icing striped in red, at the base of the tube after it went off. But most of all, I caught a glimpse of the entire contraption after the fuse was lit. Flames were shooting out the top. I couldn't see the thing well because it was behind a bush, but it looked like the stack of donuts I'd given to a family." I told him about the birthday boy and described the "cake" that resembled a skyrocket. "But those flames weren't coming from a birthday candle." I also explained that we'd used up our entire supply of dark blue sugar star sprinkles on donuts we'd given away at the picnic and that we hadn't made other donuts decorated with stars like that for several months. I added, "I know for certain that we gave two other bags that size to people at the picnic. I'll ask Jocelyn if we used more bags that size on the Fourth."

"We'll check with Jocelyn," Rex said. "I know you've already gone over all of this with Brent, but can you refresh my memory about who you gave the other two bags to?"

I held up one finger. "One went to the deceased, with only one donut in it, and that one was decorated with dark blue sugar stars. She very likely didn't aim a firework at herself and light it, but she could have given that donut and the bag to someone else, like her boyfriend, Nicholas, whose hand had been close to where the lighter ended up." I held up another finger. "Another bag, also containing only one star-decorated donut, went to Gabrielle, who was the duchess on the Fourth. The two women were supposedly best friends, but they didn't speak about each other the way best friends usually do."

Rex asked, "How did they speak about each other?"

"Nastily. Gabrielle was in my car in the parade the morning of the Fourth. She seemed jealous of Taylor, who had made spiteful remarks about Gabrielle over a megaphone before the parade began."

Brent stopped scratching in his notebook. "Would either of the bags that you gave Taylor and her best friend have contained pieces of red icing, Emily?"

"It's possible that some came off one of the other donuts before or during the picnic. However, I definitely saw part of a red-striped donut at the base of that burnt-out firework."

Rex asked if I could tell him anything else about the birthday boy and his family.

"The smallest boy had his fifth birthday on the Fourth of July. All four kids were blond, but he was the blondest. There was a girl about nine, a boy about eight, another girl about six, and the boy who was turning five."

Rex looked at Brent.

"We'll try to find that family," Brent offered, "from birth records from five years ago."

For the sake of the officers who would be assigned that task, I hoped the blond boy had been born in or near Fallingbrook.

Rex showed me another photo.

Before he could ask if I recognized the object in it, I told him, "That dark blue birthday candle is either the one I stuck into the boy's stack of donuts or one just like it. It had been in the glove compartment of our 1950 Ford and must have gotten too warm and melted slightly. It was curved like the one in your photo. If it is the same one, it will have my fingerprints on it. My fingerprints should be on file from when I was a 911 dispatcher."

Rex set the picture down. "Okay, we've got pieces of donuts that you admit came from your shop, a bag that someone claims you threw out, and a candle that you admit probably has your fingerprints on it. It's fortunate that you have very loyal friends."

I had a feeling I was supposed to smile at this. I didn't.

Rex explained, "They all say, independently, that you would never knowingly harm anyone. And they're honest. Want to know how I know?"

Not really. Guessing he was about to tell me anyway, I shrugged.

"The four friends who attended the fireworks with you have told us that you left them after the fireworks display had been going for some time and returned to them a few minutes later, only moments before the firework behind Ms. Wishbard exploded. If they'd been trying to cover up your activities, they wouldn't have said that."

I objected. "None of those four would *ever* lie to cover a friend's activities. They spoke the truth. I did leave them for a few minutes. I went back to my car for my sweater."

"And that's all you did?"

"Yes." He didn't expect me to explain all the details of unlocking, opening, closing, and relocking car doors, did he?

"You didn't plant a lit firework behind the victim before returning to your friends?"

"Certainly not. Did they tell you which direction I came from when I returned?"

"From the hill above them, from the direction of the parking lot."

I just looked at him.

Apparently, I couldn't intimidate him with my calm stare. He pointed out, "That doesn't rule out your lighting the firework, going up the hill, and then returning."

I ran my fingers through my curls, undoubtedly messing them up. "How long *was* that fuse?"

"Different materials burn at different rates." Rex nodded toward Brent. "My colleague here says he's known you for a long time and he also does not believe you would knowingly harm anyone."

"I wouldn't."

Brent added, "And all four of your friends who were at the fireworks with you have confirmed that you weren't carrying anything besides your backpack and a bag of donuts when you arrived at the fireworks that night and that they ate all of those donuts. They also say you didn't have a sweater with you when you left them, but when you returned after a minute or two, you were wearing one. When I got there, you were wearing a red sweater. And your backpack, which you've already told me is big enough to hold the bag of six donuts plus the birthday candle."

I gave him a wan smile. "It is, but I didn't take the birthday boy's stack of donuts to the fireworks. Someone else did."

Brent nodded. Rex's expression was inscrutable.

Although I'd already told Brent about everyone I'd seen leaving the fireworks before the explosion, Rex had me describe them again. I pointed out that whoever injured Taylor might have gone down the hill afterward, not up to the parking lot. "There are other routes into and out of the fairgrounds."

Rex reminded me that the smaller Deputy Donut bag containing blue sugar stars, donut crumbs, bits of red icing, and a slightly melted birthday candle had been found in a trash can near my donut car in the parking lot. "It seems likely that whoever lit the firework that injured Ms. Wishbard did go up to the parking lot afterward."

I nodded. Thinking about Philip Landsdowner lurking in the parking lot after nearly everyone else had left for the night, I pointed out, "That bag could have been thrown into the can near where my car had been *after* I drove away. The person who fatally injured Taylor could have hung out on the hill looking innocent after he lit the fuse. He wouldn't have to have been among the people I saw leaving the fireworks when I was returning with my sweater."

"Granted," Rex said. "Are you positive that *you* did not throw out the bag in the photo, the one that you say is smaller than the one you admit to discarding?"

"Absolutely," I said firmly. "I'm guessing that the person who reported seeing me throw out that smaller bag also told you that he saw me light the firework. He couldn't have, because I didn't. Either he mistook someone else for me, or he's making things up." I glanced toward Brent. "I know I'm not the only person who was wearing blue pants and a red top on Thursday night. Probably about three-quarters of the people on that hill were dressed like that. And I'm betting that Philip Landsdowner, the man who claims he saw me light that firework and throw out that bag, also said I was wearing a hood. My red sweater doesn't have a hood."

Rex had perfected a stare that could make people doubt their own stories.

I had facts, sort of, to support mine. "There's a picture of me in yesterday's paper that was taken after the explosion. It shows me holding the larger paper bag before I scrunched it up and shoved it into my pocket. I had a blanket around my shoulders, so you might not be able to see that the sweater I was wearing didn't have a hood, but I was definitely not wearing a hood when the picture was taken."

Brent looked up from his notes. "I don't remember seeing a hood on her sweater that night."

I suggested, "If you haven't already, you should search the trash can that was closest to the unmarked cruiser that Brent parked in that lot. I put a larger bag than the one in your picture in that can. When I brought that larger bag, it did not contain any dark blue sugar stars. The donuts I brought to the fireworks to share with friends were decorated with tiny light blue sugar balls. Some of them might have fallen off into that larger bag."

Rex glanced at Brent but didn't confirm or deny that investigators had found that bag and that it had contained a tiny light blue ball or two and was maybe smeared with blueberry jelly.

I added, "If your forensics lab tests the smaller bag, the one that I did not take to or have at the fireworks, they might find traces of gunpowder or black powder or whatever was inside the thing that killed Taylor. But they won't find any in the larger bag, the one I brought and threw out near Brent's cruiser."

Rex asked me, "When the explosion occurred, had you already scrunched the bag you brought into your pocket?"

"No. Could traces of gunpowder or whatever have landed on that bag, on people's clothes, and in their hair during the explosion?"

Rex threw the question back at me. "What do you think?"

"I think it's possible."

Rex nodded.

I told him, "I have copies of the papers with pictures of the Fourth of July activities in it. They might show that my sweater didn't have a hood, and they might show that the bag I was holding was bigger than the one you found near the car I drove to the fireworks on the Fourth. You could come to Deputy Donut to see the pictures."

Rex said, "We have those newspapers."

"And I hope you have any other pictures that Philip Landsdowner took, including one of someone lighting that firework, because whoever it was, it wasn't me."

"We have this." Rex pulled another photo out of his folder.

The picture was clearly of me. I was standing immediately behind Taylor Wishbard at the fireworks, and I was holding a stack of jelly-filled donuts, carefully, using both hands.

A dark sticklike thing was poking out of the top donut, a sticklike thing that was also a *fuse*-like thing. . . .

Chapter 14

✼

I scooted forward on the faux leather for a better look at the photo Rex was holding. "I never stood right there behind Taylor before the explosion," I said. "And I did not carry a stack of donuts like that when I was at the fireworks." I glanced over at Brent.

His face was almost expressionless, but I thought I glimpsed a touch of warmth in the gray depths of his eyes.

I gave Detective Rex Clobar the full force of my most earnest expression. "Someone tampered with that photo. He cut me out of a different picture and pasted it into the image with Taylor in it. He even drew a fuse over the birthday candle. The original of that picture is in today's paper and was taken at the picnic that started around noon on the Fourth. I'm wearing food handlers' gloves and carrying that stack of donuts. I'm sure that if your forensic investigators enlarge the original image, they'll see that the object sticking out of the top is a birthday candle, probably the one you found in the Deputy Donut bag, and not the fuse of a homemade firework. In both pictures where I'm carrying the stack of donuts, I'm wearing my Deputy Donut uniform. They're only from the waist up, so you can't see my black shorts." I touched my collar. "But you can see my white polo shirt." I folded my hands on my lap. "And you can see a Deputy Donut apron and hat." I took a deep breath that wavered only slightly. "But if you look at photos taken during and after the fireworks and published in both yesterday's and today's papers, you'll see that in the evening I was wearing blue pants and a red and white striped blouse, which was later covered by a red sweater. I did *not* instantly change into my Deputy Donut uniform, carry donuts behind Taylor, and then change back into my long pants and blouse while the fireworks were going on." Maybe I was being too vehement. I added more calmly, "I'm guessing that Philip Landsdowner doctored the photo to make it look like I brought a stack of jelly-filled donuts to the fireworks display."

Rex asked me, "If that's true, how did *he* know that the firework was inserted in a stack of donuts? That's not general knowledge."

"He could have put the firework into the donuts himself, or he could have seen the bulky thing after it was lit, like I did. Having photographed that stack of donuts earlier in the day, he could have recognized it the next time he saw it or one like it. He must have been hanging around that hill. Also, after the explosion, there was a fair amount of chaos and people running all over the place. My two police officer friends who were assigned to the event were understandably more concerned at first about injured people than about keeping the crime scene pristine. When none of us were paying attention, Landsdowner could have looked at the burst tube, seen parts of donuts around it, and guessed the rest."

Rex said, "If the photo was taken during the afternoon, the colors would be bright and the sun would be shining."

"Whoever tampered with that photo made it look like night, but he didn't quite hide the highlights where the sun was shining on me."

Rex suggested, "Those highlights could be from the fireworks overhead."

I argued, "This photo and the one that was in today's newspaper are exactly the same except that this one has been flipped left to right and darkened, and a fuse was added." I pressed on with conclusions that should have been obvious. "The perspective is wrong. Nicholas and Taylor are sitting on the ground. My picture was scaled down to approximately their size, so you'd think I was close to them, but if I was that close, my feet, or at least my knees, would be in the picture. However, I'm shown only from the waist up, like in the picture of me holding a stack of donuts at the picnic. I'm sure that the experts in Forensics will be able to determine that the picture of me was added to the one of Taylor and Nicholas."

"Could be." Rex didn't sound quite convinced.

I plunged on in my own defense. "When Landsdowner took two of the pictures from earlier on the Fourth that are in today's pictorial essay, Jocelyn, our assistant at Deputy Donut, was near me. Landsdowner cut her out and pasted in different backgrounds where she had been."

"Why would he do that?" Rex seemed genuinely interested.

"I don't know, but by removing her from the pictures, he has shown that he can use photo-editing software."

Rex looked receptive.

I admitted, "If the bag you found in a trash can near my car is the one I gave to the birthday boy, my fingerprints will be on it."

Rex slipped the photos he'd shown me into the folder. "I see what you mean about your image looking pasted into the photo of the two people who were later injured."

Even though he was obviously very close to agreeing with me, I wasn't quite ready to stop pleading my case. "I think you'll also find that this photo showing the backs of Taylor and Nicholas is the same as the one in today's paper. In that one, I'm sitting a little uphill and to the left of them and I'm wearing dark blue pants and a red and white striped blouse. I'm leaning back, and the larger paper bag was empty and on my lap. I could not have been sitting to their left and standing behind them at the same time."

Rex pointed out that Taylor and Nicholas might have been in the same positions in pictures taken at different times, but I could have moved.

Frustrated, I reminded him of the discrepancies in the perspective and my clothing.

I might have convinced him. He told me I could leave.

I slid forward on the cold vinyl couch and stood up.

Brent offered, "I have copies of those newspapers in my office. Shall we go look at them now?"

"Later," Rex said. "You'll show Ms. Westhill out?"

Brent opened the room's door. "Yes." Out in the hallway, he touched my elbow. "You and I can go look at those newspapers."

Chapter 15

✻

I had not, after all, avoided going into Brent's office. Alec's old office.

"Okay," I breathed.

Brent tossed a quick look down at me. No one else was in the hallway. He said quietly, "That night was the worst night of my life, too."

At first, I thought he meant Thursday night, the Fourth of July.

Then I realized that Brent fully understood my dread about going into his office. He meant the night that Alec was shot.

I hadn't thought about it exactly that way, that the worst night in my life was also the worst night in Brent's, but I should have known it, should have been less wrapped up in my own pain and empathized more with his. "I'm sorry," I said in a small voice. "I know you miss him, too."

He guided me through another turn in the maze of corridors. "Terribly, and like you, I go over and over that night and think that if only we'd gone this way and not that, gone sooner, gone later, if only I'd moved in front of Alec or could have gotten him behind cover, he'd still be with you."

Again, I hadn't thought of it that way. I'd dwelt on my own guilt and never considered that Brent might feel guilt of his own. "You did everything you could."

"After the shots, yes, but could I have prevented his being hit? I'll never know, but I'll always think, 'If only . . .' "

I took a deep breath. "We can't revise the past, no matter how hard we might want to try."

"And I know it's not the same. I lost one of the best friends I'm ever likely to have, but you lost the love of your life."

"I . . . yes. Thank you, Brent."

A pair of uniformed officers were coming toward us. Brent didn't say anything else until he reached for the door of his office. "You'll be okay, Em," he said softly.

I couldn't answer except to nod.

The office had barely changed. Two battered oak desks were covered by stacks of papers and file folders. There were computers on the desks and two more on a table.

One thing was different, though. A picture of Alec, smiling in sunlight, hung on the wall.

Tears warmed the backs of my eyelids.

Brent shut the door. No one else was in the office. "I could tell that the photo of you behind the deceased and that bush was created by merging one photo with another."

Turning my face so he couldn't see the emotions that the photo of Alec had caused, I nodded. "Did Detective Clobar know?"

"I suspect he had an inkling."

"Then why . . . ?"

"Probably to gauge your reaction."

"Strange."

"Detectives can do things that seem strange to others."

I let out a shaky laugh. "You sure can."

"Plus, we, especially Rex, weren't sure how Landsdowner knew about the stack of donuts. If it was real, the picture of you with those donuts could have been a convenient answer to that question."

"Too convenient," I said dryly.

"Yes. Luckily, we don't stop searching after the first convenient answer occurs to us, and I don't think Rex was about to stop there, either." Brent pulled a couple of newspapers toward the side of the desk we were on. "Show me the other two doctored images?"

He stared for a long time at the one that Landsdowner had taken in Deputy Donut. "Hmmm. I don't remember exactly where your espresso machine is. I'll have to come over and take a look."

"Anytime." I had more or less tamped down the grief that had surged through me when we entered Alec's old office. Touched because the Fallingbrook Police Department detectives displayed Alec's photo in their office, though, I still had to fight tears.

Together, Brent and I looked at the picture in the paper of me with the stack of donuts near our table at the Fourth of July picnic. We agreed that it was the original of the one that Landsdowner had pasted behind the backs of Nicholas and Taylor when they were watching the fireworks. I described where our table had been.

I didn't have to tell Brent about the image of the police station replacing the original background of that photo. He noticed it himself. Then he also discovered the photo that showed the identical image of the police station where it belonged. "Mr. Landsdowner is going to have to answer a few questions," he said. "Did you see him at the fireworks before you noticed the flaming fuse sticking out of a stack of donuts?"

"No, but like most of the crowd, I was looking up. And Nicholas and Taylor must have been watching the sky when someone slunk behind them and planted that stack of donuts. The fireworks were so noisy that they probably didn't hear the person, either."

"Also, whenever we're in a crowd, we're not as aware of people around us doing unusual things as we would be if we were alone or almost alone."

"And people at fireworks can't help making those appreciative ohs and ahs."

He laughed. "It can be noisy." He thanked me for my help. "I'll walk back to Deputy Donut with you now, if it's okay, to see the location of your espresso machine in relation to where you were standing in that one photo." Instead of leading me back past where we'd met with Rex, Brent took me out of the police station the way I remembered, past the open area where Misty, Hooligan, and other cops were sitting at desks. They seemed to be discussing something serious, so I merely waved. In return, I received a smile from Hooligan and a questioning look from Misty.

The late-afternoon heat outside was welcome after I'd nearly developed hypothermia inside the building.

Brent asked me to show him where the Deputy Donut table had been on Thursday, where I'd been, and where Landsdowner had snapped the photo of me with the stack of donuts. I led him up the east side of the village square and stopped about where I'd stood.

Brent asked, "Do you mind if I take your picture?"

"As long as you don't put it in the paper. I've gotten enough notoriety this year, and it's only July."

Grinning, he took out his phone and snapped a couple of shots from where Landsdowner had been. The police station was behind Brent, not behind me.

Crossing the square, I wanted to thank Brent for making me go into Alec's old office, but I also didn't want to talk about it. I barely said a thing all the way to Deputy Donut. Brent was quiet, too, probably mentally reviewing evidence concerning Taylor's murder. We went in through Deputy Donut's back entrance, straight into the office.

Dep was sleeping on the newspapers. She blinked, stood, and stretched, clawing little holes in the top newspaper. I picked her up, stroked the soft fur above her upper lip, and told her, "It's a good thing that Brent has copies of those newspapers in his office and wasn't counting on having a really good look at the ones you've decided are a kitty bed."

She wriggled. I set her on the floor. She immediately rubbed against the ankles of Brent's navy blue slacks. He scooped her up and held her close to his jacket as if he wanted to distribute cat hair more evenly over his clothes.

The kitty claws hadn't punctured all the way through to the paper's centerfold pictorial essay. I pointed at the first picture. "Here's where the espresso machine should be."

Brent set Dep down. "Can you show me where you and Landsdowner were when he took this picture?"

Without too much difficulty, we left my affectionate cat inside the office.

I led Brent to the serving counter. He stayed where Landsdowner had been, and I moved to the other side of the counter. "Here's where I was. Tom was here, and Jocelyn was behind us. From there, it would have looked like she was between us."

"And from this angle, the espresso machine would have been behind her?"

"Yes."

He snapped photos. "What do you know about this Philip Landsdowner?"

"Only his name. And that he began taking pictures that had me in them early on the morning of the Fourth, especially when I seemed to be in conflict with others. It was like he was planning to commit a crime and frame me for it. But how could that be? He didn't know me. The first time I saw him was right here, that morning. It doesn't make sense."

"He could have known *of* you."

"Did Alec ever confront or arrest him?"

"We have no record of any Landsdowners."

"Maybe Landsdowner planned to harm someone with a homemade skyrocket during the fireworks when lots would be going on and very few people would notice an extra explosion. Maybe he didn't know who he was going to harm or who he might frame for the crime, and the first thing that day, he started snapping pictures of people who could have been angry. It just happened that he caught me frowning at least a couple of times, so when he saw me at the fireworks, he planted the five-year-old's skyrocket birthday cake near where I was sitting."

I detected a glimmer of amusement in Brent's eyes. "You have quite an imagination."

"You can't tell me that you detectives don't brainstorm all sorts of ideas."

"I can't?"

I heaved a dramatic sigh. "Unfortunately, I can't say that Landsdowner was the one who lit that skyrocket cake. I wish I'd been watching Taylor and Nicholas instead of the fireworks. I'd have seen the culprit, whoever he was. Or she was."

Brent put away his phone and took out his notebook. "Tell me again who you saw in the vicinity that evening who might have had a grudge against Ms. Wishbard."

"There was Duchess Gabrielle, who was obviously jealous of Taylor. And I saw Felicia, a hairstylist. Using a megaphone at the parade-marshaling grounds, Taylor claimed Felicia was jealous of Taylor's hair and wanted to make it as ugly as Felicia's. Which is as silly a motive as me supposedly being murderously angry at Taylor for refusing to ride in my car and calling it a clown car, and probably smelly, besides."

Brent asked what Felicia's hair was like.

I had to laugh. "It's a lot like mine, actually."

He glanced at my head. "Definitely not ugly."

Flustered, I thanked him. "Well, she's older than Taylor was, and unlike mine, her dark hair is dyed, all one shade of black. She keeps it in place with so much hairspray that it doesn't quite look like real hair."

"Maybe it isn't."

I spluttered with a sudden and uncontrollable laugh. "Taylor preferred softer waves."

"Did Taylor criticize any of the other people you saw at the fireworks?"

"No, but I wonder about Ian, who was elected king. As I told you before, Gabrielle said Taylor dumped Ian. But I might not have mentioned that when Taylor was late for the parade and the rest of us were waiting for her, Ian acted nervous and jittery, like he couldn't stand still."

Brent wrote in his notebook. "Who else did you see that night who might have had connections to Taylor?"

"You know Freeze, the ice cream shop just east of the square that I like so much?"

"Everyone likes it."

"When I went there Thursday morning to see if Taylor was at work, the clerk, Kelsey, hinted that Taylor was often late. But Mama Freeze, the ice cream shop's owner, gushed about how hard Taylor worked and how gorgeous she was. I wonder if Kelsey was jealous because Mama Freeze seemed to prefer Taylor. But I'd never seen Taylor working there, so I don't know who was right about Taylor's work ethic. I saw Mama Freeze at the fireworks, too, but I don't know of any grudges she might have had against Taylor. One thing for sure—Kelsey didn't need to be jealous of Taylor's looks."

"Women don't always understand that about themselves."

He was right, but he was also staring at me too intently. Not eager to discuss women and how they viewed themselves, I changed the subject completely. "Would you like a donut? They were fresh this afternoon."

He pointed at one in the display case. "What are the ones with the gooey-looking orange icing?"

"Filled with lemon and topped with gooey orange icing."

"Sounds good."

"They all are." I plated one for each of us, drew him an espresso, and made myself a mug of chai. To be sociable, and also to quiet Dep, who had been yowling the entire time since we left her in the office, we took our treats into her playground, set them on the coffee table, and sat beside each other on the couch with Dep between us.

She stretched, sniffed in the direction of my donut, and stalked away. She jumped onto the desk and prodded my phone. Afraid she was about to knock it onto the tile floor, I picked it up. Someone had left a message. I apologized to Brent, checked, put the phone down, and explained, "That was one of those spam recorded messages saying that I supposedly won a contest that I didn't enter. I was hoping it was my parents."

"Are they back?"

"No. They're usually in Fallingbrook long before the Fourth of July. I don't know where they are."

Dep raced me to the couch and curled up in the center cushion. The office was, after all, her space. I returned to the end of the couch where I'd been sitting before Dep reminded me to move my phone farther from the edge of the desk.

Concern in his eyes, Brent asked me, "Do your parents still drive back and forth to Florida?"

"Yes, in a humongous RV. They're good drivers, but they're in their early seventies." I had come into their lives, they'd always told me, as a delightful surprise when my mother was forty-one and my father was forty-three.

"Do they share the driving?"

"They share everything, including a very basic old flip phone that they never turn on, conserving the battery for emergencies, they say. I've offered to get them new phones and show them how to use them, but they always tell me that the one they have is perfectly fine."

"When did they last get in touch with you?"

"A couple of months ago."

Wrinkles appeared between his eyebrows. "That's a long time."

I shook my head in mock exasperation. My parents had some peculiar quirks. Being too independent was only one of them. "Not for them. They'd call if they needed my help." *If they could.* "They don't usually contact me until they get back to Fallingbrook in the spring. Or, the past few years, in the summer. They figure I should know that they won't call me when they're on their way or about to start out. They always gave me lots of freedom when I was growing up and were fond of telling me they hoped I would never have to act like a parent to them, especially—hint, hint—an *overbearing* parent. 'Feel free to let us make our own mistakes, just like we let you make yours,' they told me frequently."

He grinned. He didn't know them well, but he'd met them several times, enough to recognize some of their hippie-flower-child traits and philosophies. "Do they still park their RV at the campground near the falls?"

"They rent their space year-round."

"Don't they e-mail you?"

"They've managed to avoid using computers at all, ever. And they don't send letters or postcards when they're on the road, or right before they leave, either." I couldn't help sighing.

"Want me to run out to the campground and look for them?"

That was sweet of him. He really was helpful and support-ive. "I'm not that worried. Besides, I can drive there myself."

"If you need company . . ."

"I'll be fine. They'll be fine. They've been lengthening their winter stays as they become more and more acclimatized to hot weather. Lately, they've been finding July and August up here a little chilly."

"Would you like me to file a missing persons report?"

I raised my hand above my dozing cat as if I might stop Brent by grabbing his wrist, but instead of letting my hand land on him, I settled it into Dep's warm fur. "It's not neces-sary, really. I'm sure they're having a grand old time touring routes they've never explored before. They don't like super-highways. Too fast and no scenery, they say. But if I had to drive a rig like that . . ." I shook my head. "No, I wouldn't drive it on superhighways. I'd abandon it and hitchhike home. Or if I was in Florida and didn't like the so-called chill of July and August in Wisconsin, I'd stay in Florida. I might inform someone of my decision, though."

He smiled at my joking, but I could still see concern in his wary expression. "I hope so. Let me know if you want me to do anything, need company going out to check on them, or anything. Meanwhile, thanks for the donut. I'll go back to the office and show Rex the pictures I took of you on the square and here, with your espresso machine."

He picked Dep up and rubbed noses with her. "Look after Emily, okay?"

"Meow," Dep said.

He put her down, slung one arm around my shoulders, gave me a quick squeeze, and let me go before I could reciprocate. "Call if you need me, Em. Anytime."

"Thanks. For everything." *Like forcing me to think about how Alec's death affects you, too, and also showing me that I can face his old office* . . . I didn't say it, but I thought Brent understood. I let him out, watched for a second as he headed down the driveway toward Wisconsin Street, and then I snapped Dep's halter and leash on.

When Dep and I got to Wisconsin Street, Brent was almost at the square, but instead of heading toward the police station, he was standing still and looking our way. I waved. He waved back and stood there as if planning to watch us until we were no longer in sight.

Chapter 16

✺

Dep and I started south. A couple of blocks later, we were about to leave Wisconsin Street and go into our neighborhood. I looked back.

Brent was where I'd last seen him, still facing us. I waved again, and Dep and I turned the corner. We were out of Brent's sight and he was out of ours.

Did he think we weren't entirely safe? I considered walking faster, but Dep apparently decided it was too nice an evening to do anything more energetic than amble along checking for beetles in the grass next to the sidewalk.

Despite the beautiful weather, I wanted to cocoon inside my house—or in my walled-in backyard—and not go anywhere else. I was hungry and emotionally wrung out.

After Dep and I both had fish for dinner, Misty called. "Was Brent giving you a tour?"

"Have you met Detective call-me-Rex Clobar?"

"Briefly. He seems okay."

"He wanted to talk to me, at police headquarters. And I agree with you. He does seem okay, but a little scary. Thank you for telling him you were sure I wouldn't intentionally harm anyone. That seemed to help my case."

"Was Brent at your interview?"

Did she think that her frequent mentioning of Brent was so

subtle that I wouldn't guess she hadn't given up trying to throw Brent and me together?

"Yes." She probably heard my smile and believed it was about Brent and not about her matchmaking pipe dreams.

"That's good. He would also say that you would never intentionally harm anyone."

"He did. With me right there."

"I'm not surprised." Now she was the one with a smile in her voice, as if she were about to say that Brent's defense of me made him perfect for me. She didn't, quite, but she did say, "After Hooligan and I saw Brent with you, Brent was gone for a while. Did he walk you home?"

"Only to Deputy Donut to check on something related to the case."

"Well, don't you sound like a wannabe police officer!"

"Show-off. And no, because I don't wannabe."

"Show-off donut monger."

Both laughing, we told each other good night.

I looked down at Dep, who was gazing, wide-eyed, up at me. "Sorry, Dep. Misty isn't coming over."

"Meow."

"She's still matchmaking. Me and Brent."

"Meow!"

"You saw him only a few hours ago."

"Mew."

"I invite him over a lot, you know," I said sternly. "Just to please you."

Tail up, she trotted upstairs.

"It's true," I muttered, following her. "You and Brent are especially fond of each other. I'm merely your go-between."

The next morning, minutes after Misty, Hooligan, and a couple of other officers seated themselves at a table in the middle of our donut shop, a woman came in and sat at the next table, so close that she could have turned halfway around in her chair and touched Misty.

It took me a second to recognize Gabrielle. Instead of a duchess gown and fur capelet or a pomegranate-red minidress and apron, she wore pink and lavender plaid shorts, a pink T-shirt, and lavender sandals. And her hair wasn't pinned up. It fell in dark brown waves and curls around her shoulders in a style similar to the one that Taylor, a blonde, had worn as queen.

Jocelyn served the police officers, and I welcomed Gabrielle to Deputy Donut.

Gabrielle asked, "Did you enjoy our Happy Hour? You should come earlier and stay longer next time. And bring friends so you won't have to sit alone."

Carefully, I didn't point out that she was sitting alone, at least at the moment, in Deputy Donut. I told her, "I liked that nut mixture and your selection of draft beers."

"We're good at Frisky Pomegranate, even down to the lowliest waitress—me."

"And now I get to be *your* waitress. Are you cashing in one of your coupons?"

"How'd you know?"

I smiled at her. "It was a wild guess." Fallingbrook merchants had awarded the members of the Fourth of July royal court gifts and prizes. Tom and I had given each of the four winners coffee and donuts for a year—fifty-two coupons for a coffee and a donut. They could use them any way they wanted. They could cash in one per week, treat themselves and fifty-one of their best friends all at once, or do anything in between.

Gabrielle ordered a cappuccino and an apple jelly–filled donut.

When I brought them to her, I asked how she was doing.

Although I hadn't been certain on Friday evening at Frisky Pomegranate that Gabrielle had yet heard about Taylor's death, she now obviously knew about it. Her shoulders sagged. "I can hardly stand it! Poor Taylor. She should have had a long and wonderful life." She picked up a Deputy Donut napkin and dabbed at her eyes. "And now she can't." Jerking her head back, she sniffled and then raised her voice. "I'm absolutely devastated. I'll miss her forever. She was my best friend!" Gabrielle spoke so loudly that Hooligan, who was across the table from Misty, stared at her.

Tom was getting ahead on donut production, and Jocelyn had given the police officers their donuts and coffee and had gone to the front of the shop to take orders from other customers. I seized the chance to talk to Gabrielle a little longer. I asked with genuine sympathy, "You knew Taylor for a long time, didn't you?"

Gabrielle wailed, "Ever since we were little tiny girls! We were best friends and we were rivals, too, but in the best way, the way that helped each other. Maybe if I'd been elected queen, this wouldn't have happened."

Startled, I asked, "Do you think someone harmed her on purpose because she was elected queen?"

Gabrielle dabbed at her eyes again. "I don't know what to think. But maybe if I'd been elected queen and someone went after me the way they went after her, I'd have noticed and put a stop to it. Anyway, best friends are willing to take each other's place."

"Even if they know they'll die?"

"How would I have known that?" she demanded. "I didn't know my best friend was going to die!" Then she must have realized that she'd still been talking loudly and that, to the police officers at the next table, her words might have resembled confessing that she had lit the firework but hadn't believed that Taylor would die of her injuries. Gabrielle practically shouted, "I had no idea anyone was even being threatened on the Fourth. If I'd known what was going to happen, I would have told my bestie not to go to the fireworks that night."

Customers kept glancing curiously at her. In an attempt to

calm the atmosphere to the usual Deputy Donut camaraderie, I spoke quietly. "Would she have listened?"

"Of course she would. If I'd known, I'd have told her, and she would have believed me, and she would be sitting at this table this very minute." She kicked at the leg of the chair beside her, moving it slightly as if someone were on it.

Hooligan had stopped staring at Gabrielle, but he had turned his upper body toward her.

Aha. He was aiming his body cam at her. People at nearby tables were laughing and talking. Cutlery clattered against ironstone mugs and plates. The microphone on Hooligan's camera would have to be sensitive to pick up all of Gabrielle's words. Right behind Gabrielle, Misty was sitting very still, as if listening.

Gabrielle pointed the uneaten half of her donut at Jocelyn. As if she now wanted to prevent the police officers at the next table from hearing anything she said, she asked quietly, "What's *she* doing here?"

"She's our new assistant."

Gabrielle nodded slowly. "Watch out," she murmured. "She was a couple of years behind Taylor and me in school, but everyone knew who she was because she was, like, always winning awards. No one believed she got those perfect grades fairly. Plus, she worked with Taylor at Freeze, only I shouldn't say that Jocelyn *worked* there. She was *paid* there. But she's a celebrity." She drew the word out, putting a sneer in her tone. "People treat celebrities better than they treat ordinary people."

I wasn't able to control a surprised widening of my eyes. "But you're a celebrity."

"I only just became one."

"Do they treat you differently at Frisky Pomegranate?"

"They're okay, but they don't spoil me. I'm not like Jocelyn, famous since she was a baby. Some people get everything." The bitterness in her voice did not come from her coffee or her donut.

I had to defend our new employee. "Actually, Jocelyn is a very hard worker. She's good with customers, and she's talented at decorating donuts. With her brains and persistence, her good grades aren't surprising."

Gabrielle gave me a sour look. "She's good at faking it. Taylor told me all about her."

I offered a dry little smile. "At the moment, she's doing more than her share, so I'd better go help." I hurried to the kitchen.

Misty and her friends left. Wearing a smug look on her face as if she'd accomplished a goal, Gabrielle followed them out. I didn't see which way she went.

Working in the kitchen later, I heard children's voices near the front. Jocelyn called out, "Look who's here, Emily! The birthday boy!"

Chapter 17

❧

The cute little blond boy had barely gotten inside Deputy Donut with his family when he burst into tears.

Jocelyn and I both rushed to him. The bigger sister hugged the boy. His older brother patted his shoulder. The other girl's eyes welled with tears.

Jocelyn and I asked at the same time, "What's wrong?"

The boy sobbed, "My birthday skyrocket!"

The mother explained, "We'd like to buy six donuts, please, like the ones you gave us on Thursday."

The longer I can keep this family here, the more I can find out about them. I asked, "How about if you sit down at a table, and we'll decorate some?"

Smoothly, Jocelyn added, "Since it's not the Fourth of July, how about rocket ship sprinkles instead of stars?"

I grinned in silent praise for her quick and brilliant suggestion.

Tearfully, the boy nodded.

Jocelyn glanced at me. "I'll go put them together."

I thanked her. With a surprising amount of discussion, the kids and their parents chose a table and decided who would sit in which chair. I asked them what they'd like to drink. The kids opted for lemonade. The father wanted tea, and the mother wanted our special coffee of the day, a smooth organic brew from Bali.

I hurried into the kitchen and told Tom I needed to call Brent. Tom raised an eyebrow but went across the kitchen to the counter where Jocelyn was injecting blueberry jelly into three partially hollowed donuts. He whispered to her. She handed him the injector, washed her hands, and went to the dining area to wait on customers.

I followed her out of the kitchen and then headed for the office. Dep woke up, leaped to one of her carpeted pillars, and climbed to a tunnel near the ceiling. Waiting for Brent to answer his personal number, I slipped outside to the parking lot. About a dozen cars were in the section near our shop.

"Hey, Em." Brent's voice was warm. Apparently, he wasn't in a meeting.

I spoke quickly, anyway. "The family we gave the stack of donuts to on Thursday just came into Deputy Donut. They wanted donuts like the ones they had on the Fourth, so it's taking a little time to prepare them, but I don't know how long we can keep the family here."

"Thanks, Em. Don't make any attempt to keep them there longer than they want to be. I'll see you in a few minutes." He disconnected.

The only vehicle in our parking lot big enough to hold a family of six was a minivan. Quickly, I walked past it and glanced inside. Colorful toys and books were spread around the two back seats. I snapped a picture of the license plate.

I returned to the kitchen and whispered to Tom that Brent was coming over in a few minutes, and then I poured the family's drinks.

I set the little boy's lemonade in front of him. He looked up at me. Tears filled his blue eyes. "I losted the skyrocket cake you gave me. It was the best birthday cake ever and I losted it."

This was potentially huge news to pass on to Brent, but I tried hard to look like a caring adult, not an excited amateur sleuth. "Thank you. That's a very nice thing to say about the donut cake, and I'm very sorry it got lost. How about if we make the six donuts that Jocelyn is decorating right now into another skyrocket cake?"

He said in a heartrendingly sad voice, "Yes."

I glanced at his parents to see if they minded my talking to their small son. The mother smiled, so I asked the boy, "How did it get lost?"

He sniffled. "I don't know! I put it in a safe place and then I went into the bouncy castle. I bounced and bounced. Then they told me I had to stop bouncing. I went to put on my shoes." Tears spilled over his lashes.

His mother asked him, "Was that when your cake got lost?"

The younger of the two sisters, who was not much older than the boy, said, "He had that bag with him when you went to make your hair appointment, Mom."

The boy nodded vigorously.

Fallingbrook hair salons must have been busy on the Fourth. At least two of them had been open that morning before the parade.

The mother tilted her head. "I don't remember. I was concentrating on talking to Felicia and getting out of there before any of you tipped over one of those giant hair dryers."

Felicia.

The older sister's eyes flashed. "That's not fair. We wouldn't do that."

The bigger boy said, "Maybe he took it to the restaurant where we ate dinner. Remember? Before we got a table, we went into that little room, and Dad put some of the stuff we'd been carrying up on a shelf where only big people would see it."

The mother looked up at the ceiling for a second. "We could have left it in the coatroom."

The five-year-old jumped up and down in excitement. "That's what happened! Let's go get it!"

Almost positive that the donuts had been blown up and that the bag they'd been in had been thrown out near my donut car, I told the boy, "By now, that donut cake wouldn't be very good." If my conjectures about its fate were correct, that was an understatement. "The one we're making for you now will be much better." I asked the father, "Which restaurant was it?'

"A new one. A pub, really, but the food is good. It's just north of the square."

The smaller of the two girls said, "And it had a funny name, like a puppy."

"Pomegranate," her big sister corrected her, "not Pomeranian."

Her mouth an O, the littler girl stared at her big sister for a second. Then she stated, "I don't care. When I get a puppy of my own, I'm going to name her Pomma . . . Pomma . . . what you said."

The restaurant had to be Frisky Pomegranate, where Gabrielle worked. Had she dropped in there before the fireworks and found the stack of donuts in a bag? Had the candle sticking out of the top donut given her a deadly idea?

Or maybe the family had actually left the bag at Felicia's.

The mother said, "I hope someone found those donuts in time to eat them while they were fresh. Otherwise, what a waste!"

Another understatement . . .

She added, "Who can resist donuts?"

I smiled. "No one."

Not even Brent, although he hardly ever visited Deputy Donut with other police officers during breaks. He was coming in now, though. His summer-weight gray suit and white shirt could have given him away as a detective.

The boy's parents, if they noticed Brent at all, did not seem concerned.

I asked the boy, "Would you like us to package your new stack of birthday donuts for you to take with you, or would you rather have it served now? We can light the candle, and everyone in here can sing 'Happy Birthday.' "

Walking past me as I delivered this long and involved speech, Brent didn't greet me or hesitate. Even if he hadn't guessed who the family were, he had to have heard enough of what I said to figure it out.

The birthday boy leaped down from his seat and tugged at his dad's arm. "In a bag, just like before! You promised we could take it home and sing 'Happy Birthday.' And open presents."

The father ruffled his hair. "You already opened your presents."

"But there could be more. If we sing."

His two oldest siblings quickly and succinctly informed him that wasn't how it worked, but he seemed unconvinced. He was adamant about taking the donuts home in a bag. I asked the mother if the family had gone to the fireworks on the night of the Fourth of July.

The two youngest kids answered for her. "Yes!"

The birthday boy put his hands over his ears. "Noisy."

His slightly older sister scoffed, "You fell asleep."

"Did not."

"Did. And the fireworks were pretty."

I asked the boy, "Did you see anyone else with a skyrocket cake like the one you lost?"

He stuck out his lower lip. "No one else could have one like mine."

His mother grinned. "I'm sure those first six donuts were quickly devoured by whoever found them."

The father was watching me as if wondering whether to stop my questioning of his children. I couldn't blame him. He answered quietly, "I didn't see one."

I excused myself. "I'd better go see if the frosting being put on those donuts is hard enough not to smear when we stack them."

Tom was on the kitchen side of the serving counter, pouring coffee into a mug for Brent.

I breezed past them and picked up a bag, a birthday candle,

toothpicks, and the platter holding the six specially injected and decorated donuts. I put them all on the counter in front of Brent. Inserting a toothpick into the bottom donut, I quietly told Brent about the places the family thought they might have lost the donuts. His eyes gleamed slightly for a second when I mentioned Felicia and again when I mentioned Frisky Pomegranate. I slid a donut on top of the first one, stuck in another toothpick, and eased another donut onto the other two. "I don't think the kids are making up tales to hide the fact that they're vicious murderers." Brent grinned. With the help of more toothpicks, I stacked the rest of the donuts while I told him about photographing the license plate in the parking lot.

"E-mail the picture to me later?" he asked quietly. I wondered if a new girlfriend was encouraging him to suddenly start wearing whimsical ties. Tiny gray goats were kicking up their heels all over this one.

I stuck the birthday candle in the top donut. "Sure." Tom helped me slide the stack of donuts into the bag. I said just loudly enough for both men to hear, "I was going to give these to the family for free, but if they pay with a charge card, we'll know at least one of their names."

"Don't charge them anything," Tom said. "Let Fyne work for the money the fine folk of Fallingbrook are paying him."

I took the bag with its top still open to the birthday boy and held it where he could peek inside. He crowed, "That's the best cake *ever!*"

The father asked for a bill, but I said it was all on the house. We argued about it until Tom joined forces with me. Acquiescing, the family stood to leave.

I didn't need to watch to see if the family got into the van I thought was theirs. Tom let Brent into the office where Brent would get a good view of the van.

Helping me clear the family's table, Jocelyn asked me, "Who's the suit playing with Dep?"

"A friend of Tom's and mine." She'd probably find out

eventually, so I added, "He's a detective." It didn't seem to faze her.

Tom opened the back door. Brent put Dep down, went outside, and disappeared from my view.

Later, after Tom, Jocelyn, and I closed and tidied the shop for the night, Dep and I walked home and ate dinner—fishy for her and beefy for me. I still hadn't heard from my parents. I was debating whether to drive out to the falls right then or wait until the next day, my first planned day off other than Christmas and New Year's since Tom and I opened Deputy Donut a couple of years before.

Misty called and made the decision for me. "Can I talk to you, Emily?"

Chapter 18

✿

I invited Misty to my place.

"I'll be there in fifteen minutes. Is it okay if Samantha comes, too?"

"Of course. Does that mean you're not coming on police business?"

Her usually musical laugh sounded a little strained. "Hardly."

In the kitchen, I took three yummy cheeses—Amber Mist, Manchego, and Camembert—out of the fridge and arranged them on a large tray with crackers, cheese knives, and sweet pickled baby cucumbers. I placed the cheese tray, three plates, three wineglasses, and some cute cocktail napkins on the granite-topped island where we'd all be able to reach everything.

Fingers tapped on the front door. Making a funny chirping noise, Dep bounded to the living room.

I was sure my visitors would be Misty and Samantha, but I peeked outside, anyway.

Misty and Samantha were each holding a bottle of wine up near the peephole where I'd be sure to see it.

Laughing, I opened the door and invited them in. Both were in shorts, cool tops, and sandals. For a second, I thought that Samantha's hair was its original brown, but then I saw the subtle navy streak in front of her left ear.

"None of us has to work tomorrow," Misty explained. "Let's party!" Did I detect wariness in those blue eyes?

Samantha cast a quick glance up at our tall friend and then looked at me. *By the second glass of wine,* I thought, *Samantha and I will hear about whatever is bothering Misty.*

I'd already thanked Misty for telling Rex Clobar that I wouldn't harm anyone, so I thanked Samantha, too.

Both of them shrugged it off. "You'd say the same for either of us," Samantha said.

Misty added, "I'm only sorry that you left us for those few minutes to go get your sweater and we couldn't say for certain that we knew where you were every second."

Samantha's grin reminded me of her impish smiles back in junior high. "Too bad Brent wasn't with us during the fireworks. You could have cuddled up to him."

"Or sent him for my sweater," I said.

Samantha did a little dance step. "She doesn't deny the cuddling."

"Alleged cuddling," I corrected her. "Why would I deny something that can't happen?"

Misty and Samantha giggled. I did my best to ignore them, helped by Dep, who galloped into the kitchen. We followed her and feasted on cheese, crackers, pickles, and wine. Dep wandered into the sunroom and sat on a windowsill where she could keep track of the yard outside.

After about the seventh time that Misty sighed, I asked, "Is something wrong, Misty?" We were only on our first glasses of wine.

She broke a cracker in two. "I think I know why Scott doesn't like me."

I contradicted her. "Of course he likes you."

Samantha added, "Scott likes everyone."

"That's just it." Misty sighed again. "And that's one of the reasons I'm crazy about him. He's just about perfect. But he likes me the same way he likes everyone else, and I was hoping he'd automatically be as interested in me as I am in him. He likes *you*, Emily."

"In the same way he likes everyone else," I argued. "I'm just a friend. I'm sure he knows I don't want to go out with anyone."

"But you're always nice to him. I'm not."

Samantha moved the wine bottle farther from Misty. "You're cut off."

I said, "Misty, you're nice to everyone."

Misty ran her fingers through her long blond hair. "Not when I'm on duty."

I contradicted her. "I've seen you on duty. You're always kind."

Samantha remained very noticeably quiet and watchful. She had to have witnessed Misty at more emergencies than I had.

Misty scowled. "Not always. Like the night of the Fourth of July, and last October, too, out at Little Lake Lodge. When I have to manage a scene and take statements, I'm bossy and treat everyone, including Scott, like potential criminals. I order Scott around. No wonder he doesn't like me."

I eased a slice of Amber Mist onto a cracker. "When you're doing crowd control at a fire or a collision that Scott's attending as fire chief, how does Scott treat you?"

Still obviously annoyed with herself, Misty muttered, "Not like a criminal."

"Misty, I've seen him at fires and collisions lots of times," Samantha reminded her. "He's businesslike and abrupt, and he's not afraid to order people to move back. I'll bet he's told *you* what to do at times, like when there's a fire or other hazard."

"That's different," Misty claimed. "He does that to protect us."

Samantha slanted a look at her. "Misty, do you like him any less because he's doing his job?"

"Of course not. He's always kind. I'm not."

Samantha and I just looked at her.

"I guess I could change," Misty admitted. "Or try to. If it's not too late."

I suggested, "You don't need to change, but why don't we all get together again when none of you are on duty and no one has to order anyone else to move back or get out of the way? We could all go to the Fireplug or to the new pub, Frisky Pomegranate. Or we could have a nice, casual potluck barbecue at one of our houses. We had lots of fun together on the Fourth before the tragedy."

"We did have fun," Misty agreed. "Are you free tomorrow night?"

Samantha and I both said that we were.

"Let's have a barbecue at my place, then," Misty said. "I'll try the guys, too, but even if they can't make it, we three will have fun together."

Samantha grinned. "We always do. And you might even try flirting with Scott. I flirted with Hooligan, and look where it got me."

Misty and I both asked, "Where?"

Samantha's sly smile turned into a very happy one. "Going out together every chance we get."

Misty and I cheered, and there were high fives all around. And more wine.

Misty said to Samantha, "Wait, Hooligan's not working tonight. You two should be together."

With one hand, Samantha dusted cracker crumbs off the granite countertop into the other hand. "He's picking me up in . . ." She glanced at my kitchen clock. The big hand was a knife and the small hand was a fork. "Three minutes, actually."

That statement provoked more cheers from Misty and me.

Samantha must have thought she needed to add, "So, that means that Scott and Misty have to get together, and then there's you, Emily." She dumped the crumbs into the sink.

I held my palms out toward her. Halt. Double halt. "I was already paired off with someone perfect. I've had more than my share of happiness."

"But maybe Brent hasn't." Samantha could be very sassy. She climbed back onto her stool, picked up her wine, and watched me over the top of her glass.

I had to resist. "Maybe he has. He's never seemed to have difficulty finding gorgeous women to date. Gorgeous *tall* women."

"That was then," Samantha said.

Misty added, "Haven't you noticed how he looks at you, Emily?"

"No!" Flustered, I corrected it to, "He doesn't look at me any differently than he looks at other people." I glared at my two best friends. "Stop snickering! He doesn't look at me any differently from the way he looks at *Dep*."

Samantha and Misty laughed harder.

"Anyway, Samantha," I informed her snootily, "your three minutes are nearly up."

She slid off her stool. "So they are. Excuse me, ladies, I'm off to spend the rest of the evening with my darling Hooligan."

Misty and I looked at each other. Between giggles, I managed, "Way back in junior high, we pinky swore to avoid dating hooligans."

Samantha flounced out of the kitchen. "You two are jealous."

Misty looked wistful. "Maybe," she admitted.

The front door closed. Misty and I traded glances and then ran to the living room and peeked out the window.

Hooligan, in a nice shirt and jeans, had his arms around

Samantha. He let her go, opened his passenger door, and gallantly handed her into the front seat.

Misty breathed, "True love." We watched Hooligan's car pull away from the curb. "I'd better go, too," Misty said. "So you can get your beauty sleep in case Brent wants to see you tomorrow."

"So I can suffer through another interview with DCI Agent Rex Clobar? No, thanks."

Misty became serious as she let herself out. "Try not to hurt Brent."

Bewildered, I shook my head. "I'm not . . . he's not . . ." But she was gone.

"Meow."

I picked up my cat. I didn't mind cuddling *her*. "He doesn't look at me any differently than he used to, Dep, does he?"

She wriggled.

I set her gently on the floor. Trying not to remember that, before the interview with Rex Clobar in that freezing meeting room, Brent's and my relationship had seemed to change, I went into the kitchen and wrapped the remains of the cheese and crackers.

"Meow."

"Okay," I admitted to Dep. "Brent was attentive during and after the interview, too."

"Meow."

I put the pickles away. "He can't help being empathetic."

"Meow."

"Yes, Dep, Alec was, too. And I do like Brent. A lot." I shook my head to clear it. "As a *friend*."

"Mew."

I washed the glasses and put the empty wine bottle in the recyclables bin. "I think I had too much to drink tonight. And besides, Brent was all business today in Deputy Donut."

"Meow."

"Okay, you're right, he was businesslike except during those few seconds of playing and snuggling with you, but you don't have to brag about it."

Without answering, Dep trotted upstairs. Reminding her that we had the next day off and could sleep in if we wanted to, I followed.

Chapter 19

As usual, Dep made certain I was awake in time to get ready for work, even though it was my day off. Grumbling about her early-morning enthusiasm, I showered and dressed in fuchsia shorts and a matching blouse with a scalloped hem.

After breakfast, I sat outside on a chaise longue with Dep purring on my lap and a mug of complex and exotic coffee grown in Papua New Guinea. It would have been more relaxing if I'd been able to stop thinking about how Tom and Jocelyn were getting along without me. What if the shop became crowded and Jocelyn felt overworked and wanted to quit?

For me, being there might be less worrisome than not being there.

However, I had other things I needed to do. As soon as I thought that Felicia might be at her hairdressing salon, I called her. She had a cancellation in only a half hour.

Even though I had to leave Dep at home, it was a great feeling to go out in the middle of the morning for a walk. The day was sunny and already warm. I zigzagged south and east through our residential neighborhood to Felicia's cozy salon.

"Emily!" Felicia cried when she saw me in the entryway. "Long time, no see!"

I made a rueful face. "I know. I'm overdue for a cut." I

pulled at one of my curls and let it spring back more or less into place.

Nearly everything inside the salon was brilliant lime green. Cloaked in a lime green nylon cape, one patron sat underneath a hair dryer that could double as a UFO on a stilt, and I understood the birthday boy's mother's concern about her children knocking it or others like it over. Felicia wore a smock, lime green tropical flowers and leaves, with matching leggings and shoes. Even her short curly hair was lime green. On the night of the Fourth of July when I'd glimpsed her leaving the fireworks display only moments before that homemade skyrocket exploded and fatally injured Taylor, Felicia's hair had been its usual jet black. Had she changed the color to go with the décor of her salon, or did she hope that anyone who saw her now would not realize she was the woman they'd seen at the fireworks, perhaps with a homemade skyrocket hidden inside a stack of donuts?

Felicia covered my fuchsia outfit, which didn't *quite* clash with everything else in her salon, with a lime green cape. "Is your mom home yet?"

I followed Felicia to the shiny black porcelain sink. "I haven't heard from her. Have you?"

Felicia turned on the water and helped me and the voluminous cape into the chair. "Not a word. She goes to someone in Florida who just ruins her hair! I wish she'd get back here so I can attempt to fix the terrible cut she always gets down there."

Suspecting that the "someone" in Florida who cut my mom's hair was my dad, I didn't say anything. Both of my parents were inveterate do-it-yourselfers. The wonder was that my mother ever let a professional cut her hair. She had to like Felicia's haircutting a lot. Or my father's not so much . . .

Felicia reclined my chair until the back of my neck rested on the comfortably indented and curved edge of the sink. Warm water sluiced over my head. I relaxed and let Felicia massage my scalp and then wrap it in a warm, fluffy towel. That treatment alone could have been what kept my mother returning to Felicia.

Back at the cutting station, Felicia removed the towel and looked at my reflection in the mirror. "How much are we taking off?"

My drenched curls drooped halfway down my neck. "Lots. If it's nice and short, I won't have to bother you again for a long time."

"Aren't you a chip off the old blockette?"

For a second, I thought Felicia said *blockhead*. My mother would have laughed.

Felicia tilted my head down and started snipping.

Raising my eyes without raising my chin, I looked at her in the mirror. "I heard that the Fourth of July queen had her hair done in here on Thursday morning."

Felicia made a clicking noise with her tongue. "What a pity." She glanced over her shoulder toward the other patron, who was paging through a magazine. With that UFO roaring around her head, the woman probably couldn't have heard what Felicia and I were saying. Nevertheless, Felicia lowered her voice. "It's sad when anyone dies, especially a young person just out of her teens, and far be it from me to speak ill of the dead, but that queen was a piece of work. I fixed her hair up all nice and pretty that morning, and then she refused to pay me." *Snip, snip, snip.* "She said I should bill the Fabulous Fourth Festivities Committee! Of all the nerve! Then she flounced out of here and went across the street to that fancy-schmancy place and had her hair done all over again. I saw her come out of there with her hair in an absolute mess, like she just got out of bed."

To me, Taylor's hair had looked lovely, but I didn't tell Felicia that.

I hoped that Felicia hadn't heard what Taylor had said about her—broadcast through a megaphone, no less—at the parade-marshaling grounds.

No luck. With her scissor blades clashing against each other, Felicia launched into a diatribe about how Taylor had defamed her. "In front of the whole world! She told everyone I was jealous of her hair. Now, *that* was certainly never true. I can be a blonde anytime I want." She gave her lime green curls an approving smile in the mirror. "That queen was mean, so mean to everybody that I wonder if someone killed her just to get back at her, you know?"

"Who would do that?" I asked.

"I wouldn't know." *Snip, clash, snip.* "I certainly wouldn't."

"Who was she mean to?"

"She complained about nearly everyone in town. She actually gloated about beating out her so-called best friend in the competition to be queen." Felicia was so worked up that I was afraid her scissors might slip. "Your mother," Felicia told me, "never complained that time I slashed her neck."

I almost jumped. "What?" I squeaked without moving my lips more than I absolutely had to.

"It was totally an accident, and your mother forgave me. *And* she let me give her first aid." *Snap, snip.* "She paid me, too. Not for the first aid, which I did for free, but for the cut and styling."

After that, I was afraid to say much, afraid to move. However, Felicia managed to cut my hair without severing an artery, and she did a good job, too, although it was always hard to tell with curls that had minds of their own.

While coaxing those curls into place, Felicia told me, "I saw you at the fireworks. You were with a handsome guy in a uniform."

Oh, great. When Felicia finally saw my mother, Felicia would tell her about the handsome guy in the uniform, and my mother would borrow every wedding magazine in the Fallingbrook library. I quickly set the record straight. "I was beside him, but not *with* him. I was with a group. He was actually with one of my friends." It wasn't a huge fib. It was sort of true, too, even if Scott didn't know it yet.

I'd seen Felicia when she was leaving the fireworks and I was returning to Scott and the others, so Felicia must have seen me earlier. I hadn't noticed her, but she could have passed the five of us when we were laughing and talking together, totally focused on one another.

If Felicia was willing to admit that she'd been at the fireworks, did that mean she was innocent of harming anyone there? I asked, "Did you enjoy the fireworks?"

"Naw. All that noise and light gives me a headache. You know Mama Freeze?"

"Yes. She makes the best ice cream."

"Doesn't she? Every year, I say I'm not going to the fireworks, and every year, she persuades me to go. We've been friends for years, so we end up going lots of places together. Oops, there's a naughty little curl that escaped its fate." *Snip*. "There. Now it's perfect."

While I was paying Felicia and no longer in danger from those clashing scissor blades, I asked if anyone had left a Deputy Donut bag full of donuts in her salon recently.

She was digging around in her cash drawer and didn't look up at me. "Why would anyone do that?"

"I gave a family a half-dozen donuts at the community picnic on the Fourth, and they managed to lose the entire bag somewhere. They thought it might be here."

She broke a roll of quarters on the edge of the drawer. "I didn't cut a family's hair on the Fourth. I would've remembered that."

"I think they stopped in for the mother to make an appointment."

Felicia slid quarters into their compartment in the drawer. "Those donuts would be stale by now, wouldn't they? Or do you use preservatives?"

"They'd be stale."

"Then I don't know who would want them after all this time."

I glanced at the appointment book lying open on the counter. Reading upside down, I saw a scratched-out name and my name scrawled in the margin beside it.

Felicia turned her head and called to the woman under the hair dryer, "I'll be right with you!"

I quickly asked, "Could one of your other customers have picked up the bag of donuts that day?"

Felicia made a slightly disgusted face. "Why would anyone do that?" She dumped change into my hand. In those lime green shoes, she hurried toward the other woman.

I walked out feeling almost light-headed. I'd probably lost a pound of hair. Maybe that was an exaggeration.

Felicia hadn't really solved my problem. By now, Brent had probably figured out who the birthday boy's family was, and he might have questioned them and found out other places where they might have "losted" the birthday cake.

Meanwhile, who had taken that bag of donuts to the fireworks?

Chapter 20

❧

Walking north, I brainstormed ways of sneaking peeks at the page for July fourth in Felicia's appointment book, but my ideas weren't subtle enough to keep me out of possible danger if Felicia, not one of her clients, had found those donuts and taken them to the fireworks.

Mama Freeze and Felicia could both have been angry at Taylor for insulting Felicia, and the two old friends could have worked together. They could have lied to give each other alibis. It was hard to imagine, but nearly everything about Taylor's murder was.

On the patio in front of Deputy Donut, Jocelyn was chatting with customers. She obviously noticed me walking up the other side of the street. Smiling, she called out, "Checking up on us?"

"Yep! How are you doing?"

"Perfect! Enjoy your day off!"

"I am!" I kept going.

Farther north, I took one of the diagonal pathways across the sunny and neatly landscaped village square. Since it wasn't yet lunchtime, very few people were on Frisky Pomegranate's patio.

I went inside and stopped to let my eyes adjust from the bright sunlight. I didn't expect to find a bag containing six stale donuts and a slightly melted birthday candle, but what if I did? A lot of my theories would unravel and I'd have to rethink how some of our donuts got from the picnic to the fireworks.

In her ruby-red minidress, Gabrielle appeared right beside me. "Hey, welcome! Sit wherever you want."

"Actually, I came to apologize. I think someone might have accidentally left donuts they got from us at the picnic on the Fourth of July in your coatroom, and the donuts might be attracting ants or something. I could clean it up for you, if you like." Right, there I was, with no cleaning supplies. Maybe Gabrielle would think they were in my backpack with my wallet and phone. I probably did have some tissues. . . .

Gabrielle gazed off toward my left. "Ugh. I hope not. Let's go check."

I followed her into a small wood-paneled room lined in closet rods. Most of the hangers were empty, but a raincoat and a droopy sweater hung from two of them. The birthday boy's older brother had been right that only big people could see what was on the shelves. In hopes of seeing as much as a taller person might, I backed up as far as I could. My shoulder bumped hangers. They clattered.

Gabrielle jumped. "You scared me."

"Oops. Sorry." If Gabrielle hadn't killed Taylor, she might think that I had, and being alone in this tiny room with me was making her edgy. Her possible nervousness wasn't proof that she was innocent, however.

Pointing at a short folded ladder in a corner behind a couple of umbrellas, I asked, "Mind if I climb up on that to look?"

Gabrielle shrugged. "Go ahead. I've got to go see if any patrons have arrived on the patio. How come you're not working today?"

"It's my day off."

"Lucky you."

I asked, "Do you work long hours?"

"Very. But that's how you advance, right? By doing a good job and impressing the boss."

Could she have been at work when the birthday boy's family left the skyrocket birthday cake here? I quickly asked, "Didn't you have the Fourth of July off?"

"I had to work as soon as my duties at the picnic finished so I could have that night off." She lowered her voice. "I told my boss that another of my duties as duchess was going to the fireworks." She spoke normally again. "While I was working here that afternoon, though, I could barely hear what people were ordering over kids screaming in the bouncy castles."

"Did you get a chance to eat the donut we gave you at the picnic?"

"Too fattening." She turned to go. "Let me know if you need help, but if there are bugs or dust bunnies up there, I don't want to hear about them."

"Okay." She was gone before I could ask her what she'd done with the donut from the picnic. Or perhaps more important, what she'd done with the bag we'd put it in. That bag was the same size as the one we'd later given to the birthday boy with his skyrocket cake inside it. I also hadn't asked her why the donut from the picnic had been too fattening when the one she'd eaten at Deputy Donut must not have been. Maybe it had something to do with her wanting to sit near police officers in Deputy Donut so they could hear her proclaim that she'd loved Taylor and was devastated by her loss. Maybe I was being cynical.

I opened the ladder and climbed up it. Frisky Pomegranate was too new for dust bunnies. Except for the abandoned clothing and umbrellas, the coatroom was spotless. No donut crumbs, no forgotten bag of donuts pushed to the back. No ants. No bugs.

Bracing myself with one hand after checking the final shelf, I wondered if someone had taken the bag of six donuts from one of these shelves and, if they had, if they'd left fingerprints. And if the fingerprints would still be there . . .

I hadn't seen any fingerprint powder, which didn't prove that the police hadn't already dusted the room for prints. Someone could have cleaned.

I hoped the police weren't about to check that room for prints. Now they'd find quite a few of mine. I wasn't about to try to wipe them away, though. If Gabrielle came back and found me doing that, she'd be certain the room was full of crumbs and critters. Deciding to take my chances on having to explain to the police why my prints were in that room, I folded the ladder and tucked it back where I'd found it.

Gabrielle was on the patio. "Find anything?"

"Nothing. Sorry for bothering you."

"No problem. We've got lunch specials today. The soup's French onion, and the meat pie is steak and stout."

"Sounds good, but I'd better get home to my cat. Another time."

"Hey, did you just get your hair done? Who did it?"

"Felicia."

"Felicia's good. Too bad Taylor didn't appreciate her talents."

I agreed and crossed the street. I was about a quarter of the way down the kitty-corner path on the square when I turned and looked back. In that red dress and apron, Gabrielle was standing still, just about where I'd last seen her, and she was watching me.

Like she'd seen through my story about donuts still being in the coatroom and attracting ants. After the picnic on the Fourth, Gabrielle could have carried her one donut inside its bag into Frisky Pomegranate. Then, after the birthday boy's family left their bag of donuts in the coatroom, Gabrielle could have taken it with her and no one noticed, especially if she'd tossed out the first bag.

I'd seen her leaving the fireworks shortly before the skyrocket cake exploded. If she was the one who had taken the bag of six donuts to the fireworks, she might have figured out why I'd been asking questions about her one donut, the family's bag of donuts, and the hours she'd worked on the Fourth. If Gabrielle was a killer, I could have put myself in danger.

Maybe she had never seen that bag of six donuts. She could have been watching me walk away because she didn't have anything else to do at the moment. Or maybe she'd merely been watching those two squirrels chase each other around the trunk of a huge oak tree.

I had told Brent that the birthday boy's family thought they might have left the donuts at Felicia's or Frisky Pomegranate. Brent or another investigator could have already asked at those two places about the bag of donuts. That could explain Felicia's avoiding giving me direct answers and Gabrielle's possibly watching me walk away. Both Gabrielle and Felicia could be innocent of harming Taylor. Or, I reminded myself, either of them could be guilty. I walked faster.

At home, I made a sandwich of Gouda, avocado slices, and bean sprouts on thick multi-grain bread and ate it outside underneath the pergola while Dep padded through the grass searching for anything that might creep, crawl, or slither. After lunch, I took Dep inside, grabbed the key for the padlock on my parents' shed, went out to the driveway, and got into my bright red sports car.

I thought about Brent's offer to go to the campground with me. Company would have been nice, but he probably needed to work long hours to figure out—under Detective Rex Clobar's direction—who had intentionally harmed Taylor. Besides, it wasn't like going to my parents' campground was difficult or painful.

Unlike the morning of the Fourth of July, I had time to take County Road G, my once-favorite scenic route. However, I'd been avoiding it for nearly seven years, ever since the body of the man who'd owned my favorite gourmet grocery store had been found near that road. And then, five years later on that same isolated road, I'd had a chilling encounter with a murderer. The memory still gave me nightmares.

I took the quicker way. About a half mile before the parking lot for Fallingbrook Falls, I turned down a wooded lane and into the Fallingbrook Falls Campground. It had been carved out of the forest when my grandparents were in their twenties. Underneath a shady canopy, narrow roads looped through the campground. The campsites were separated by thickets of trees and shrubs, which made them cozy and private, but the campground was also a sociable place. Whenever campers wanted to be neighborly, they could stroll along dirt roads and stop to chat with new folks and old friends. At this time of year, the campground was a green glen. RVs and trailers occupied most of the sites. I spotted only one tent. People waved as I passed, and I waved back.

Except that the grass had grown, my parents' site looked exactly like it had when I'd last cut their minuscule lawn. The concrete pad for the RV was still bare.

My parents had rented the same site since before I was born. When I was a kid, we'd spent summer weekends and vacations in a series of ever-larger tents, tent trailers, and camping trailers. Misty, Samantha, and I had clambered over every inch of the trails, including the ones we weren't supposed to, the dangerous and slippery ones next to the falls and close to the quickly flowing river above them.

I wrestled the push mower out of the shed and rolled it through the grass. Shaded by birches and white pines, the lawn wasn't particularly lush. The smell of cut grass and the sounds of the mower's quiet blades and of neighboring children's laughter brought back happy memories.

Although the lawn was small, the site was large, hedged in by cedars and junipers, and there was a pit big enough for the bonfires that my parents loved to host, with lots of room around the fire for other amateur musicians and their instruments. A huge boulder had been my favorite climbing structure and perch until I was old enough to explore the campground and the trails around it by myself or with Misty and Samantha.

I slotted the mower between garden tools and lawn furniture in the shed, closed the door, and padlocked it.

On the dirt road beside the campsite, a vehicle slowed.

I turned around.

Spraying gravel, a small black car sped up and disappeared beyond cedars, but not before I caught a glimpse of the driver.

I was almost certain he was that photographer, Philip Landsdowner.

Chapter 21

The small black car went out of sight. The driver had not been, as far as I could tell, taking photos.

I wasn't sure whether I should rush away, stay where I was, or drive slowly around the campground in case the man I'd seen was Philip Landsdowner and he was living here. If I saw him in a campsite—maybe the one with the tent?—I might learn which part of the campground to avoid.

Searching for him would be creepy, though, and I wasn't sure about hanging around, either, in case he returned.

After a swift check to assure myself that my parents wouldn't have much to do when they arrived besides park their rig, level it, and connect everything, I jumped into my car and drove away.

Halfway back to Fallingbrook, I noticed a black car keeping pace behind me.

Other vehicles got between us, but no matter how many vans, trucks, and cars came and went, the black car maintained its two-block distance behind me all the way to the outskirts of Fallingbrook.

I loved my bright red sports car, but I was beginning to regret having chosen that color. It was easy to spot.

And easy to follow.

Maybe I had no reason to be alarmed. Still, I wasn't about to lead that black car to Dep's and my home. I continued north through downtown Fallingbrook. Patios in front of Deputy Donut and the Fireplug Pub were crowded.

The black car was still two blocks behind me.

It was time for some diversionary tactics. I drove up the west side of the village square and turned right at the north end of the square. Lots of people were enjoying a break on Frisky Pomegranate's patio. I didn't see Gabrielle. I turned right again and drove down the east side of the square.

The black car made both of those right turns. Not only that, it had moved up and was only about a block behind me, and no vehicles were between us.

I figured I could drive around the square again and again, and the black car would probably stop following me.

I had a better idea.

I continued beyond the south end of the square, made a sharp right, zoomed past a sign that said AUTHORIZED VEHICLES ONLY, and stopped in the police department's parking lot.

My back was to the street I'd just left. I looked at my side-view mirror. The black car sped past. I craned my neck around to see out. Tires squealing, the black car turned east at the next street.

I hadn't been able to see the driver.

Slowly, I released my grip on the steering wheel.

Maybe the driver had not been Philip Landsdowner. Small black cars were not exactly unusual. However, if the unknown driver had wanted to go east, he hadn't needed to drive around three sides of the square. He could have turned east at the south end of the square and driven past the fronts of the fire and police stations.

Reminding myself that the driver could have been daydreaming and temporarily lost his way, I backed out of the police department's lot, parked near Freeze, phoned Misty, and asked if I could bring ice cream to the evening's barbecue at her place.

"Sure. Samantha, Hooligan, and Scott are definitely coming."

"Great!" My matchmaking was progressing nicely. She added, "I'm not sure about Brent."

As if I didn't know him, I asked, "Brent?" Hadn't we discussed a get-together that included only Misty, Samantha, Hooligan, Scott, and me? But Misty was hosting the dinner. She could invite anyone she wanted.

She explained, "I thought even numbers would be nice."

It could have been worse. Brent was better than some random person she might have found for me. Brent understood my reluctance to become attached to anyone, except as a friend.

Misty and I said our goodbyes. I tucked my phone into my backpack and checked my windows and mirrors. No small black cars seemed to be hanging around. I headed to Freeze.

On the Fourth, Kelsey had seemed critical of Taylor's sometimes being late. I'd caught a glimpse of Kelsey in the crowd leaving the fireworks display before the stack of donuts exploded. How could I get Kelsey to discuss Taylor?

I didn't have to. As soon as I went into the cute shop, Kelsey asked me quietly, "Did you hear about Taylor?" Her eyes were red.

"It was horrible." I meant it.

There must have been a bell or buzzer in the kitchen that alerted workers that the front door had opened. Again, Mama Freeze backed in from the kitchen with a cardboard tub of ice cream. "What was horrible?" she asked. "Not our ice cream, I hope."

I didn't feel like joking about her ice cream, which she had to know I loved. I said, "What happened to Taylor."

Mama Freeze set the barrel down and wiped her eyes with the back of one hand. "Such a terrible tragedy. And to think, I was there only minutes before she was hit. If I'd only known, I'd have done something to prevent it."

"Me, too," Kelsey said.

Unsure whether or not these two knew Gabrielle, I didn't

tell them that Gabrielle had said the same thing. Instead, I clumsily changed the subject. "Felicia told me she was at the fireworks with you, Mama Freeze."

The ice cream shop owner had a wonderful belly laugh. "Felicia always complains that she hates fireworks, but she always goes with me."

Kelsey's smile was wan. "That's because you bring ice cream."

Mama Freeze waggled her eyebrows. "Bribery will get you nearly anywhere."

I asked, "Doesn't it melt, even in a cooler?"

"Bribery?" Mama Freeze demanded.

I could tell she was teasing, but I clarified my question anyway. "Ice cream."

"Not if the cooler has dry ice in it," she explained. "Wonderful invention."

Kelsey sniffled.

I felt a little guilty. Our bantering was obviously making Kelsey feel worse, but I needed more answers, so I continued the joking, with a hidden agenda that I hoped I could keep hidden. "I see why Felicia likes to go places with you, Mama Freeze, even if they give her headaches."

Mama Freeze raised her chin and opened her eyes wide. "There's my wonderful personality, too, don't forget."

I smiled back at her. "Who could forget that? Felicia didn't tell me what she brings." Keeping my agenda hidden wasn't exactly easy.

"Nothing. Nothing to eat, that is," Mama Freeze said with a fond smile. "But she goes absolutely nowhere without her battery-powered hair dryer, curling iron, and straightening iron. For emergencies, she says. The bag she carries is about twice the size of my cooler, and my cooler is not petite, let me tell you!"

So . . . the evening of the Fourth of July, both Felicia and Mama Freeze must have carried containers large enough to conceal six donuts and a homemade rocket that could shoot out a marble or two. . . .

Mama Freeze took an empty barrel from the display freezer and put the new one in. "Triple chocolate," she told me. "Swirls of milk and white chocolate with semisweet chocolate chunks mixed in. One of Taylor's absolute favorites." She wiped at her eyes again. "What would you like, Emily?"

"A quart of that, a quart of mint chocolate chip, and a quart of French vanilla."

Mama Freeze prompted, "Kelsey?"

Kelsey was still standing with a stunned expression on her face. Rivulets of tears running down her cheeks, she opened the back of the display freezer and dug her paddle into a tub of French vanilla. "I'll pack them for you, Emily." Her voice sounded muffled. Both she and her boss, when her boss wasn't joking about bribing Felicia to go to fireworks with her, seemed to be actively mourning Taylor.

Mama Freeze, however, seemed to want to be sociable despite her grief. "I saw your pictures in the paper, Emily, but I almost didn't recognize you. You're usually so cheerful and smiling, but you looked angry or maybe even accusing in those pictures."

"In one of them, I was only teasing my business partner, Tom. In the ones taken at the fairgrounds after Taylor was injured, I was upset."

"Were you there?" Kelsey asked me. Although I'd seen her when I was coming back from the car with my sweater, I'd been fairly certain that she hadn't glanced my way.

"Yes. Didn't I say?" *No, Emily*, I scolded myself, *you certainly did not.* Kelsey and Mama Freeze were going to know I was up to something. I hoped they hadn't heard that I might have helped solve crimes a couple of other times.

Mama Freeze explained, "Emily was definitely there. Some of her pictures in the *Fallingbrook News* are from that night." She wrapped her undoubtedly cold hands in the skirt of her ruffled pink and white apron. "It was like who-ever took those pictures was trying to make you look like you were"—she let go of her apron and shrugged, palms up—"I don't know. Guilty or something, Emily."

I didn't admit that I'd thought the same thing when I saw those pictures. I asked, "Do you know anything about that photographer? His name's Philip Landsdowner."

Mama Freeze shook her head.

Kelsey turned toward us and plunked my quart of vanilla on the counter next to the old-fashioned bronze-toned cash register. "Isn't that the guy who kept coming in here and just sat staring at Jocelyn like she was his long-lost daughter or something?"

"That guy!" Mama Freeze exclaimed. "I'm not sure he was old enough to be her father, but he was definitely older than she is, and I could see why he made Jocelyn want to leave."

Kelsey rinsed a paddle in hot water and pushed it into the mint chocolate chip ice cream. "That wasn't it. He stared at Taylor when she was here, and at me, too, but the real reason that Jocelyn quit was because she felt like she was doing Tay-lor's job for her." Kelsey didn't look up from scooping ice cream.

Mama Freeze began packing the triple chocolate. "That doesn't make any sense. Nobody worked as hard as Taylor did." She stabbed the paddle down into the ice cream. "No-body," she repeated. She topped up the triple chocolate and closed the carton. Muttering that she needed to look after a new batch of cappuccino ice cream, Mama Freeze wiped her eyes, pushed the swinging door open, and disappeared into the kitchen.

I paid Kelsey.

"You hired Jocelyn, right?" she asked me.

"Yes."

"Good luck," Kelsey said. "She does make a fuss about oth-ers not doing their share. I'm not sure how Jocelyn defines her own share, but most people probably wouldn't agree with her about it."

And Gabrielle had confided that Taylor had told her that Jocelyn didn't work hard enough at Freeze.

I suspected that both Kelsey and Taylor had either made up stories or exaggerated some tiny fault of Jocelyn's that Tom and I would dismiss if we even noticed it. I defended Jocelyn. "She's worked very hard, so far."

Kelsey handed me a sturdy paper bag with all three quarts inside it. "There are only three of you working there, right? Her and her two bosses?"

"Right."

"How long has she worked for you two?"

"About a week and a half."

Kelsey nodded like a wise old person. "Just watch, is all I'm saying. As Mama Freeze said, Taylor worked hard, so I don't know what Jocelyn was going on about. She probably did leave because Philip Landsdowner was staring at her, not because of anything Taylor did or didn't do."

I thanked Kelsey, took the ice cream home, and put it into the freezer. I pre-chilled a cooler with a couple of ice packs and then went upstairs, showered, and changed out of the fuchsia shorts and blouse and into a casual and comfy navy and white striped T-shirt dress. When it was nearly time to leave, I slid a bottle of wine into my backpack with my wallet and phone. Only the top of the bottle's neck stuck out. I traded the possibly melting ice packs in my cooler for a couple of solidly frozen ones and tucked the ice cream into the cooler with them.

Misty lived less than a mile away. If I walked, wearing the backpack and lugging the cooler, I could justify eating more of that ice cream. . . .

Chapter 22

My white sandals were almost as comfortable as sneakers. I walked.

Misty's house was in a newer neighborhood than mine, one that had sprung up around 1930. Her home's entryway had its own little roof. One side of the roof was short, a straight slant. The other side was longer, not as steep, and had a jaunty upward curve at its lower edge. With that whimsical roofline, the diamond-paned leaded glass windows, and the door's wrought-iron hardware, the house looked like a larger version of one that elves might design for themselves.

Misty answered my knock. In a frilly white blouse, skinny white pants, and high-heeled sandals, she looked very feminine. Her long blond hair curled around her shoulders.

"Wow," I said.

"Is it too much? I could change into jeans."

"Or you could just put on your uniform, bulletproof vest, and clunky boots. That would impress him."

She pulled me inside. "You're terrible."

"You look fabulous. Don't even think of changing."

Smiling, Scott arrived a few minutes later. I was certain that Misty noticed how yummy he looked in his jeans and navy blue T-shirt. He handed her a bouquet of yellow roses. "From my garden," he explained. He also brought a bottle of wine and a stack of thick steaks, which he said he'd grill. "Fire extinguisher in hand," he joked.

Misty thanked him, found a perfect cut-glass vase for the roses, and put them and some water into it.

When the doorbell rang again, Misty was drizzling dressing over her garlicky green bean and tomato salad. I answered the door.

Samantha was on the narrow stoop with a big bowl of potato salad and a bottle of wine. Her short hair was tinted in pastel blues and aquas that coordinated with her floral-printed summer dress. I peeked past her. Hooligan was nowhere in sight.

A few minutes later, he showed up looking adorably boyish with his freckles and auburn hair and in his cutoffs, polo shirt, and sandals. He brought a shrimp ring appetizer and another bottle of wine.

We set up Misty's kitchen island as a buffet, and Scott poured us each a glass of wine. We toasted each other. Samantha and Hooligan stood side by side, bare arms touching. The baby blue of his shirt coordinated nicely with Samantha's dress. They kept throwing smiles at each other. *Yes!*

"Brent probably can't make it," Misty told us. "He said to eat without him."

In a way, I was relieved. In another way, I was disappointed. As long as the numbers were uneven, Scott would probably divide his attention equally between the rest of us, and there would be no chance for him to show Misty that he preferred her.

Then I realized that, in the back of my mind, I was actually considering pretending that Brent and I were more interested in each other than we really were, only to throw Misty and Scott together. That might be okay, as long as Brent understood why we were doing it. But I had no idea how I could go about suggesting such a thing to him without sounding really peculiar.

Try not to hurt Brent, Misty had told me.

Telling someone that I was pretending to be romantically interested in him in order to do some matchmaking might not be the best way of not hurting that particular someone. Saying it to a friend, even a good friend . . . well, I wasn't going to. Brent's friendship mattered to me. A lot.

Still, I was almost glad that he hadn't come. Maybe the others would have tried to throw the two of us together more than either Brent or I would have liked.

Hooligan and Scott went out to Misty's patio with the steaks. From inside, we could hear the rumble of their deep voices.

Misty beamed at Samantha. "I'm happy for you," she said.

I agreed.

Samantha blushed. "Thank you, Misty, for making certain that we met and for not minding spending your time off with your work partner."

Misty dismissed her thanks. "He's easy to be around. We work well together, partly because of the structure of the police department. There's no question about who's boss in our relationship. I have seniority, and *I'm* boss." She let out a devilish cackle, which made the other two of us burst out laughing just as the men brought the steaks in.

They gave us funny looks but didn't say anything.

We loaded our plates and took them outside to Misty's patio. Her large round umbrella table was set for six, with pretty turquoise quilted place mats and matching cloth napkins on the glass surface.

Samantha and Hooligan sat beside each other. Misty was between Hooligan and Scott, and I was between Scott and the empty chair. Flushed, Misty was charming and not at all abrupt, and I had a feeling that if Scott hadn't already noticed how attractive she was, he was seeing it now.

It was getting late when the five of us carried the dishes into the kitchen.

The doorbell rang. Misty left to answer it.

She came back with Brent.

Misty might believe that even numbers were good, but I felt suddenly awkward. Brent knew about my matchmaking. The other four seemed to be pairing off the way I'd hoped, which left Brent and me as a pair of non-dating singles. We might look like we were dating when we weren't.

I told myself I was making a big deal out of nothing.

And I was right. There was no problem. Brent came into Misty's kitchen smiling at everyone and with his hands full of gourmet flatbreads, cheese, grapes, strawberries, and yet another bottle of wine, which meant that we could all smile and greet him without worrying about hugs, handshakes, and backslaps. He wore a white shirt untucked over khakis. No shoulder holster in sight.

We had already devoured the shrimp ring. Brent's offering worked as an appetizer for him and a pre-dessert for the rest of us. There was no way we would drink all of the wine we'd brought, but no one minded having just a little more.

Scott took the last steak out of Misty's fridge. We all went outside and joined forces, teasing Brent that the rest of us were going to help ourselves to his steak. After the meat and salads were on Brent's plate, we all sat at Misty's outdoor table again, but not where we'd sat before. I ended up across from Brent.

Absently watching him while he ate, I thought about what I'd learned from Felicia, Gabrielle, and the women at Freeze.

Brent caught me staring at him. My face heated. With his slightly unnerving detective expression, he stared right back. I looked away. Maybe, sometime when we were alone, I might discuss the murder investigation with him. At the moment, I needed to relax and enjoy being with these friends.

When Brent was ready for dessert, we dug into the ice cream.

We joked, laughed, and teased one another until my face hurt from smiling. Needing to go to work, Samantha left first. Hooligan stayed another half hour and then drove off in his own car. Scott, Brent, and I helped Misty clean up.

I glanced at the clock on her wall. How did it get to be almost ten? Dep usually made certain I was awake about five in the morning. "I should go," I said.

Brent asked me, "How did you get here?"

"Walked." If he offered me a ride, I would take it. Misty and Scott would be alone together.

"I'll walk you home." Brent's tone left no allowance for refusal.

"I'll come, too," Scott said. "I need to go into work."

That wasn't part of my matchmaking plan.

We all hugged Misty and then left for my house. Brent carried my cooler. Walking between the two tall men, I took my longest and quickest strides, but I suspected they both had to slow their normal pace for me.

Scott asked Brent how the murder case was going.

"We're making progress. Have you heard from your parents yet, Em?"

For a second, I considered commenting on his abrupt change of subject. Instead, I answered, "No. I went out to their campsite this afternoon. They hadn't arrived there yet, either."

Scott seemed very concerned until I reassured him that my parents almost never contacted me during their rambling journeys to and from Florida.

Both Scott and Brent came up onto my front porch with me. I opened the door.

"Me*ow!*" Dep ran outside to greet Brent. Quickly, he set down the cooler and scooped her up. I plunked the cooler on the living room floor and held out my arms. Dep wriggled. Brent handed her to me. He and Scott said goodbye and jogged down the porch steps. Dep and I watched as they turned toward downtown Fallingbrook and the police and fire departments, and then I carried Dep inside and deadbolted the door.

"Meow!"

I held her up to my face and looked into her eyes. "Brent will be back another time."

"Meow!"

"How could I give either of them goodbye hugs when I was hugging you?"

"Mew."

I cradled her like a baby. She purred.

Chapter 23

✼

The next day was Tom's first day off since Jocelyn had begun working with us. Dep and I arrived at Deputy Donut before Jocelyn did. My one day away felt like several. I went into the kitchen and punched down the yeast dough that Tom had made the night before and had placed in our temperature- and humidity-controlled proofing cabinet to rise overnight. The dough was perfect.

Singing, Jocelyn danced in. She rolled and cut out the yeast dough while I mixed the dough that used baking soda and baking powder as leavening agents.

I fried donuts. Filling milk and cream pitchers and making certain that every table was ready for guests, Jocelyn raced around the dining room. She was like a ball of energy, possibly about to do backflips over tables. Fortunately for the tables, she didn't attempt it.

Standing beside each other at the high marble work counter in the kitchen, we started the part of the job she seemed to like best, frosting and decorating.

"I love working here while I'm saving for college," Jocelyn confided. She had taken the year since high school to train and attend competitions. She was scheduled to start college in the fall. "If you and Tom need more time off this summer, I could work seven days a week, and put in overtime, too."

Summer was busy at Deputy Donut. "Would you like to

skip your day off tomorrow? With your gymnastics, you must not have much free time."

"I can handle it."

"Tom and I will both be here tomorrow, but you can come in, also, and see how you feel about working here seven days a week." I was certain that Tom wouldn't mind. "Did you work lots of hours at Freeze?"

"Yes, and sometimes at very short notice when . . . um, when one of the employees didn't show up."

I carefully did not look at her. "I got the impression from Kelsey that Taylor was often late for work."

Jocelyn sighed. "She was almost never on time, and she took days off without warning anyone, which was why I sometimes had to drop everything and go in to work. It was okay, but being able to plan ahead is better. And I really wouldn't mind being called in on short notice, as long as I get to my coach when I'm supposed to. That's another reason I like it here. You two let me go at five thirty, and sometimes before."

"Mama Freeze told me that Taylor was a very hard worker."

Jocelyn didn't say anything for a heartbeat, and then she muttered, "She worked hard when Mama Freeze was looking."

"But you and Kelsey and other clerks often took up the slack?"

"Yes, although I worked in the kitchen more than out front with the other clerks."

"Why was that?"

"I like making good things to eat."

"Did Taylor work in the kitchen, too?"

Shuffling her feet, Jocelyn shifted her position. "Not much. I probably shouldn't say this, but she only worked in the kitchen or worked hard when she needed to make a good impression."

"On Mama Freeze." I stated it like fact.

"On Mama Freeze. Taylor had no problem making a good

impression on people buying ice cream. She was really good at dealing with the public."

"You are, too."

Jocelyn drizzled lines of chocolate icing over the vanilla frosting on raised vanilla donuts. "I have trouble smiling when I don't feel like it, but Taylor could smile no matter what. A kid drops an ice cream cone? No problem. *Taylor* would clean it up after the kid left."

I thought I heard doubt in that last sentence. "And did she?"

"Not when I was around. I usually did the cleaning and tidying during the hours we were open. The Jolly Cops Cleaning Crew came in at night. I only met them once, but they truly are jolly. You and Tom said they clean here, too. Are they also cops?"

"They were. They retired from the police force."

"That would be a good cover for someone who liked to snoop or for plainclothes policemen."

I laughed. "It would. But we have our own retired policeman working here most days."

"Tom's nice, isn't he." It wasn't a question.

"Very." I slid a tray of donuts into our display case and then returned to the work counter. And to my questions. "Did you ever see anyone threaten Taylor?"

In a playful tone, Jocelyn accused, "You sound like a police officer. I told them, too. I never noticed any threats to her."

"What about from Kelsey and the other clerks at Freeze?"

Jocelyn slathered pink icing on plain raised donuts. "They never made any threats. And of course Mama Freeze wasn't threatening. She was going to promote someone to manage all of the clerks, and I think Taylor was the one Mama Freeze was planning to promote."

"What made you think that?"

"Little things. Comments like we should all treat customers like Taylor did, and we could learn a lot from Taylor, and soon Taylor would be in a position to help us be better employees. It was pretty obvious." Jocelyn quickly added, "It didn't bother me, but when I heard that you might be looking for someone to work here for the summer, I applied and was happy to get the job."

"And we're glad you did."

"Thanks." Humming, she dotted the pink-frosted donuts with multicolored sprinkles.

My phone rang. Another scam number. I didn't answer. Sighing, I thrust my phone back into my apron pocket.

"Expecting a call?" Jocelyn asked.

I told her about my parents' long silence and that I had expected them back sooner than this.

"No news is good news when people go missing. They'll turn up." Jocelyn sounded about sixty instead of nineteen. It was cute.

"Soon, I hope, so I can stop worrying about them."

"You talk like you're the parent and they're teenagers." We weren't facing each other, but I heard a smile in her voice.

"I often feel that way." Wondering how much consternation a girl like Jocelyn, who could probably hang by her ankles from chandeliers, must have caused her parents, I unlocked the front door and turned our WELCOME sign to face the sidewalk.

Later, after the Knitpickers had been served, I was frying donuts. Jocelyn came into the kitchen and picked up a carafe of coffee for the retired men. She glanced toward the front of the store, thrust the carafe onto the marble counter, and scurried away, into the storeroom.

Philip Landsdowner opened the front door and came inside.

Chapter 24

Luckily, the donuts were perfectly golden on both sides and ready to be lifted out of the oil. I quickly hung the basket to drain, grabbed the carafe of coffee that Jocelyn had unceremoniously left on the counter, and headed toward the front of the store.

I must have resembled a mama bear protecting her cub. Philip Landsdowner glanced at me barreling toward him, opened the front door only enough to slip out, and left. Without stopping at one of our patio tables, he kept going to the sidewalk and turned south on Wisconsin Street.

Maybe he had noticed Jocelyn's flight into the storeroom, and he was going up our driveway and around to the back of Deputy Donut in hopes of . . . what? Taking a photo of her and then cutting her out of it?

Both of our back doors, the one from the office and the one from the storeroom, were supposed to be locked whenever we weren't using them. I was certain that the office door was, but had Jocelyn relocked the storeroom door that morning after she arrived?

I poured coffee into the retired men's cups and returned to the kitchen. With a clean carafe in one hand and a too-innocent look on her face, Jocelyn strolled out of the storeroom.

"Did you go outside?" I asked her.

She lifted the carafe. It partially hid her reddening face. "I went to get this."

"Philip Landsdowner came in, just barely, for less than a minute, and left when he saw me coming. He turned south on Wisconsin Street. I was afraid he might go up the driveway and come around to the back and try to get inside."

Jocelyn's blush deepened. "Why would he do that?"

I looked steadily at her. "I don't know, but I don't trust him. I'm sure the office door is locked, and besides"—I glanced into the office—"with all of those windows, we'd see him. Just to be safe, I'll go check the door near the loading dock."

"I'm sure I locked it this morning, but . . ." She pointed at the fryer. "Want me to put those donuts you just fried on racks to cool?" I loved that she didn't have to be told what to do. She offered or went ahead and did it. Her shoulders looked stiff, not her usual graceful posture. Then again, a gymnast might tense up like that if she was about to do a few handsprings.

"Yes, please."

To my relief, the storeroom door was still locked. I went back to the kitchen and told Jocelyn. She didn't look at me, but her shoulders lowered to their normal level. I peeked through the office to the portion of our parking lot that I could see. Philip Landsdowner was nowhere in sight.

All morning, I missed Tom and his expertise at quickly frying and decorating donuts, but Jocelyn and I worked well together, and I didn't notice any of the slacking off that Kelsey and Gabrielle had warned me about.

In the afternoon, Duke Nicholas came in by himself. Except for his left arm being in a sling, the twentysomething with the spiky platinum hair and the deep tan looked not only healthy but also as strikingly handsome as he had when I'd first seen him in the sunlight at the parade-marshaling grounds.

By the time I made it to him, one of his coupons for coffee and a donut was lying on the table beside him.

I asked how he was doing.

"Okay." He touched his bandaged arm. "Almost the worst part for a lefty is learning to do everything right-handed."

Was that worse than losing your girlfriend to an early and probably painful death?

I was being unfair. He probably couldn't bear to discuss Taylor with people he didn't know well.

He wanted our special coffee for the day, a smooth, slightly fruity light roast from El Salvador. He ordered a cherry cheese-cake–filled donut to go with it.

I returned to the kitchen and let Jocelyn serve him. She spent a long time at his table. He was smiling at her and talking in a much more animated way than he had on the Fourth of July in my car or later when the royal court made their walking tour of the square. He'd barely seemed to notice Jocelyn that time. To be fair, he'd been with Taylor.

Jocelyn moved off to wait on other customers.

Nicholas finished his donut and coffee and beckoned me to his table. He asked me quietly, "Do you know if Jocelyn's dating anyone?"

Ordinarily, I might have suggested that he should ask her himself, but in case he had murdered his previous girlfriend, I wasn't about to encourage him to find more reasons to talk to Jocelyn. "She is."

After I went back to waiting on other customers, Nicholas stood and headed toward the front of the shop. I helped him with the door and watched him walk away.

I wasn't paying him much attention.

I was thinking about the night of the Fourth. His left arm had been around Taylor before the firework went off behind them. The lighter we'd found had been close to where his left hand had been. Lighting a fuse behind the back of the person seated next to one would be difficult at any time. But in that situation, it would have been easier for a left-handed person than for a right-handed one.

Shortly after four thirty, the last of our customers left. Jocelyn and I cleared the tables. She made a disgusted face. "Nicholas is *creepy*. How can he go around making passes at people right after his girlfriend died?"

I rolled my eyes to show that I didn't know the answer to that question. Glad that Jocelyn did not seem about to fall for Nicholas, I said, "You knew Taylor from high school and also from Freeze. Did you know Nicholas from school, too, or Gabrielle or Ian?"

"I didn't know any of them very well. They were in lots of clubs and the two guys played football. I was more of a bookworm, and my free time was taken up by ballet and gymnastics."

"Were the four of them popular?"

"I guess."

"Were they friends with each other?"

"Gabrielle and Taylor seemed to be, but I don't know about Ian and Nicholas. Maybe they were, because of football. I don't remember seeing them together, but I didn't notice."

"Was Kelsey in their class?"

"Yes. All three girls—Kelsey, Gabrielle, and Taylor—were cheerleaders. Taylor was head cheerleader."

"Were you a cheerleader?" She'd had the gymnastic skills even then.

"I didn't want to be one. Most of them, like Kelsey, Taylor, and Gabrielle, were snarky, including about one another. Which I guess is how you and I are acting right now . . ." She gave me a sidelong glance.

I turned a chair upside down on top of a table. "It's only gossip if someone else is doing it."

She laughed.

I asked, "What did you think of Ian and Nicholas in high school?"

"They were okay. Ian was president of Student Council and often made the honor roll. Nicholas was laid-back, like having lots of friends was more important to him than doing well in school. Maybe he was afraid that if he got good grades, he wouldn't be popular. Or maybe he was afraid that even if he tried, he would still get only Bs and Cs."

"Did any of those four date each other back in high school?"

"Ian and Taylor were already a couple when I started at Fallingbrook High, and they were still together when they graduated. Everyone thought they'd get married. I don't know when they broke up."

"Gabrielle said it was after the royal court was elected. Did Gabrielle ever date Ian or Nicholas?"

"I don't think so, but I don't really know."

"What about Kelsey?"

"I'm pretty sure she had a crush on Ian in high school."

Maybe, if neither Kelsey nor Ian was guilty of harming Taylor, the two of them could find happiness together. And Gabrielle and Nicholas? Gabrielle had flirted with Nicholas when they were in my donut car, but Nicholas had been rude to her as if he didn't like her. However, when it came to romance, people could do surprising things.

Although knowing that Jocelyn might not want to discuss my next subject, I commented, "Kelsey said that Philip Landsdowner, the photographer, often came into Freeze and stared at you."

Jocelyn didn't say anything for a couple of seconds. "She's right. He did. I hated it. And that's partly why I wanted to leave there." She sighed. "It didn't take him long to find me."

"If Philip Landsdowner or anyone else bothers you, tell me or Tom or one of the officers who come in here. We'll make certain he stops."

"Okay."

"I'm serious. I don't want you to quit working here because a customer is making you uncomfortable."

"Don't worry. I'll tell you."

"And you'll be extra careful and observant, like when you're riding your bike? I think he drives a small black car."

"He does. And I'll be careful."

"Promise?"

"Promise." She didn't smile. Her face was unusually pale.

Chapter 25

All the way home with Dep on her leash, I worried about Jocelyn and how to keep her happy and safe.

Brent always told me to call him if I had concerns. As soon as Dep and I were locked inside our house, I phoned his personal line.

He answered right away.

"I'd like to talk to you about a few things that might or might not be related to Taylor's murder," I told him. "I'm not sure they're important."

"Doesn't matter. Where are you?"

"At home."

"I'll be over. I was just about to take a break. Can I bring dinner?"

"Sure!" I disconnected and looked down at Dep. Her pupils were enlarged and her ears were turned almost backward, giving her an owlish look. "Brent's coming." I probably hadn't needed to tell her. She must have heard his voice and guessed.

Pretending something like indifference, she sashayed into the kitchen to her food and water bowls, but after a few bites of kibble and a couple of dainty laps at her water, she ran to the living room and sat down with her nose almost on the front door. She stayed there until footsteps sounded on the wooden porch. Then she stood up, sniffed at the crack between the door and the jamb, turned toward me, and meowed loudly.

"I'm coming, Dep," I said.

The doorbell rang.

I peeked out. It was Brent.

I opened the door. He handed me several paper bags and smiled, but that detective watchfulness lurked behind his gray eyes, as if he was worrying about the information I'd said I had.

In the kitchen, I opened the bags. He'd brought a meal from a new restaurant in town that featured foods from India—chicken tikka, spinach with Indian cheese, and spicy chickpeas, all to be served with basmati rice and tangy, salty Indian pickle.

The dishes had been flavored with delicate and different combinations of freshly ground spices, many of which I couldn't name, but which were delicious. We mopped up the sauces with yummy chunks of yeast-leavened naan.

After we ate, Brent took his notebook from a jacket pocket. "What did you want to tell me?"

"I had yesterday off. I drove to my parents' campsite. Something peculiar happened." I told him about the small black car staying at a distance behind my car all the way back to Fallingbrook and described how I'd encouraged it to stop following me.

"Why didn't you tell me this yesterday?"

"I wasn't sure it was important."

"And are you sure now?"

"No, and I didn't get a good look at the driver, but I thought it was Philip Landsdowner."

"Did you come into the station?"

"No, merely driving into your lot was enough. And there could be an explanation for someone following me around three sides of the square, like bad navigational advice." I took a deep breath and smiled a little sheepishly. "Also, I didn't want to take the time. I needed ice cream to take to Misty's last night."

He obviously understood the reason for my sheepish smile. "You needed ice cream from Freeze, where you knew Taylor used to work." It wasn't quite an accusation about possibly interfering in a police investigation.

"Freeze makes the best ice cream."

"Granted." I saw a twinkle in those gray eyes. "And what you brought last night was good. So, tell me what you learned at Freeze."

"Probably the most important thing is that both Kelsey and Mama Freeze needed to control tears when discussing Taylor. Also, Kelsey said that someone who was probably Philip Landsdowner used to come into Freeze and stare at Jocelyn and also at other clerks. And then, today, Jocelyn and I were working at Deputy Donut alone, and Landsdowner came in. Again, Jocelyn rushed into the storeroom where she would be out of his sight. I headed toward the front. And that's when Landsdowner did something strange. I know he saw me coming toward him, but he left without talking to anyone or ordering anything. It was like he wasn't going to stay if he couldn't talk to Jocelyn."

"Or Tom."

Knowing that Brent sometimes liked to play devil's advocate, I grinned. "I didn't *think* he was looking for Tom, but I could be wrong. And he definitely did not want to talk to me. He seems much too interested in Jocelyn, while it's obvious, at least to me, that she does not want to be around him. Or even to be seen by him."

"We'll have another talk with him. Is anything else worrying you? It doesn't matter how small it seems. Anything might be the piece that puts the puzzle together and solves a murder."

"Maybe you know this, but Mama Freeze told me that she

carried a cooler of ice cream to the fireworks, and that Felicia always carries a large tote of hairdressing supplies. Both of them could have hidden that homemade skyrocket and stack of donuts in things they were carrying."

Brent wrote in his notebook.

I probably hadn't learned anything at Frisky Pomegranate that Brent didn't already know. Investigators would have questioned Gabrielle about where she was and what she did on the Fourth of July. Brent would know that, if the family had left that bag of donuts in the coatroom, anyone who'd been in Frisky Pomegranate that evening could have picked it up. He might also have looked inside Frisky Pomegranate's coatroom and determined, as I had, that if a bag containing several of our special Fourth of July donuts had been left there on the Fourth, it was long gone.

I suspected that, in case investigators found my fingerprints in Frisky Pomegranate, I should tell Brent about my visit there, but I didn't want to admit that I'd been snooping.

There were a couple of other potential clues that Brent might not know, though. I told him, "Jocelyn said that Taylor was often late to work at Freeze, often missed days, and worked hard only when Mama Freeze was watching. Jocelyn told me she was almost positive that Mama Freeze was planning to promote Taylor to supervise the other clerks."

"Interesting," Brent said.

"Also, Deputy Donut customers sometimes don't realize that they're revealing possibly incriminating information about themselves. Today, Taylor's boyfriend, Nicholas, came into Deputy Donut. He didn't seem to be grieving over Taylor at all. When I asked how he was doing, he only answered that his arm wasn't too bad. Maybe it's a coping mechanism, but he flirted with Jocelyn, and later he asked me if Jocelyn was dating anyone."

"That could be a reaction to losing someone. Twenty-somethings can be socially inept."

"But losing his girlfriend to death. To *murder*."

We stared at each other, both of us undoubtedly thinking about Alec and our own reactions to his death. To his *murder*.

Breaking the staring contest by looking away, Brent conceded, "That's a little extreme."

"There's more. Nicholas is left-handed. Lighting that homemade skyrocket from the position he was sitting in wouldn't have been as difficult for him as it would have been for a right-handed person."

Again, Brent wrote in his notebook.

Not having brought any donuts home, I served us each a couple of scoops of lemon sherbet from Freeze.

After we finished eating, Brent didn't seem in a hurry to end his allegedly quick break and return to work. He carried Dep into the living room and relaxed on the couch with her on his lap. She purred.

I sat in the armchair across from them. Staring into the distance beyond the street outside, Brent stroked Dep's warm fur.

"Jealousy." Brent's one word broke into the purring quiet and startled me. "Felicia might have been jealous of Taylor's hair. Gabrielle might have been jealous because Taylor was elected queen and Gabrielle came in only second. Kelsey might have been jealous because Taylor was about to be promoted. Same goes for your assistant." Sitting on my hands, I resisted the urge to defend Jocelyn. "Nicholas might have been jealous of Ian. Even if Nicholas hadn't really cared about Taylor, he might have decided he had to prevent her from returning to Ian. Or maybe Ian was jealous of Nicholas and had tried to aim that skyrocket at Nicholas, not at Taylor. Jealousy can be a strong motive."

"Detective Clobar can stop suspecting me, then," I teased. "According to Philip Landsdowner, I was angry at Taylor for insulting my car."

Brent winked. "You could have been jealous of Taylor's convertible."

I snapped my fingers and gave my head a haughty shake.

"I have my own car, and it's fast and bright red, not a girly pastel. Besides, even if I had killed Taylor, how would I have ended up with her car? She didn't know me, and I couldn't be in her will, if she had one."

"She didn't, and that car is actually her mother's. All that Taylor left behind was a walk-in closet full of clothes and shoes plus about fifty-six dollars in the bank."

Those personal details made her death seem even sadder. "So, no one killed her for her possessions."

"I doubt it, but we haven't ruled out anything or anyone."

"I couldn't have craved her car. Besides my fast red car, I own one half of a vintage police car with a donut on top. Everyone in the *world* should be jealous of me."

He grinned. "We are."

"What about Philip Landsdowner? What would be his motive for killing Taylor?"

"Until you told me he used to go into Freeze, I didn't know he had a connection with Taylor."

"I did manage to tell you something useful this evening."

He had a really nice smile. "You often tell me useful things. And I probably don't thank you enough."

"Sure you do."

"I'm most interested in Landsdowner, thanks to all you've told me about him that he didn't mention to us and that we wouldn't necessarily have noticed. It sounds like he could be stalking both you and Jocelyn, and we take stalking seriously. But that's not all that concerns me. Maybe he had a good reason for editing Jocelyn out of photos, like he thought she and her parents would be stickier than other people about her photo being published, but I don't understand why he gave us that clearly doctored photo of you carrying the donuts. He's either up to mischief or trying to protect someone."

"Like himself."

"Exactly." Brent's hand on Dep's back stilled. "Thank you for the break."

"I didn't exactly give you a break from thinking about your latest case."

His smile was warm. "It was a break from other police officers. And with a purring cat." Dep had become a boneless lump of contentment in his lap. "You know why I don't want you playing amateur sleuth, don't you?" Those gray eyes focused on my face.

I had to look away. "So I won't compromise the police investigation."

"That, too. I also don't want you putting yourself in any sort of danger."

I still didn't look at him. Once, almost two years before, he'd said something similar and then he'd added *for Alec's sake,* and I had snapped at him because I'd been hurting too much to discuss Alec with his best friend. This time, I didn't have the least desire to snap at Brent. "Or Jocelyn," I said. "Or Tom."

"Or anyone."

I wanted to remind him that by keeping my eyes and ears open I might prevent a killer from striking again, but I knew that argument wouldn't work, not with Brent.

Probably figuring out what I was trying hard not to say, he sighed. "I suppose I should go back to work."

"Don't go," I teased. "You'll upset Dep." Having lightened the atmosphere a little, I risked looking at him.

He was staring down at my cat. Gently, he lifted her, brought her to me, and deposited her in my lap. "I'll see myself out, but don't forget the dead bolt as soon as she lets you get up."

Dep barely stirred. "Yes, sir," I said.

Because I was in the armchair, my back was to the door. Brent was behind me. A strong, warm hand gripped my shoulder for a second and then let go. I didn't hear Brent walk to the door, but I figured he was putting his feet down extra quietly so he wouldn't disturb Dep.

Then I felt warm breath riffle through the curls on top of my head, and there was the lightest of butterfly touches on my hair, like a kiss. Unsure how to react, or even if I could or should react, I sat still, not breathing.

The floor creaked. The door latched.

I heard Brent's footsteps as he trotted down the porch steps.

I remained sitting in a sort of shock.

What just happened?

Dep's purring gradually brought me back to a semblance of consciousness, and then, without moving, I mentally replayed and analyzed parts of Brent's short visit.

When he'd arrived with the bags of food, I'd used both hands to take them from him the way I always did, which prevented the casual and impersonal sorts of hugs we often gave each other as greetings when neither of us was carrying anything.

Usually, whenever Brent left we managed a semblance of a hug, or Brent gave Dep, me, or both of us knuckle-rubs. Sometimes, Brent ruffled my hair.

Tonight, though, Dep had been sleeping. Brent had eased her gently into my lap, and I hadn't been able to get up. And Brent had squeezed one of my shoulders and then . . . What?

Calm down, I told myself. *Nothing happened.*

Nothing in our relationship had changed. Brent had not kissed the top of my head. That had been a light knuckle-rub. That was all.

Try not to hurt Brent, Misty had said.

I wasn't sure I *could* hurt him. For all I knew, he was dating someone, and the affection he showed me was only because Alec had been his best friend and we both missed Alec.

Dep yawned, stood up, stretched, and hopped off my lap.

I remembered to shoot the dead bolt.

Chapter 26

✤

By morning, I'd convinced myself that the touch I'd felt had been a gentle pat, not a kiss.

Dep and I arrived at Deputy Donut before six thirty, the time that Jocelyn usually parked her bike and breezed into the kitchen. I told Tom that I'd given her permission to work that day.

Tom didn't mind. Although he had no grandchildren, his smile was grandfatherly. "She's a great help. As long as she doesn't burn out or miss any of her gymnastics, we're good."

Jocelyn didn't arrive at six thirty. At seven, after Tom had made dozens of donuts to be decorated, he asked if I was sure she was coming in.

I tried to remember exactly what we'd said. "Maybe I didn't make it clear that she could work today. I thought I did. But I'm not sure she actually said she would."

At nine, I tried her phone number. She didn't answer. I left a message for her to call me. When she'd applied for the job, she'd also given us her parents' numbers. I tried them. No answer. Maybe her parents were like me and usually ignored numbers they didn't recognize.

Misty, Hooligan, and Scott met for their morning coffee break and sat out on the patio in the sun. They seemed to have a great time together, and while Scott was his usual attentive self toward me during those short periods when I was beside their table, he was smiling a lot, mostly at Misty. I'd have liked to sit down and enjoy their company, but the patio and the shop were full, not that I was about to complain about having to rush around chatting with happy customers. Or about Scott and Misty seeming more than usually aware of each other. They were subtle and restrained about it, and I might have been the only one who noticed, though I did catch Hooligan watching them. A little grin twitched at his mouth. Recently having fallen for Samantha, he was probably super-alert to signs of budding romance in others, especially people he liked.

Not long after Misty, Scott, and Hooligan sauntered away together, I was in the kitchen, right behind the serving counter. Philip Landsdowner opened our front door only enough to slip in sideways. His gaze darting back and forth through the shop, he ambled in his loose-kneed way to the serving counter.

Again, he was wearing jeans, sneakers, a photographer's vest, and a long-lensed camera on a strap around his neck. His wandering gaze drifted beyond me into the kitchen. He asked quietly, "Where's Jocelyn?"

My spidey senses went on such high alert that I could almost feel the spideys crawling around in my curls underneath my Deputy Donut hat.

Philip Landsdowner knew Jocelyn's name. He wanted me to tell him where she was. I was almost glad she hadn't come to work.

But where was she? Did this droopy-looking man know, and was he only pretending that he didn't in order to establish an alibi for the approximate time when she disappeared?

Trying to keep my suspicions from showing, I said between almost clenched teeth, "I don't know."

"She works here, doesn't she?"

I turned my head. Tom was watching us. He looked casual, dipping donuts in brown sugar glaze, but I knew his retired police chief antennae were extended to their highest, and I was glad he was there. "Not at the moment." If anything, my teeth were more tightly clenched. I wanted to send Landsdowner away, but I didn't want to cause a scene. I also needed to learn as much as I could from him, especially if he had something to do with Jocelyn's not having come to work that morning.

Landsdowner leaned forward and asked in an even softer voice, "What's going on with the investigation into Taylor Wishbard's murder?"

Why would he think I could or would answer that? Had he noticed that I'd been with uniformed police officers at the fireworks even before Taylor's fatal injury? Maybe before he came inside just now, he had been watching me joke and chat with Misty and Hooligan, who had both been in their police uniforms.

"I don't know." I forced my teeth apart and tried to relax my face into a more natural expression. "You should give the police investigators all of the photos you took that night. And earlier in the day, too."

He made a disagreeable smirk. "I did."

"The original, unedited files," I stated sternly.

The smirk became a sneer. "When's Jocelyn coming in again? I'd like to do a feature on her."

"I don't know."

"Tomorrow?"

"I don't know." My jaw was nearly clamped shut again.

"Tell her she needs to talk to me. It's for her own good." He turned around.

A pocket spanned the lower half of the back of his vest. That pocket, pleated at the bottom and elasticized at the top, was definitely big enough to hold the bag containing six donuts that Jocelyn and I had given the birthday boy.

Landsdowner sidled through the dining area and went outside.

The spideys were holding a gymnastic event all over my scalp. *Tell her she needs to talk to me. It's for her own good.*

That had sounded like a threat. Would Jocelyn and her parents even want Philip Landsdowner to do a feature on her?

I joined Tom, now tending the fryers. He lifted a basket of perfectly fried unraised chocolate donuts out of the shimmering oil. "What was that all about?" he asked.

My face heating, both from being beside the deep fryer and from a combination of fear and anger at Philip Landsdowner, I told Tom what the man had said.

Tom lowered another basket of donuts into the fryer. "We're going to have to keep an eye on that girl."

"When she's here. Do you think we should call the police and report that she didn't show up for work?" It would have been a ridiculous idea if Landsdowner hadn't oozed in here and started asking questions about her.

"It's too soon," Tom answered, "considering that you're not sure she actually meant to come in today."

"Do you remember suspecting Philip Landsdowner of anything when you were on the Fallingbrook police force?"

"I don't remember that name."

I questioned him about other people I suspected of possibly having harmed Taylor, but he didn't know if any of those people had ever been involved in criminal activities, either. His eyes twinkled. "It might help if you told me their last names. Duke, Duchess, and King don't quite work for me."

I grinned back at him. "I don't know their last names."

He glanced past me. "Isn't that guy one of them?"

His handsome face a study in suppressed despair, Ian came into Deputy Donut and chose a table near the window.

"Yes, that's King Ian," I told Tom.

Sitting on the office windowsill overlooking the kitchen, Dep stared at me with a demanding look on her face, obviously requesting my presence in the office.

I wiggled my fingers at her and went to Ian's table. "How are you doing, Ian?" I tried to sound sympathetic without brashly inserting myself into a tragedy that was obviously affecting him.

He fiddled with his Deputy Donut coupon book. I could just make out the edges of a folded piece of paper crammed into the back of it. "Can I redeem one of these today?"

"You can redeem them any day in any way you want." I wondered what had become of the coupon book that had been destined for Taylor. Had she picked up her prizes before she was killed? Our fifty-two coupons weren't worth killing over, but were any of the prizes, assuming that her killer could obtain them, valuable? "What can I get you?"

He ordered the day's special coffee, a medium roast from the slopes of Mount Kilimanjaro in Tanzania, and a raised donut with vanilla frosting and chocolate sprinkles.

I brought him the coffee and donut. He fingered the mug as if testing how hot it was and then blurted, "I know you helped find out who the real killers were a couple of times."

Dread flickered deep in my mind. I'd achieved quite a reputation, mostly undeserved, and it wasn't a reputation I wanted. And it was one that Brent definitely did *not* want me to have. Remembering the way Brent had parted from me the night before, I felt myself flush. "You give me too much credit."

"Yeah, but can I talk to you?"

Chapter 27

✺

Despite my reluctance to be known as an amateur crime solver, I was certainly interested in anything that Taylor's ex-boyfriend might say about her murder and possibly about suspects. "Of course."

"You asked how I was, and I didn't answer. Sorry for being rude."

I dismissed that with a shake of my head. "You weren't."

"I was."

"Even if you were, I would understand." Hoping that Ian would tell me more and unwilling to explain my own long-term grieving, I stayed quiet and waited for him to explain.

He took a large bite out of the donut. "Taylor and I dated for years. I was sure I could win her back from that . . . from that . . . well, he didn't love her. Taylor and I had quarreled, so the timing was right for him to steal her from me. He just wanted to prove that he could."

I told him I was very sorry about her death.

"I'll get over it." A second bite almost demolished the donut.

Silently, I corrected him. *No, you won't. Not completely. Not if you loved her.*

He grabbed a coupon, gave it a vicious jerk, and tore it almost in half before it came out of the book. He swore under his breath and then apologized. "Should I give you a different one, instead?"

"That one will do."

With two long fingers, he guided the torn coupon across the glossy table toward me. "The police suspect me of harming Taylor. Why would I do a stupid thing like that? I was sure she would see what kind of guy Nicholas was and come back to me. And the quarrel that Taylor and I had was nothing. But the police won't believe that." Unlike Nicholas, Ian was obviously in pain. Emotional pain, not physical pain.

"They must have better suspects." I wasn't sure if it was true. I wasn't about to tell Ian that Philip Landsdowner was at the top of my list of suspects.

"They got a search warrant, and they took *my* computer and *my* phone."

I braced myself with one hand on the back of the chair next to his. "Does that worry you?"

As if taking a moment to rehearse his answer, he sipped at his coffee. "They'll find all the e-mails and texts I ever sent to Taylor. Most were totally innocent, like 'meet me after work' or 'call me tonight.' I was angry and hurt when she dumped me for that . . . for *him,* but I never threatened her. Never. Except they think I did. They think the e-mail I sent her on July third was a threat. I printed a copy to give her on the Fourth, in case she hadn't read the e-mail, but I chickened out, so I still have it. I wanted to see what you thought of what I wrote."

I could barely contain my curiosity as he pulled the folded piece of paper out of the back of the coupon book and started opening it. He must have read and reread his e-mail many times during the week since he printed it. Its edges were already ragged. Its creases were worn, and a couple of them looked about ready to split.

He handed me the tattered sheet of paper. "Here. This is identical to the e-mail the police have." Drinking his coffee and pinching donut crumbs into piles with his fingers, he watched me read.

The e-mail was addressed to Taylor Wishbard. It said: "You promised you would always be mine. It's time for you to stop pretending you prefer him. You succeeded. You made me jealous. Stop playing around. Leave him and come back to me. If you don't, I'm going to do something that will make you very sorry."

It was hardly romantic, and certainly not worded to make an estranged lover come running back. I understood why the police had interpreted it as a threat. I hoped, for Taylor's sake, that she hadn't read it and hadn't felt threatened on the last day of her life.

Barely breathing, I eased down into the chair beside Ian. "Did she read it?"

"I don't know. I was afraid to ask."

"What were you planning to do to her?"

"I wasn't going to do anything to her, but I know that's what it sounds like."

Wondering if he'd been trying to harm Nicholas, not Taylor, I nodded.

A new group of customers came in. Tom gestured with one hand to show that he'd look after them and headed toward their table.

Ian looked at the paper as he refolded it along its creases. "I was going to move away from Fallingbrook, go where I wouldn't see her with someone else. I was going to start a new life. I was giving her one last chance to come back to me. That's all. I wish I'd written it that way instead of the way I did. Maybe she would have come back to me. Maybe she'd be alive right now." Without seeming to realize how incriminating his words sounded, he poked the e-mail message into the coupon book and looked up at my face again. His mouth worked like he was trying to gulp down sobs. "You must have connections in the police force from the other times you solved murders. I saw you out on your patio earlier this morning talking to that woman who drove Taylor's car in the parade. Can you tell her or other police officers what I really meant?"

He wanted me to believe his one-sided story. I said as gently as I could, "I think you should tell them."

"I did. They didn't believe me. And there's more that makes them suspect me."

This was getting worse. Strangely, though, my spidey senses weren't sending out warnings about Ian. Maybe Philip Landsdowner had exhausted them.

Or Dep was taking over for them. She was still in the office, but she'd moved to the windowsill next to the dining area, and she was puffed up with her back arched. She was staring straight through her window at Ian.

I looked at him again and asked as kindly as I could, "What else makes the police suspect you, Ian?" The approximate ten-year difference between his and my ages was making me feel ancient.

"I left the fireworks before Taylor was hurt, and I didn't find out about her death until the next morning. I stopped in at Frisky Pomegranate for a coffee before work on the fifth. You know who Gabrielle is, don't you?"

"The duchess."

"She's a waitress at Frisky Pomegranate. She told me flat out that Taylor had been . . . was gone, and that Nicholas had been beside her when a firework exploded close to them, and that he was only slightly hurt."

Reeling in sympathy at the painful way he'd heard about his ex-girlfriend's death, I shut my eyes for a second until the room stopped whirling. Later that same evening, I'd gone to Frisky Pomegranate's Friday Happy Hour. Gabrielle had been smiling and talking to patrons. She hadn't mentioned Taylor's death, and the only indication that she knew about it was her smudged eyeliner. I supposed I had to be fair. She'd been in Ian's grade in high school. She knew him better than she knew me. I didn't discuss my grief with strangers, either, especially when I was at work. Besides, maybe as the hours passed on Friday she had become more used to the death of her best friend and less willing to talk about it.

I said softly, "Hearing it that way must have been horrible. Gabrielle probably didn't mean to be insensitive."

"I'm not sure Gabrielle can help it. She was born that way. I never knew what Taylor saw in her, but I guess Taylor was loyal to her childhood friend."

I thought, *And I don't know what you saw in Taylor.*

"But here's what I said that I wish I hadn't," Ian told me. "Without thinking, I said that the wrong person died. I meant that if either Taylor or Nicholas *had* to die, it should have been Nicholas, not Taylor. It wasn't a nice thing to say, and even though Nicholas stole Taylor from me and I never liked him, anyway, neither of them should have died. I never would have said such a thing if I'd been myself, but hearing about Taylor that way upset me, and I said the first thing that came into my head." As if the logo of the cat in the Deputy Donut hat didn't belong on his plate, he scraped at it with a fingernail. "I'm sure that Gabrielle went running to the police with that information the first chance she got. I'm sure she spun it to make it sound like I admitted to her that I planted the firework that killed Taylor but had actually been trying to kill Nicholas. I didn't do either of those things." He took a deep breath. "Gabrielle was behind me in the parking lot that night, and I didn't see what she was doing when she was farther down the hill, where I'd seen Taylor with Nicholas. Gabrielle was always jealous of Taylor. She could have lit that firework."

I didn't want to rile him, but I couldn't help asking, "How do you know that Gabrielle was *behind* you?"

"I turned around when I was almost at my car, and she was right behind me. I guess she lit that firework and then got close to me so if anyone saw her near the firework that killed Taylor, Gabrielle could say I was also there. I can't prove it."

"Or she hoped you'd see her and give her an alibi."

"Or both." His Adam's apple bobbed as he gulped down more coffee. "I saw her, but I don't know when that firework went off, and I don't know if it was lit before I drove away, so I can't give her an alibi and I can't say she did it. I don't know if I even heard the one that hurt Taylor. The fireworks were still going off when I was on my way out of the fair-grounds. It was like, *bang, bang, bang!*" With the last *bang*, he opened his fists and spread his fingers out as if his hands were starbursts.

I asked him, "What was Gabrielle wearing?"

"I don't know. I was trying to ignore her. I pretended I didn't see her and got into my car. I didn't want her starting another conversation and going on and on again about how sorry she was that Taylor dumped me. She didn't care. She just likes to rub things like that in."

I suspected that, in those conversations, she'd also been suggesting herself as Taylor's replacement in Ian's heart, and Ian might not have noticed. I asked, "Did you see if she was carrying anything big enough to hide a large firework in-side?"

"I did notice that. She had a shiny silvery bag like one of those insulated cooler bags, and maybe a purse, too."

"And you told the police this?"

"Yes. But there's another reason they suspect me, not her. I didn't tell them at first that I'd had a six-pack cooler with me. I didn't want to be in trouble for bringing beer to the fireworks display, which was supposed to be alcohol-free. Someone, probably Gabrielle, told them, so I had to admit later that I'd had it, which made me look even worse for not telling them at first. See, whoever brought their own fire-work to the town display probably hid it in something like a cooler."

I couldn't help heaving a huge sigh. I thought Brent was most suspicious of Philip Landsdowner, but Ian could be right up there on Brent's list. "You really know how to make trouble for yourself, don't you?" I asked.

He hung his head like a little kid. "Yeah."

I couldn't help feeling sorry for this pained and, it seemed, rather open young man, and my probing was undoubtedly making him feel worse. But he had asked for my help, and I went on with my questions. "When did you see Taylor and Nicholas at the fireworks?"

He winced. "When I was leaving. They were cuddled together."

"Did you see if either of them had brought anything resembling a firework? Or did you see fireworks near them? Or a picnic basket or cooler?"

"No. I couldn't stand seeing them like that and him smirking like he thought he was about to get away with something, so I looked away. But I would never have done anything to harm Taylor. I always loved her. And hurting the guy she was dating, even if she didn't really care about him, could have hurt her. What if he'd been killed? She could have been blamed. She could have spent the rest of her life in jail, and what would that have gotten me? I just plain would not have harmed either one of them. Or anyone else. I'm not like that. You believe me, don't you?" The dark eyes in that handsome, chiseled face looked at me pleadingly.

How was I supposed to answer? I wanted to tell him the truth, that I didn't know him well enough to tell if he was being honest. But what if the truth angered him and endangered me? I avoided answering by asking another question. "Before you sent that e-mail message to Taylor on July third, did you tell anyone else about your plans to move away from Fallingbrook?"

He looked down at his hands, gripping his emptied mug so tightly that his knuckles were white. "Too embarrassing, like ripping open your heart and letting people see inside it."

I was touched that he had let me, a stranger, see inside that ripped-open heart. Maybe a stranger who gave him hot and delicious coffee and a super-yummy donut seemed almost like family. I suggested, "Did you research other towns? Apply for jobs? Update your résumé? If the police have your computer, they might find your search history and job applications, and then they might believe that you were only doing what you said, planning to move away."

He suddenly looked less devastated. "I was looking into Milwaukee. And Minneapolis. Chicago, too. I didn't write a résumé, but I'll tell them to look at my search history. I knew you could help me." Blushing, he stood. "Thanks."

Watching him leave, I wondered what had drawn him to Taylor in the first place. Unless she'd changed a lot since tenth grade, it probably hadn't been her personality.

And I also wondered when it might occur to him that researching moving away could be seen by the police as a premeditated escape plan. . . .

I probably hadn't helped him at all. The trouble was that I wanted to believe him. Although I'd observed him for a total of only a few minutes on the Fourth of July, he'd clearly been hurting. Had that been because Taylor had dumped him or because he was planning to harm her or Nicholas?

It seemed to me that Ian's grief over her death was genuine.

Knowing firsthand how grief could tear one apart, I was probably too susceptible to giving him the benefit of the doubt.

Besides, trusting people even when they appeared innocent was not a particularly good idea, especially when a murderer was roaming around free.

I wasn't scratching Ian off my list of suspects.

Chapter 28

✂

By the time we closed Deputy Donut for the night, Jocelyn had not called or shown up. "I must have misunderstood," I told Tom. "She'll be back tomorrow."

"Probably," he answered.

Walking home with Dep, I considered telling Brent about Ian's visit to Deputy Donut.

The police had confiscated Ian's computer and phone. If they didn't already know everything that Ian had told me, they soon would.

I convinced myself that there was no reason to call Brent.

I felt almost relieved. I didn't know how to act around him after that possible kiss on my hair the night before. "I guess I'll have to pretend that nothing happened or, if it did, I didn't notice," I muttered to Dep. She batted a pebble off the sidewalk and into the grass, as if she were reminding me that I had decided it hadn't really been a kiss.

After dinner, I went upstairs to the computer in my guest room and found the page of prizes awarded to this year's Fallingbrook Fabulous Fourth Festivities royal court. Deputy Donut's fifty-two coupons were at the top of the list. Other local businesses had given gift cards, pens, mugs, and T-shirts emblazoned with logos.

Sitting on the guest room windowsill, Dep watched the flag flutter from its pole on the porch roof. I shut off the computer and told her, "I don't think Taylor was killed for a collection of advertising T-shirts."

Dep led me downstairs. In the living room, she sat with her nose to the front door and lobbied for Brent or another friend to appear. I took her out to the garden beyond our patio. She played in the grass and I read until the evening started becoming chilly.

I didn't hear from Brent and I didn't call him. And that was fine with me.

Jocelyn was scheduled to work on Thursdays. She didn't arrive at six thirty.

At seven, the always punctual nineteen-year-old still had not shown up.

I made the first pot of the day's special coffee, a light and tasty roast from, appropriately, Java.

At seven thirty, I asked Tom, "Should we call the police?"

"She lives with her parents. They're the logical ones to report that she's missing, if she is."

"What if they don't know she's missing, like they're out of town or something?"

"Call her again," he suggested.

For privacy, and also to spend a little time with Dep, I called from the office. Jocelyn didn't answer. I left a message and then tried her parents' numbers and received no answers from them, either. I disconnected and had a closer look at the information that Jocelyn had given us. She had listed her parents' work numbers.

The person who answered the phone at Jocelyn's father's office told me he wasn't available.

"Is he in town?" I asked.

There was a silence, and then a prim, "I can't divulge information about our employees."

I didn't have much better luck at the vast tree farm where Jocelyn's mother worked. The man who answered put me on hold for a few seconds and then came back on the line and said, "She's probably out on the grounds somewhere. What's your number? I'll have her call you when she comes back."

I gave him my number and asked, "Is she at work today?"

"She should be."

Disconnecting the call, I thought, *So should her daughter.*

Jocelyn had commented to me that no news from my parents was good news. Maybe she knew that she might not make it into work someday and she'd been telling me not to worry if she didn't turn up. That thought didn't reassure me. If she'd been planning a trip, wouldn't she have simply asked for time off?

Back in the kitchen, I told Tom about my lack of success. He asked if I knew who Jocelyn's coach was. I didn't.

"We can find out," he said. "Can you keep an eye on the donuts while I go make a few calls?"

"Sure."

Through the window into the office, I saw Dep greet Tom and then try to keep him from paying attention to anything besides her.

I turned the donuts in one basket over, raised another basket out of the hot oil, and sifted cinnamon over a tray of old-fashioned donuts.

Tom came back into the kitchen and handed me a slip of paper. "Here's Jocelyn's coach's name and phone number. I'd have called the woman, but more customers are coming in."

I thanked him and pocketed the information. "I'll try her when I get a chance."

After the lunch crowd left and before most people's afternoon coffee break, I tried Jocelyn, then her parents' personal phones. Nothing. I tried the coach. She didn't pick up, either.

I returned to the kitchen. Tom asked me, "Could they all be at a gymnastics meet?"

"Jocelyn didn't say anything about one, and she did tell me she wanted to work lots of hours to save for college."

After we closed the shop, I said to Tom, "That photographer, Philip Landsdowner, didn't come into the shop today.

Yesterday, he did, and he wanted to talk to Jocelyn." Fear grabbed at me. "I wonder if he found her. The way he doctored those pictures makes me think he might have something to do with the death of Taylor Wishbard. I think Brent is suspicious of him, too."

"You have Brent's number, don't you? Maybe Brent knows where Landsdowner is."

"Arrested, I hope."

Tom's smile was brief and grim.

I had a thought that was only a little better than my previous one about Landsdowner finding Jocelyn. "I hope the DCI detective hasn't arrested Jocelyn."

Tom said gently, "They could be questioning her. That could explain why we haven't heard from her or her parents."

"I'll call Brent."

In the office, Dep ran up one of her twisty staircases to a shelf of toys and peered down at me.

Brent answered curtly, "Fyne."

"Sorry to bother you at work, Brent. I need to tell you something that might be connected to the Taylor Wishbard case."

"Let's hear it."

Imitating his businesslike tone, I explained as briefly as I could, concluding with, "I wondered if you might know where Jocelyn is. Or where Landsdowner is." I held my breath, waiting for his answer.

"You're wondering if they're here."

I answered in a voice that barely made it out of my throat, "Yes."

"They're not. Can you give me a list of the names and numbers you called about your assistant?"

I did.

He thanked me. "I'll check here for any reports we might have about her, and I'll put out an alert for her and for Landsdowner. Meanwhile, let me know if any of them contact you."

In the kitchen, I told Tom what Brent had said.

Nodding, Tom raised a basket of fragrant strawberry cake donuts from the boiling oil.

The boy who had fetched Taylor's car for her at the start of the Fourth of July parade came in and sat fidgeting with sugar packets at a table near the front windows. Unless he'd been driving without a license on the Fourth, he had to be at least sixteen, but he barely looked it. He shoved the sugar bowl aside and ordered iced tea and a donut.

When I brought them to him, his eyes shifted back and forth like he was afraid that someone besides me was looking at him. He mumbled something so quietly that I had to ask him to repeat his question. He did, only slightly louder, but I managed to catch the words.

"I might have done something bad. Can you give me advice?"

Chapter 29

Did this nervous boy know where Jocelyn was?

I sat in the chair next to him. "What do you think you might have done?"

He nodded toward the kitchen. "When I was in grade school, Chief Westhill used to come talk to us."

"He's a good man," I said. "He retired."

"Were you a police officer, too?"

"No, but I know some. None of them are in here at the moment, but lots of them take their breaks here. Would you like to talk to one?"

"Maybe you can help me. I don't want to be in trouble."

I couldn't guarantee that, but I offered, "I'll try."

"I didn't think it was stealing," he started. "Friends and I were at this new place to eat, Frisky Pomegranate, on the Fourth of July. My friends left before I did, and I saw this bag that someone left behind in the room where people put their coats and stuff. I peeked inside the bag, and it was full of donuts."

I managed not to squeak, squirm, leap about, or shout.

The teenager went on with his story. "The bag said it was from your shop. I thought that whoever left the bag behind didn't want the donuts. I squeezed one, and they were already getting hard, as if they'd been there awhile. But you never know when you'll be hungry, you know?"

With a little smile, I nodded.

"I shoved them into my backpack. I thought I could share them with friends later that night at the fireworks."

Although my brain felt like it was buzzing, I tried to keep my face neutral. "And were they good?"

A blush spread across his cherubic face. "I don't know. I was just leaving that coatroom when this family with little kids came in and took jackets and things off hangers. The dad grabbed a blanket from near where the donuts had been. They didn't say anything about donuts, but I wondered if they were the ones who'd left the bag there. I was kind of rushing away, and I heard a kid talking about going for ice cream before the fireworks. If the donuts were theirs, I thought I should give them back, but anonymously, you know? I was embarrassed about taking them."

I said encouragingly, "I get that. What did you do?"

"I went to Freeze and left the bag on a table there, so if that was where they were going, they'd find it."

"Did they?"

His flush deepened. "I don't know. The place was really crowded. I kind of stood sideways to a table and put the bag of donuts on it. I was hoping no one would notice me, so I got out of there as fast as I could. See, at first, I didn't think anyone wanted those donuts. But now I feel bad because if those donuts belonged to those little kids, they probably did want them even if they were going stale, and I don't know if they found them." He looked me in the eyes for a second before glancing away. "Do you think I'll be arrested?"

"No." I knew that the police would like to hear his story, but I couldn't tell him why. As far as I knew, the general public, except for Philip Landsdowner and the murderer, who might well *be* Philip Landsdowner, didn't know about the donuts surrounding the homemade skyrocket. Besides, telling the teenager to call a detective would probably scare him. Instead, I gave him the number for Crime Stoppers. "You can leave an anonymous tip."

"They'd know my phone number."

"That wouldn't put you in trouble. They don't give out identifying information."

"Not even to the police?"

I said firmly, "Not even to the police."

The teen gazed around the room as if he were hoping to find an escape route through a wall.

I suggested, "How about if I ask my police officer friends if you would be in trouble? I'm sure they'll say no. If they said anything to you, they'd only remind you about not picking up things that don't belong to you unless you are certain that someone lost them and you're trying to return them to the rightful owners."

He mumbled toward the donut on his plate, "That's kind of what I did."

I smiled to show I appreciated his attempts at being polite and respectful. "Kind of. Next time you come in, I'll tell you what they say."

"Okay. Thanks for the advice."

I stood. "Anytime. And you can always ask Chief Westhill or any of the officers you see in here anything you want. They like to help. And think about calling Crime Stoppers. They offer rewards for tips that help solve crimes."

"But, like, wouldn't I be, like, reporting myself? I'm the one who took the donuts."

Oops. Considering that he didn't know the whole story, he had an excellent point. "Other times." My explanation probably didn't make much sense to him.

I went back to waiting on other customers, and the next time I looked, he was gone. He'd left cash on the table, so I wasn't able to learn his name from a credit card. However, he had been one of the Fabulous Fourth Festivities volunteers. If Brent and Rex wanted to talk to him about people he might have seen at Freeze, they should be able to get a list of the teen volunteers from the committee.

Thanks to the teenager, I was almost positive that the crucial half-dozen donuts had gotten as far as Freeze after the birthday boy and his family had dinner on the Fourth. That family didn't find the donuts at Freeze, though. Where had that bag gone after the teenager dropped it off?

Had Mama Freeze or Kelsey picked it up? Either one of them could have quickly stowed it in a tote or cooler. Or they could have tossed it in the trash, donuts and all, and someone else could have retrieved it. Maybe Philip Landsdowner had been following Taylor or Kelsey around, also, and had continued spending time in Freeze after Jocelyn stopped working there. Maybe he had stuffed the bag of donuts into the large back pocket of his photographer's vest.

Maybe Felicia had met Mama Freeze there so they could go to the fireworks together. Gabrielle could have gone to Freeze after she finished her shift at Frisky Pomegranate. Had Taylor, like Gabrielle, gone to work between the picnic and the fireworks, and had Nicholas picked her up at Freeze that night, along with a bag of slightly stale donuts? Even Ian could have dropped in at Freeze that evening before the fireworks.

Any one of them could have taken that bag, along with a homemade skyrocket, to the fireworks.

The first chance I got, I joined Dep in her playroom and called Brent. He always recognized my number when it came up on his screen, but work sometimes prevented him from answering. This must have been one of those times. I left a message for him to call me.

At five, while Tom was putting things away in the storeroom and I was turning chairs upside down on tabletops, my phone rang. I didn't recognize the number, but hoping that the caller might be Jocelyn, her parents, her coach, or even Brent calling from someone else's phone, I answered.

"Emily honey?" Static clicked through the words.

The only woman who called me Emily honey was my mother.

"Mom! Am I ever glad to hear from you!"

"What?" Her voice faltered. ". . . bad connection."

I spoke more loudly. "I'm having trouble understanding you, too. Where are you?"

"We're . . . *Click, buzz* . . . this evening."

"What? Did you say you're coming back this evening?"

"We . . . *click, click, buzz, click* . . . evening."

Knowing how much she hated spending more than a few seconds on a long-distance call, I rushed through my next question. "Did you say you are or are *not* coming back this evening?"

"Sorry. Bad . . . *buzz, click* . . . bye."

The call ended. Had she been apologizing for the bad connection, for not having contacted me sooner, or for not being able to get back to Fallingbrook this evening?

She hadn't called from the phone she and my father shared. Hoping to get her, I tried the unfamiliar number. No one answered. My mother must have found a pay phone or borrowed a phone from someone she'd met at a rest stop. I could easily see her returning the phone to its owner, rushing to climb on board the RV, and driving off again pell-mell.

I found Tom in the storeroom and told him that my parents had finally touched base, more or less.

"You can go," he said. "I'll finish here and lock up."

"That would be silly. I'm not even sure they're coming this evening."

"Are you going out there later, in case they are?"

"Probably."

He headed toward the kitchen. "What are their favorite donuts?"

I followed him. "Grape jelly–filled."

"Perfect. We have a couple left. Quince jelly, too. Do they like those?"

"Who doesn't?" They were among my favorites, but the list of my favorites was about five pages long. Single-spaced.

We packed a half-dozen quince- and grape jelly–filled donuts into a bag and finished tidying, and then Tom left.

In our office, I tucked the bag gently into my backpack. With Dep's exuberant help, I logged on to the computer and did a reverse lookup of the phone number my mother had called from. All I could find out was that the number belonged to a cell phone issued in the area code for southwest Wisconsin. My parents could be anywhere. However, if they were actually in southwest Wisconsin, were in the northern part of that area code, and stopped only a few times, they could be in Fallingbrook in a couple of hours. If my mother had called from somewhere else, including the south part of that vast area code, though, they probably wouldn't make it back until tomorrow, if then.

My parents almost never took the straightest route. Those two could spot a sign advertising an attraction they would *have* to visit. *We might as well see it while we're here,* they used to say when I was a kid traveling with them. Back then they'd had jobs they'd needed to return to, and we hadn't been able to make frequent or long stops. Now that they were retired, those intriguing side trips could last for days.

I tried Brent again. Apparently, he was still very busy, and probably on his phone. My call went immediately to message. "I wondered if you've heard anything about Jocelyn," I said into the phone. "I haven't. Also, as I mentioned in another message, I found out something more about those donuts, maybe. Call me?"

I disconnected and tapped my fingers on the desk. Surely I could accomplish something useful while I waited for Brent to return my call.

I gazed down at the hopeful kitty sitting at my feet and obviously ready for the fun of pouncing on things all the way home. "I'll be back for you in a few minutes," I told her.

I walked quickly to Freeze.

To my surprise, Mama Freeze was at the front counter. "What can I get you, Emily?" she asked.

"Nothing, unfortunately. I can't keep up with what I buy."

"It will stay delicious in your freezer."

I grinned. "My freezer is just about full."

"Take it to your parents and put it in their freezer. Or aren't they back yet?"

Felicia must have told her that, on Monday, I'd said they weren't back. "They might get home tonight."

"Welcome them with ice cream!" In the kitchen, Kelsey walked past the window in the door, saw me, and waved.

Wondering how she could be warm enough in a tank top in a room where ice cream was being made, I waved back and smiled at Mama Freeze. "I would do that if I was sure they were here." I lifted one shoulder and turned slightly to display my backpack. "I've got donuts for them, just in case. I actually stopped in to apologize. I heard that someone might have left a Deputy Donut bag with some donuts in it here on the Fourth of July."

"Who?"

I should have been prepared for that question. I didn't want to cast blame on the teenage boy, but now that I'd said I'd heard that someone had left the bag here, I couldn't very well pretend I didn't know who I'd heard it from. I had told Felicia about the family. Even if Felicia had not told Mama Freeze that I'd been asking about a family leaving a bag of donuts behind, she still might. "A family," I said, finally, "with several little kids, and I thought I should apologize for being the cause of litter that someone had to clean up. Maybe that was one of the last things that Taylor did here."

Mama Freeze shook her head. "Taylor had that entire day off, thank goodness. I hope that day was absolutely perfect for her until . . ." Mama Freeze wiped her eyes. "But don't you worry, Emily. Lots of families come in here every day. I don't think anyone left a bag of donuts here, and if they did, they should do the apologizing, not you." She gave her head a couple of emphatic nods as if to show me how important it was for whoever abandoned the bag to apologize. "And donuts aren't all that messy, anyway. Now, if someone had left a bunch of melting ice cream cones in a paper bag in your donut shop, that would be a different story."

I laughed at the image, thanked her, and turned to go.

"How about a cone to eat on your way home?"

"I'll stop by for some ice cream to take to my parents when they do show up," I promised, "but now I have to go get my cat and walk her home. On a leash. That's easier said than done with an ice cream cone."

Mama Freeze let out one of her belly laughs. "I guess it would be! Well, you know where we are."

Three couples came in debating milkshakes versus sundaes or floats. Smiling at them, I went out to the sidewalk. I told myself that if Mama Freeze and Felicia compared notes, Mama Freeze might tell Felicia that I'd only been asking about the stray bag of donuts so I could apologize, and they'd probably think nothing more about it.

In our Deputy Donut office, Dep peered down at me from the upper reaches of her playground. Cooing at her, I removed Jocelyn's résumé from the filing cabinet again and wrote down the address of the house where she and her parents lived.

Dep trotted down ramps to see what I was doing with a sheet of paper. "Looking for another cat bed, Dep?" I asked.

Meowing, she flopped onto her side on the copies of the *Fallingbrook News*. I wasn't sure why I was keeping them. Maybe my parents would like to see this latest evidence of my fame. Or my infamy . . .

Dep wriggled, but I managed to snap her halter around her, and we strolled home in our usual stop-and-go fashion.

In the living room, I set my backpack down carefully to

keep it from falling over and squashing the jelly-filled donuts inside it. I followed Dep to the kitchen. She meowed imperiously while I filled clean water and dinner bowls for her. I quickly downed a peanut butter and tomato sandwich and a glass of skimmed milk.

Even this close to the middle of July, the forested Fallingbrook Falls Campground could become chilly at night, and I didn't know when or even if my parents might arrive. I changed into jeans, a red plaid long-sleeved blouse, socks, and red sneakers. I picked up the red sweater I'd worn the evening of the Fourth of July, ran downstairs, and collected my backpack.

Dep was at the front door, obviously ready to go with me. "Tomorrow morning," I told her. "I should be back tonight at a reasonable hour." *Unless my parents regale me with all ten-plus months of their adventures since they left Fallingbrook at the end of last August . . .* I locked Dep inside and headed out to my car in the driveway.

I gently placed my backpack and sweater on the front passenger seat and then drove about a mile north through my neighborhood to Jocelyn's parents' home. It was a charming three-story yellow brick Victorian with a front yard full of varying shades of daylilies, hydrangeas, and rose of Sharon. Like many houses in this vintage neighborhood, this one didn't have a garage. A long driveway ran up one side of the house.

Three or four cars would have fit, but the driveway was empty. Maybe Jocelyn's family's cars were among the ones parked beside the curb.

Feeling pushy, I marched up to the front porch and knocked on the door. I knocked again. I found a button and pushed it. An old-fashioned ringing that was more like a *zinnnng!* sounded on the other side of the door.

No one answered. I pushed the bell for a long time. I tried the bronze oak leaf–shaped knocker.

Finally, I gave up, turned around to leave, and noticed a detail I'd missed when I'd gone charging, full of determination to speak to Jocelyn or her parents, up the porch steps.

Behind the porch swing with its cheerful floral chintz cushions, a bike was chained to the porch railing.

A blue bike with coaster brakes.

Jocelyn's.

Chapter 30

Hovering with one foot about to slide off the top porch step, I gave the bike behind the porch swing a long, slow look. It appeared totally undamaged. Jocelyn must have arrived home safely Tuesday evening.

She had to be fine.

Where was she?

Brent had said he'd tell officers to be on the lookout for her.

No news is good news when people go missing, she'd claimed.

Wasn't her bike being here a good sign? And no cars in the driveway. Maybe she and her parents had taken a trip on impulse, or maybe Jocelyn had to fill in, at such short notice that she couldn't call us, for another gymnast at an out-of-town meet.

I called her number. She didn't answer. I listened for ringtones inside the house but heard nothing.

I returned to my car and sat there trying to work up the nerve to take the long way to Fallingbrook Falls. Even if my parents were coming that night, they would probably be late. I needed to drive down County Road G again, sometime. Maybe I would be able to banish some of the ghosts of horror that occasionally drifted through my mind because of everything that had happened near that road—the shallow grave of my favorite grocer, a murderer returning to the scene of the crime, and me, nearly losing my own life due to trusting the wrong person.

I would brave that road some other time.

I drove to Wisconsin Street and took the faster route.

My parents' RV was not at their site, and the grass didn't need mowing again this soon.

I climbed up to my old favorite perch on the boulder and sat there hugging my knees and soaking up the feeling of once again being in this forested campground I had loved as a kid.

In nearby sites, dishes clattered and adults laughed. Kids clamored for s'mores. "It's not dark enough yet," a man said lovingly. "We'll build a fire later." There was a chorus of protests until the man reminded the kids that an early campfire could mean an early bedtime. I couldn't help smiling. How many times had I participated in an argument like that one? The tang of woodsmoke drifted around me—someone who didn't need to be concerned about a too-early bedtime already had a campfire going.

The boulder I was sitting on became knobbier and harder than I remembered. Dep was waiting for me at home, probably not patiently. My folks liked to stop driving each night in time to make dinner. Over that bad connection, my mother must have been saying that she and my father *wouldn't* be arriving that evening. Disappointed that they had not yet made it back, I clambered down, shut myself into my car, and eased down the narrow road toward the campground exit. There were usually lots of kids in the campground. I drove slowly.

Heading toward the falls side of the campground, I was still pretty far back from one of the campground's intersections when, ahead of me, a small black car crossed the narrow road I was on and went out of my sight. I stopped. The driver's head had been turned away from me, but I'd recognized him.

Philip Landsdowner.

I was almost positive that the small black car was the one

that had accelerated past my parents' campsite on Monday afternoon. Landsdowner had probably seen my car there and had seen me locking the shed and looking toward the campground road.

Had he returned to the campground this evening to try to find me, and if so, did that mean that he was still looking for Jocelyn? My heart pounded.

She couldn't be, simply could *not* be, in his clutches.

But where was she?

Maybe I should have waited for Brent to return my call and then accepted his offer to come out here with me. That would have been silly. I hadn't known that Philip Landsdowner would show up in my parents' campground again.

I felt fairly safe from Landsdowner at the moment. When he'd crossed the intersection in front of me only seconds before, he should have looked both directions, but he'd seemed to focus only in one direction as if he'd expected to see someone—Jocelyn?—down that road. I didn't think he had even glanced toward me.

However, what if he turned around and came back? Or continued following the road he was on? He could pass my parents' campsite and then end up where I was sitting in my idling and too-recognizable car. He could be a killer, and he might believe that I was out here gathering information about him that would prove he had killed Taylor Wishbard. Searching for him, staying here, or returning to my parents' site could be dangerous.

I needed to be somewhere safe where I could call Brent.

I quickly backed my car into an unkempt site with a camper trailer on it. A faded FOR SALE sign was in one window.

I tucked my car mostly behind the trailer and hoped that if Philip Landsdowner drove along this road, he wouldn't guess that the fresh tire tracks plowing through the weeds into this campsite had anything to do with him or with anyone hiding from him. I also had to hope that he wouldn't see the nose of my car poking out behind the trailer. Because of the unmown weeds, my car should be visible only from the windshield up. Maybe the red roof was far enough back that he wouldn't see it.

He could have been driving around the campground on Monday and again today for a completely innocent reason, like he was living here for the summer. I wondered what he'd given the police as a home address.

I unbuckled my seat belt and pulled my backpack closer. Trying not to disturb the sack of donuts, I dug out my phone. My call to Brent went directly to message again.

Before I'd turned off the engine, I should have opened the windows so I could hear if anyone was near. Whispering even though the windows were closed, I left a message that I'd seen Philip Landsdowner in the Fallingbrook Falls Campground. "I'm not at my parents' site, but he was driving on a road that could take him to it. I know they're not there, so don't worry, I'm not about to go confront him if that's where he's heading." I added, "I'm parked in a different campsite near one of the trails to the falls. I'll stay in my car for about ten minutes, and then I'll take the shortest route home. I'll let you know when I get there." Or, if a small black car followed me again, I would drive straight to the police station. And this time, I would go in.

In case Brent's personal phone wasn't working, I called the police department and asked for him. A very nice dispatcher put me through to his line. I left another message.

I disconnected and slumped down in the comfy driver's seat to wait the ten minutes. Hoping for a response from Brent, I held my phone in my hand.

Across the road, in trees behind another campsite, someone moved between the trunks of a couple of white birches. I leaned forward to see better through the windshield. It was a woman, a young one, graceful, with long dark hair.

Jocelyn.

I heaved a huge sigh of relief. I didn't care what had prevented her from coming into work. The important thing was that she was okay.

Or was she? She was setting her feet down carefully as if she was trying not to be heard or seen. Wearing jeans and an oversized grayish green jacket that didn't quite blend in with the trees around her, she was heading up one of the trails that could take her to the river and the falls. She stopped, looked down the trail behind her for a second, and then flitted out of my sight beyond dense pines and a rocky outcropping.

Was she running away from someone? Philip Landsdowner?

I called Brent's personal number again and left a message that I'd seen Jocelyn alone in the campground and hiking up toward Fallingbrook Falls or the river above the falls and she'd seemed fine, but she'd looked like she was trying to escape unnoticed from someone or something. I added, "I don't know where Landsdowner is, but he's in a car, and she's on a trail where cars can't go." Not even small cars. If she was fleeing from him, she should be safe.

I had a few questions for Jocelyn. She didn't answer her phone. I left a short message. "Philip Landsdowner is in the Fallingbrook Falls Campground."

I disconnected and stared out through the windshield. It was just after eight, and that week the sun had been setting around a quarter to nine. Even in the woods, it wouldn't be fully dark for over an hour, but I doubted that Jocelyn knew the trails as well as I did, thanks to the hours I'd spent exploring them with Misty and Samantha.

Another movement beyond the campsite across the road caught my eye.

Philip Landsdowner, wearing blue jeans, a khaki photographer's vest over a light-colored T-shirt, and a camera on a strap around his neck, was walking between the birch trees where I'd spotted Jocelyn minutes before.

His movements were furtive. Unlike Jocelyn, he didn't turn

around and look behind him. He didn't seem to glance toward me and my car, both mostly concealed, I hoped, by weeds and the forlorn trailer.

He faced one direction only, toward where Jocelyn had disappeared. Walking swiftly but cautiously, he also went out of sight behind the dense pines and the rocky outcropping.

Chapter 31

✿

It was terrifyingly obvious. Landsdowner was sneaking into the woods. Following Jocelyn.

Deliberately.

She was younger and probably more fit than he was. Even moving cautiously, she should be able to outdistance him.

I again speed-dialed Brent's personal number, and again, his phone went directly to message. Breathlessly but quietly, I blurted, "Landsdowner is on foot. He's following Jocelyn up a trail that goes from the campground to the river and the falls. I'm going to call her again. If she doesn't answer, I'll try to find her before Landsdowner does. I know all of the trails and shortcuts." Guessing what he would probably say, I added, "I'll be careful."

I set my phone to vibrate only. If Brent or Jocelyn returned my calls, my phone wouldn't play its little tune and announce to Landsdowner that I was creeping up on him.

Hoping that Jocelyn had also turned off her ringtone, I phoned her.

No answer.

I murmured a message. "Philip Landsdowner is following you. Call and tell me where you are so I can find you before he does. Meanwhile, I'm going to take the trail he's on, the one you were on when you left the campground. If I haven't heard from you, I'm going to follow that trail all the way to where it ends at the main trail, pretty far up the river above the falls. If you and I haven't connected by then, I'll start down the main trail to the parking lot and look for you." I hoped she'd understand which trails I'd meant.

Wishing I'd brought a sweater in a less eye-catching color, I slipped out of the car and put on the red sweater. I needed to hurry, but I also needed to be as prepared as possible. I took a flashlight and a first-aid kit out of my trunk and tucked them into my backpack beside the bag of donuts. I hoped I hadn't squeezed the donuts. At the moment, however, cleaning sticky jelly out of my backpack was not high on my priority list.

I shoved my phone into a jeans pocket, slipped my backpack on, and crossed the road. Beyond the birches where I'd seen both Jocelyn and Landsdowner, the uphill trail zigzagged around boulders. Neither Jocelyn nor Landsdowner was in sight.

I climbed quickly. Downhill and to my right, the campground was full of happy sounds that brought back memories of staying out here on magical summer evenings, of watching fireflies and waiting for the nightly campfire. When I was really little, I often fell asleep during the campfire while the adults around me played musical instruments and sang.

The falls were uphill and to my left, far enough away that the constant rush of water was barely louder than a breeze.

A side trail branched to the left. That trail went down to the parking lot for the falls. If Jocelyn had turned off onto that trail, she could hike about a half mile along the road to the campground's main entrance. Most of the people who stayed in the campground were very friendly. They would gladly protect her from Landsdowner.

But the way Jocelyn had left the campground made me think that something in the campground had frightened her.

If she was trying to get as far away as fast as possible, she might have stayed on this trail.

In my message, I'd told her I would hike up this trail, so I needed to stay on it as long as there was a possibility that she was still on it. I probably should have warned her that it led to steeper trails, eroding riverbanks, slippery boulders, and dangerously fast water. Hoping to catch her before she got that far, I hiked upward, setting my feet down quietly and watching and listening for other people.

I passed two more side trails. One of them led to the trail running along the cliff below the falls, and the other led to the top of the falls, where water shot over a rocky lip and then fell straight down into the gorge. Had Jocelyn taken one of those trails? Had Landsdowner? Were they on two different trails, or was he about to catch up to her?

My phone remained stubbornly still and non-vibrating.

Even if Jocelyn hadn't received my message, I might be able to find her on this longest loop. If I didn't, I would go back and forth on all of the trails until dusk made these rocky trails too dangerous even for me.

The one I was on became steeper and more treacherous.

Emerging from a canyon between two boulders, I saw someone in a light-colored vest on the trail ahead of me.

Landsdowner.

He was standing still and looking farther uphill. Had he spotted Jocelyn, or was he merely searching for her?

Afraid he was about to turn around and see me, I backed out of sight until I could safely turn around. As light-footed as possible, I strode down the root-strewn path to the next trail, the one that led to the top of the falls. I started up that trail. It was one of the shortcuts that I'd mentioned in my message to Brent. It would get me to the junction of trails where I'd told Jocelyn I'd meet her, could possibly get me there as soon as or sooner than the one where I'd just seen Landsdowner.

However, it was time to call in reinforcements.

I wasn't certain that Landsdowner meant any harm to Jocelyn or that he would find her, so I couldn't justify calling 911 or even the police. And Brent was obviously busy or he would have returned my calls. However, if Misty was off duty tonight, I could use her company.

She didn't answer. I whispered into the phone, "I'm at Fallingbrook Falls, on Popcorn Trail heading away from the campground and toward the falls. My assistant is up here somewhere and so is Philip Landsdowner. I don't know if Jocelyn's in danger, but I could use help finding her before dark or before Landsdowner does. Call me back?"

As far as I knew, the trail didn't have an actual name. Popcorn was the name that Samantha, Misty, and I had given it when we were about eleven and found a line of popcorn sprinkled along it.

Glancing uneasily down Popcorn in case Landsdowner had backtracked and was sneaking up behind me, I stepped a little farther into the cover of feathery hemlock branches and called Samantha.

She answered with a cheerful, "Emily!"

"Are you working?"

"No. Why are you whispering?"

"I'm hiding from . . . that's not important. I'm on Popcorn Trail and could use Misty's help, but she's not answering."

"Is it a police matter?"

"No. Maybe. I don't know, but I need to find Tom's and my new assistant, Jocelyn. Last I knew, she was heading up Skinned Knee Trail"—the knee in question had been Samantha's—"toward the river above the falls, and a man she seems to fear is following her. If you can, could you keep calling Misty and tell her I'd like her company if she's available? Tell her that Philip Landsdowner is following Jocelyn."

"I can and I will, and I'll do something even better. I'll bring you an off-duty policeman. Hooligan has never visited the falls, and we're actually on our way. We should be there in about ten minutes."

For the first time since I'd seen Landsdowner following Jocelyn up Skinned Knee Trail, I could almost breathe. "Perfect. Climb up Noisy Cawing Crow Trail and I'll meet you near the top of the falls." Some people called the trail that ran from the parking lot up one side of the falls and then along the river above the falls the main trail. Visitors who didn't know about the trails leading to and from the campground probably just thought of it as the trail. I added, "Call or text me if you find Jocelyn."

I thrust my phone into my pocket again and peeked out between hemlock branches. No one was on the part of Popcorn Trail that I could see. I hurried up the rapidly ascending trail. Stones hurt my feet through the soles of my sneakers, and the root of a tree jutted up just high enough to catch the toe of one shoe and nearly send me sprawling.

Finally, hoping to see Samantha and Hooligan already there, I approached Noisy Cawing Crow Trail. I slowed, listening for voices. All I heard was roaring water.

I crept forward.

Due to the steepness of this part of Noisy Cawing Crow Trail, I couldn't see very far either uphill or downhill. No one was on the section that I could see.

It had been just over five minutes since I'd talked to Samantha. Even if she and Hooligan had made it to the parking lot, they would not have had time to climb up this far yet.

If Jocelyn had gone downhill from here and if she hadn't taken one of the other trails leading back to the campground, she would meet Samantha and Hooligan. They would let me know she was safe with them.

If Jocelyn was upriver from me, though, and if Philip Landsdowner was still following her, I didn't have time to wait for my friends.

I ran several feet up the trail to a level, knee-high boulder on the other side of the trail from where the Fallingbrook River streamed over the outthrust ledge of its rocky riverbed. Samantha, Misty, and I used to leave messages for each other on the boulder. We had usually arranged twigs into arrows that signaled which way the others were to go to find the hidden treasure or a clue to solve one of Misty's inventive detective games. I brushed leaf debris off the boulder, whipped off my backpack, and pulled the bag of donuts out. The donuts were only a little squashed. I squeezed grape jelly onto the boulder in the approximation of a straight line paralleling Noisy Cawing Crow Trail. Then I broke the hollowed donut into two semicircular halves and arranged them on the upriver end of the line of grape jelly to make a sort of arrow pointing uphill.

If Samantha hiked up this part of Noisy Cawing Crow, she would probably, from habit and without thinking about it, glance at the top of that rock. She would remember the amateur sleuth games that Misty used to direct up here, and she would recognize that I had left her a sign, an arrow pointing the way I had gone.

However, if Philip Landsdowner was up here searching for Jocelyn, he might pass the broken donut and see it as nothing more than biodegradable litter.

Hoping that the descendants of the original noisy cawing crow weren't waiting in trees above me to swoop down and fly off with donut halves in their beaks, I glanced toward the sky. No crows, noisy or otherwise.

I hiked along the river above the falls. Although the trail now sloped upward only gradually, it twisted around rocks and tree trunks, and there were holes and gullies to leap over or find a way around. As I went farther, the river became less tumultuous, but it still had to flow around boulders and fallen trees. Even this far from the falls, the current could sweep unwary hikers downstream, bashing them against rocks. If those rocks didn't stop them or if they couldn't wade out of the river, they could plummet over the falls and into heaps of deadly rocks far below.

The river and Noisy Cawing Crow both curved to my right, so I couldn't see far along the shore, but I knew I had almost reached the spot where Skinned Knee joined the trail I was on.

And I saw Jocelyn.

Chapter 32

✣

Upstream from me, Jocelyn was crossing the river in a way that only she could, quickly and gracefully leaping from rock to rock. She was about halfway to the far shore.

Was she fleeing from Philip Landsdowner? Where was he? I inched forward and peeked between pine branches.

Landsdowner had apparently given up, for the moment, on following Jocelyn. Still wearing his camera hanging from a strap around his neck, he sat hunched on a boulder in the river. Water dripped from the hems of his jeans onto the boulder.

Rescue could be at hand for him, however. Standing on the bank on my side of the river, a woman in black leggings and a red hoodie was shouting and waving at him. She took a couple of tentative steps down toward the river and held one hand out as if to beckon him close so she could pull him up the steep riverbank. "Philip!" she yelled.

I couldn't tell if he didn't hear her or was ignoring her. He stared unwaveringly in Jocelyn's direction.

Flying from stone to stone, her unzipped jacket flapping, Jocelyn was almost all the way across the river. About a yard from the far bank, she performed a perfect backflip, landed on her feet, and dodged between trees. Within seconds, I lost sight of her.

I hadn't explored the trails on that side of the river as much as I had the ones on this side, but I knew that she could make her way down to the comparative safety of the highway, the parking lot at the foot of the falls, or the campground.

I let out a breath of relief. I could start down toward the parking lot, also. I could intercept my friends, and we could find Jocelyn and escort her to the lovely Victorian home with the blue bike chained to the porch railing behind a floral-upholstered swing.

I was perfectly happy to leave Landsdowner marooned on that boulder while Jocelyn escaped him. The sun wouldn't set for about a half hour. He would have plenty of time to work up the courage to slide off his rock and wade to whichever shore he preferred.

The woman on my side of the river continued urging him toward her. She pushed the hood off her head. Her long auburn hair gleamed in the sky's orange glow.

She was Kelsey, the clerk from Freeze.

Landsdowner had claimed he'd seen me wearing a red hoodie and lighting the firework that killed Taylor. That night, I'd been wearing the red sweater I had on now. It didn't have a hood.

Kelsey was about my size. On the night of the Fourth, seen from the rear, in blue pants and the hoodie she was wearing now with the hood hiding her long auburn hair, she could have been mistaken for me.

Or not. Maybe Landsdowner had known all along that Kelsey lit the firework. Maybe he'd been protecting her, not himself.

Kelsey could easily have been the one who picked up the bag of donuts that the teenage boy left in Freeze. She could have added a homemade skyrocket and a lighter to the bag and taken it all to the fireworks. I didn't remember noticing Kelsey carrying any sort of bag when I saw her, but it was easy to imagine seeing straps like from a backpack across the fronts of her shoulders.

It was all conjecture. Kelsey had hinted that Taylor was

often late for work, but would she have killed Taylor because of it? Kelsey had also griped about Jocelyn. Was Kelsey a threat to Jocelyn?

Still apparently paying no attention to Kelsey's shouted pleas, Landsdowner was staring at the woods where Jocelyn had disappeared.

I did not want to stay near either Landsdowner or Kelsey. Besides, I needed to go back down Noisy Cawing Crow and look for Jocelyn. And Samantha and Hooligan, too.

I crept cautiously away until I'd gone around a curve and could no longer see Landsdowner and Kelsey, and then I hurried down Noisy Cawing Crow, skirting obstacles as quickly as I could.

Although I was fit from running around inside Deputy Donut, my heart was beating hard and my breath was coming out in ragged gasps.

If Jocelyn was on a trail leading downhill, finding her shouldn't be difficult. Kelsey and Landsdowner would probably stay where they were until Landsdowner slithered off his rock. Even if Jocelyn and I didn't encounter Samantha and Hooligan, I could take Jocelyn home and then go home myself. I would let Samantha know we were both safe, and then I would call Brent with my theories about Kelsey and Landsdowner and let him and his team sort it all out.

Panting, watching where I was placing my feet between roots and rocks, I passed the rock where I'd left the donut arrow. It was still there. Popcorn Trail went off to my left. I started down the steepest part of Noisy Cawing Crow Trail, where it was at its narrowest, running between a rock wall on one side and steep cliffs above the whirlpool underneath the falls on the other.

A woman above me on Noisy Cawing Crow called, "Emily!" I could barely hear her over the roaring water.

Samantha and Hooligan could be up here on one of the nearby trails.

I turned around.

In a tank top that matched her black leggings, Kelsey was on the trail near the top of the falls. Her hands were empty. What had she done with the red hoodie? It was a strange time of evening to be shedding long sleeves. Among the trees, the night would soon become cooler and might also become buggier.

My instinct was to run away, down toward where Samantha and Hooligan should be, but no matter how many times in the past I had raced up and down Noisy Cawing Crow, I didn't know all of its pitfalls. Hoping I could reach Popcorn Trail and hurry down it faster than Kelsey could, I jogged up toward Popcorn Trail.

It was possible that Kelsey hadn't harmed Taylor, and it was also possible that she had called out to me because she knew Jocelyn and was concerned about the girl's safety.

Kelsey glanced down toward the boulder where I'd left the donut halves and the line of grape jelly. "Leaving a trail of bread crumbs, Emily?" she yelled.

Roaring, the Fallingbrook River continued plunging into the abyss.

I sort of shook my head, sort of smiled, and sort of shrugged, all at the same time.

"Why did you run away from Philip?" she hollered.

I put as much enthusiasm into my shout as I could. "To get help for him!"

She held an encouraging hand toward me. "You and I can rescue him."

I shook my head.

She charged.

I wasn't going to beat her to Popcorn. And I wouldn't be able to go very far down the more treacherous Noisy Cawing Crow Trail before she caught up to me.

My best option was a dangerous route that Misty, Samantha, and I had never found terribly difficult in our teen years, one that Kelsey might not even consider attempting. I jumped up and sat facing the trail on the peeled-log guardrail. To brace myself, I cupped my hands behind and underneath the rough log.

Kelsey appeared to slip on loose stones. She grimaced and threw her hands above her head as if to catch her balance.

Her hands landed on my shoulders. To anyone watching, the gesture might have appeared to be an accident.

She glared into my eyes and gave both of my shoulders a good, hard shove.

That shove was definitely not an accident.

Chapter 33

❧

Was I the one who let out that high, thin scream?

Kelsey's push sent my upper body backward.

Thanks to the ninja cop tricks that Samantha, Misty, and I used to perform, I was more or less prepared. Holding on to the back of the splintery guardrail as well as I could, I managed to fling one leg over the railing in a fairly controlled manner. My momentum shot my other foot up. It struck Kelsey's chin.

After a strange sort of scissor-legged flip, I ended up on the other side of the railing, facing it with my body bent forward and my stance wide. My feet slipped toward the precipice. I shifted them, grasped the railing more tightly, and regained some of my balance.

Her hand to her chin, Kelsey stared at me with a dazed expression on her face. I hadn't intended to kick her and could not have avoided it. Maybe, considering that her shove had seemed deliberate, it had been a good move.

Kelsey's stunned look turned to anger. Her lips thinned with determination. She put her hands on the guardrail.

Before she could pry my hands away from it, I let go.

Obviously, Kelsey wasn't about to let me return to Noisy Cawing Crow Trail. Feeling for handholds and footholds, I started crawling backward down the cliff. It wasn't as easy as it had been when Misty, Samantha, and I were teens. I had to stop watching Kelsey and focus on where I was going. The cliff was slippery with spray.

Despite railings and parental warnings, kids apparently still explored this cliff. Plants that had managed to take root in tiny cracks in the rock had obviously been stunted by sneakered feet.

I crept down to a narrow ledge that slanted only slightly toward the empty space in front of the constantly falling water. Crouching, hanging on to rocky protuberances, I looked up toward Noisy Cawing Crow.

Kelsey leaned over the railing and met my gaze for an instant. She put one leg over the guardrail.

She couldn't be contemplating coming after me down the side of the almost vertical cliff. Even if she made it safely to this algae-slimed ledge, wrestling with me here could result in both of us falling to our deaths.

I wriggled my shoulders until my backpack came to rest in a more comfortable position. I didn't dare let go of the rock above me to straighten up and fish my phone out of my pocket.

Facing the trail as she cautiously climbed over the railing, Kelsey was no longer watching me.

Jocelyn had said that Kelsey went to Fallingbrook High. I hoped that Kelsey was one of the locals who didn't know it was possible to cross the river behind the falls. Maybe if I disappeared from her view, she would think that I'd tumbled off the ledge, and she'd stop following me.

I couldn't stay where I was, beneath her. If she fell, she'd knock me off the cliff.

Grasping at sharp, rocky fingerholds and pelted by water droplets, I edged toward the cascade of water. The pathway into the cave behind the falls had not eroded away completely, but it seemed narrower.

Kelsey was lower on the cliff. Like an experienced rock-climber, she was facing the rocky wall and feeling her way downward the way I had.

Panic-fueled adrenaline and muscle memory helped me slip into the tall but narrow cavern that Misty, Samantha, and I had nicknamed Shower Curtain Grotto. I stood trembling behind the wall of water where no one could see me.

I wouldn't be able to see anyone else, either, and I certainly would not hear them.

Could I make it to the side of the river that, last I knew, Jocelyn was on? I hadn't crossed all the way behind the falls since I was about a year younger than Jocelyn was now. I wasn't sure I could still do it. I wasn't even sure how I'd made it this far.

I can do it.

My feet refused to move.

I was wet and cold and rapidly becoming wetter and colder.

Kelsey didn't show up in the opening behind the noisy and constantly moving curtain of water. If she believed I had fallen, she probably wouldn't risk being seen nearby in case investigators asked difficult questions. Maybe she had scrambled up the cliff and had sensibly left the area.

By now, if Jocelyn went down the trails on the far side of the river as quickly as she'd danced across the river, she could have made it to the parking lot. Maybe Samantha and Hooligan had found her there and were giving her a ride home.

Or they'd arrived too soon to encounter Jocelyn. Maybe they hadn't seen Kelsey and didn't know she was in these woods. Maybe they were waiting for me right now where I'd asked them to, on Noisy Cawing Crow Trail near the top of the falls.

I began to hope that Samantha would *not* see my jelly-filled donut arrow. What if she and Hooligan followed the arrow's direction? Landsdowner might have come off his rock, and Kelsey could be upriver, too. What would either of them do if surprised or cornered by Samantha and Hooligan?

If I got colder, I might lose what little grip I had and plunge to the rocks below. I was going to have to choose between the side of the river that Kelsey might be on or the even more treacherous pathway behind the falls to the other side.

A shadow darkened the far side of Shower Curtain Grotto. Philip Landsdowner?

Fear tightened my windpipe until I recognized Jocelyn. I would have gone limp with relief if I'd dared.

She edged close to me. Water streamed from her jacket. She pointed toward Noisy Cawing Crow and shouted, "She pushed you!"

Nodding, I held my palms up in a *What can I do about it?* gesture. Water splashed my hands.

Jocelyn pointed toward the route I'd taken and then pointed behind her and tilted her head in a question. "Which way?"

Still unsure I could navigate the frighteningly narrow pathway that Jocelyn had taken, and hoping that Samantha and Hooligan, but not Kelsey, were nearby, I pointed toward Noisy Cawing Crow.

My courage returned. I was determined not to take a false step. If I did, Jocelyn might make a hasty move and we both might plummet off the ledge. Slowly, facing the tumbling water, I sidestepped back across the narrow stone catwalk behind the falls. Jocelyn stayed beside me.

Compared to the passage behind Shower Curtain Grotto, the sloping algae-covered ledge where I'd been crouching when Kelsey started climbing over the railing looked almost flat and dry.

But not safe. Kelsey was on it, kneeling and staring up toward the guardrail as if waiting for someone to come along and help her.

Jocelyn touched my sleeve and pointed at the section of the cliff closest to the top of the falls. The route up that part of the cliff was a steep one that I'd avoided as a teen. Other kids must have avoided it, too. Saplings grew out of crevices.

Keeping my distance from Kelsey's perch, stretching, and grabbing at small trees, I crawled upward. My wet jeans pulled at my legs.

Jocelyn scooted to the safe side of the railing right after I did. No one was in sight in either direction on Noisy Cawing Crow Trail. No Landsdowner, but also no Samantha or Hooligan. No Misty, either. I didn't know if she had received my message or if Samantha had told her that I wanted her to meet me at this spot.

Jocelyn and I went down the trail until we were where I'd flipped over the railing. Together, we looked down at Kelsey. We needed to get help for her, but I didn't want either of us to be within her reach, especially on the side of a slippery cliff. We were all safest if she didn't move until professional rescuers arrived. I shouted down at her, "Stay there!"

Glaring at me, Kelsey shook her head and pointed toward the route that Jocelyn and I had taken up the cliff. She eased toward it.

The way she'd crawled down was much safer. I shouted, "This way's better!"

Kelsey must have realized that I was right. She started up the route she'd taken down. Pointing, Jocelyn and I shouted directions. I wanted to phone for help, but I had a feeling that if I took my eyes off Kelsey and stopped encouraging her, I might witness a terrifying fall.

Whatever she was, whatever she might have done to Taylor and attempted to do to me, Kelsey didn't deserve that.

She made it to the railing. Jocelyn and I helped her over. Staying together, Jocelyn and I quickly backed away from Kelsey and from the cliff below us.

"Why did you do that?" Kelsey yelled at me. "I nearly killed myself trying to save you!" She glanced toward Jocelyn as if assessing whether Jocelyn believed her.

Jocelyn stayed next to me, out of Kelsey's reach.

I pointed down Noisy Cawing Crow Trail toward the parking lot and shouted, "Let's go where we can get dry and warm!"

Kelsey ran her fingers through her long, wavy auburn hair, now splattered and damp. "No! We have to save Philip!" She started up the trail toward where I'd last seen Landsdowner.

Chapter 34

Kelsey clambered up the trail and out of our sight. I beckoned to Jocelyn and then ran up Noisy Cawing Crow to the flat rock where I'd left what Kelsey had called my trail of bread crumbs.

The two halves of donut were now almost together in their original circle, closing in on the line of jelly I'd squeezed out on the rock.

When we were teens, if Samantha, Misty, or I came upon an arrow that one of the others had made, we sometimes moved the wings of the arrow closer to the shaft. To us, a more streamlined arrow meant speed. It would signal to the girl who had created the arrow that we had seen her message and were hurrying in the direction she'd shown us.

I'd seen Kelsey near that rock. She hadn't touched the arrow. Unless someone else had moved the donut halves, Samantha or Misty had spotted my arrow while Kelsey, Jocelyn, and I had been out of sight. And then Samantha or Misty had streamlined the arrow to tell me she was speeding in the arrow's direction.

My friends knew that Landsdowner might be up here. They would be wary around him.

They didn't know that Kelsey was dangerous. I wasn't positive that she was a murderer, but I knew what she had attempted to do to me.

I reached into my damp jeans pocket and eased my phone out. It was wet. It also wouldn't turn on. Hoping Jocelyn could hear me over the falls, I shouted, "Does yours work?"

"I don't have it!"

I pointed at myself and then up the trail and yelled, "I have to go up there!" I pointed at her and then toward Popcorn Trail. "Go back to the campground."

Shaking her head, she wagged a finger between us. "Let's stay together."

She was right. I didn't know for sure that Kelsey was returning to Landsdowner and, even if she was, whether or not the two of them would stay where I'd last seen him. I didn't want to lead Jocelyn into more danger, but I couldn't let the nineteen-year-old roam alone in the woods while I searched for Samantha and Hooligan. Misty, too, if she was up here. Besides, two sets of eyes and ears were better than one.

Nobody, with the possible exception of Jocelyn or other athletes, could actually sprint up that trail. I moved as quickly as I dared, jumping over potholes, stepping around rocks, and dodging low branches. Jocelyn stayed with me. Gradually, the roar of the falls became distant. When the river beside us merely rushed past, babbling where it was shallowest near the shore, I was able to tell Jocelyn in a normal tone, "I saw you crossing the river up there. I was coming to warn you that Philip Landsdowner was following you, but he got stuck on a rock, and I saw Kelsey." I didn't explain why seeing Kelsey in a red hoodie had made me flee.

Jocelyn leaped over a cluster of exposed roots. "I saw you, too, when I was flipping myself onto the bank. You were on the trail on this side. I peeked out from behind a tree. You were tiptoeing away, down this trail. I was planning to come underneath the falls to warn you in case you hadn't seen Philip Landsdowner and didn't know he was prowling around out here."

Her concern touched me. "That was dangerous."

She reached out a hand to help me across the bumpy roots.

"Not for me. But when I was about to go behind the falls, I looked across the empty space in front of the falls, and I saw Kelsey push you off that railing. It was horrible!"

"Were you the one who screamed?"

"I couldn't stop myself. I thought you were going to fall all the way down, but you did this weird kind of flip and landed on your feet. And then you were clinging to the side of the cliff, and I came behind the falls to do what I could for you. But you didn't need help."

My laugh was a little shaky. "I'm not entirely sure about that."

"I had no idea that Kelsey could be so nasty."

"Me, neither."

Would anyone believe that Kelsey had pushed me, even if we told them? For a second, a picture of Brent frowning in concern flashed through my mind. If he'd been with us at that very instant, I would have run the entire scenario past him. He trusted me, but our story was outlandish, and we could expect skepticism about whether Jocelyn could have witnessed, through the mist near the waterfall, what had happened across the river from her.

Besides, the first thing that Kelsey had done after Jocelyn and I helped her to safety was claim that she'd been trying to save me. No matter what either Jocelyn or I might say, Kelsey would probably stick to that story.

The path became less rocky. Jocelyn and I were nearly trotting. Could I tell anyone about my misadventure? Not Tom and Cindy. They would be horrified at the thought of possibly losing the daughter-in-law they treated as their own daughter, the woman their late son had loved.

My own parents were used to my youthful shenanigans, at least the ones they'd heard about. They probably wouldn't want to know that I might be continuing similar activities now, over six months after my thirtieth birthday. They had expected me to stay out of trouble with minimal lectures about safety, responsibility, and respecting others. Most of the time, I had obeyed.

I wasn't even sure I would tell Misty about Kelsey pushing me. I might have to, though, since I would probably tell Samantha, when and if I caught up to her and Hooligan.

Where were they? Could they keep themselves safe if Kelsey found them?

Maybe Kelsey wasn't a threat to them. Kelsey must have had a reason for trying to push me off the cliff, and it very likely had nothing to do with my refusal to go back up the river with her to help rescue Philip Landsdowner.

After she saw me tiptoe away from her down the trail, she had removed her telltale red hoodie.

I had guessed, from questions Brent asked me, that the person Landsdowner claimed he'd seen near the donut skyrocket was about my size and dressed like I was, except that the potential killer might have worn jeans and a hood.

Had Kelsey also gleaned from the detectives' questions that they were particularly interested in anyone who'd been wearing a red hoodie the night of the Fourth?

And then, because of my reputation for helping the police solve murders, she could have believed that the police told me more than they actually did, so she'd ditched the hoodie before she chased me down Noisy Cawing Crow Trail.

She hadn't seen me at the fireworks and didn't know that when I saw her I hadn't paid attention to what she'd been wearing. I'd been surprised that her hair was long, that was all. She wouldn't know that I hadn't seen her when a hood was covering her hair.

But when she noticed what she called my trail of bread crumbs, she must have been certain that I'd left a secret message. She could have jumped to the conclusion that I'd made that arrow *after* I'd seen her in the hoodie and that I was directing someone, possibly police investigators, to her.

Knowing that she was guilty, she must have believed her

guilt was obvious to everyone. An innocent person probably would not have jumped to so many conclusions. But if I was right, she had jumped to them. And she wasn't innocent.

Assuming that I might have figured out that she'd killed Taylor, she had attempted to silence me.

That alone made me certain that she was guilty of killing Taylor. I wasn't sure how I could prove it, though.

Maybe, like Kelsey's, my thinking was too self-centered.

What else might Kelsey be planning?

Maybe Kelsey was also a threat to Philip Landsdowner. He could have seen her light that firework and thought she was me, and then he had tried to prove that I was the culprit by giving the police that doctored photo and claiming that he'd seen me throw out a bag that I hadn't touched since earlier that afternoon. Maybe his only motive had been to collect a reward for giving the police information leading to the arrest of a killer.

That didn't explain why he'd begun taking pictures of me early that morning.

The police would have had no reason to show Kelsey the doctored picture of me with the stack of donuts behind Taylor. Unless Landsdowner had shown the picture to Kelsey and told her about his attempts to finger me as the killer, she might suspect that Landsdowner knew she'd lit the firework. She could have seen him hanging around that night with his camera. She could have feared he'd taken incriminating photos of her.

Maybe she had removed the hoodie because she didn't want *Landsdowner* to see her in it. When I first saw her calling to him from the riverbank, she was wearing the hoodie, but he'd obviously been focused on Jocelyn. Maybe Kelsey had been certain that he had not seen her wearing the hoodie when she was near the river, so she had tossed it to prevent him from seeing her in it, either when she was leaving him to chase me down the trail or when, as she'd seemed to want to, she took me back to help rescue him.

Later she'd asked Jocelyn and me both to help.

Did Kelsey really intend to rescue Landsdowner?

Maybe she had planned to "accidentally" make Landsdowner, Jocelyn, and me fall into the river during the attempted rescue and she had hoped that the current would be strong enough to carry all three of us downstream and over the falls.

It didn't sound like a workable plan, but that didn't mean that she wouldn't have tried.

Or that she wouldn't try something similar with Samantha and Hooligan.

The trail narrowed and the riverbank beside it steepened. I wanted to walk faster, but the setting sun cast long shadows that alternately exaggerated and disguised dips and bumps in the trail.

I asked Jocelyn, "Do you know what sort of relationship Kelsey and Landsdowner have? She wanted to take me with her to rescue him in person. I refused, and she pushed me over the railing."

Jocelyn swung herself around the slanted trunk of a cedar. "I should have told you about him when you first asked. He spent hours at Freeze, just sitting by himself at a table and not saying anything, like he could never decide what flavor to order. When I was behind the counter, he stared at me in this icky way, so I tried to avoid him, but I couldn't hide in the kitchen all the time, so I quit and went to work at Deputy Donut. I thought he was completely creepy, but Kelsey said he was mysterious and romantic." Helping me around another tree trunk, Jocelyn shuddered, probably only partly due to her wet clothing. "She developed this huge crush on him. She must have told him where I was working. He showed up at Deputy Donut and at our table at the picnic. And then, Tuesday night, I was home alone, and I saw him outside our house on the sidewalk. He was pointing his camera at the window where I was."

Horrified, I stopped walking. "Is that why you didn't come to work the past two days?"

She kicked a pinecone. "Yeah. My parents live in their trailer in the campground all summer and commute to work. I was staying in our house so I could bike to work and gymnastics. After I saw Philip Landsdowner spying on our house, I got my dad to come get me. I didn't tell him why. I said I had time off from my new job. I'm sorry I worried you."

"As long as you're okay," I said. "I kept leaving messages on your phone."

"It's at home. I was afraid that Kelsey had given him my number. What if he had some way of tracing my phone's location? It wouldn't be where I was."

"And you turned off the ringtone."

She jumped over a short outcropping. "I didn't want him standing outside and calling me and hearing my phone ring. My parents wouldn't have liked it if he broke in, even if I wasn't there."

I walked around the outcropping. "Your parents wouldn't like someone stalking you, period."

She strode ahead. "Which is why I didn't tell them."

"Jocelyn . . ."

She said over her shoulder, "I know. I should have." She stopped, turned toward me, and tilted her head in question. "How did you know I turned off my ringtone?"

I gave her an apologetic smile. "You might think I'm as bad as Philip Landsdowner."

"I doubt it."

"I stood outside, called your number, and listened. And just now, you told me you'd left your phone at home." I passed her as the trail widened. "I wish you had called the police when you saw him outside your house." *Peering into windows with his telephoto lens . . .*

She caught up and walked beside me. "It's one of those things, you know? Like happens to lots of women. It would be my word against his, and no one might believe me."

I skirted around an eroded hole in the riverbank. "I do."

I stumbled over the end of a log and went down headfirst into ferns.

My hand touched cloth.

Chapter 35

Jocelyn helped me stand. The garment I was clutching came up with me.

If I'd been deeper in the darkening woods, I might not have been certain what the garment was or what color it was, but the still-milky sky reflected on the river, brightening everything nearby.

The garment was a hoodie.

A red one.

Farther down the sloping riverbank, close to the water, something rustled in underbrush behind a juniper. I caught a glimpse of something more solidly black than nearby tree trunks.

Startled, I asked, "Who's there?"

No answer.

My hand tightened on the hoodie. Could someone be lying injured on the riverbank?

Jocelyn and I traded concerned glances.

I called out, "Are you okay?"

Silence.

Jocelyn whispered, "A bear?"

The black I'd seen had not resembled fur. I asked in a tone that could be heard on the embankment below me, "Aren't we supposed to make lots of noise if a bear's around, to scare it?"

Turning the corners of her mouth down, Jocelyn glanced up toward the pine beside her as if wondering if she could climb higher than a bear could.

I clapped my hands, and shouted, "Shoo!" No bear, or anything else, went splashing into the river.

Okay, whoever or whatever it was knew I was coming. Still carrying the hoodie, which I would fling at any ferocious wildlife I might encounter, I climbed over the log and side-stepped down the slope toward the river. I heard Jocelyn right behind me. Teetering on stones that were partly sub-merged in an eddy at the edge of the river, I clutched at a prickly branch of the juniper and peeked around it.

In her black tank top and leggings, Kelsey was crouching among the juniper's exposed roots next to the river. She jumped up. "Bear?" she asked.

"I heard something, but maybe it was you." I backed a step away from her. "Where's Philip Landsdowner? Does he still need our help?"

She pointed up the river. "Up there, past some trees, but you can't see him from here."

I wasn't about to take my eyes off her to turn around and check.

She looked at the hoodie in my hand. "What are you doing with that?"

"Is it yours? It's getting cold out here. Maybe you'd like to put it on." I tossed it to her.

She swatted it as if it were a pesky bug. It landed in the eddy and circled lazily, a red blob among floating bits of veg-etation.

I stepped away from Kelsey again. My backpack bumped into Jocelyn. I pushed gently, hoping she'd take the hint and run up the bank.

I'd be right behind her.

Kelsey had other ideas. As if her knees were springs, she leaped over roots and gave my shoulders a hard shove. Again.

I lost my balance and staggered into the shallows. Cold water flowed into my sneakers and resoaked the ankles of my jeans. I slipped on algae-covered rocks. My arms flailing, I managed to stay upright and steady myself enough to remove my backpack and hold it in front of me where I might have a chance of keeping it dry. "Run farther up the trail," I told Jocelyn in a voice that was, considering my emotions, surprisingly calm. "One of our regular customers should be up there somewhere. Find him." *And bring him and Samantha back here.* I didn't say it.

Jocelyn shook her head. Obviously, she wasn't leaving me alone with Kelsey. And I wasn't sure I wanted her venturing up there alone. Samantha and Hooligan might not be anywhere around. And if Landsdowner was still on that rock and saw Jocelyn, he might suddenly discover that he could wade back to shore.

As I'd hoped she might, Kelsey jumped to the wrong conclusion about the regular customer. She snarled at Jocelyn, "Philip's *my* boyfriend, not yours!"

Jocelyn retorted, "You're welcome to him."

I sloshed toward the bank and Jocelyn.

Kelsey blocked me, obviously not about to let me climb out of the river.

I asked her, "Why aren't you rescuing him like you said you would?"

"I had other priorities." *Ambushing Jocelyn and me, perhaps.* "And a couple of other people are up there staring at him. Hey, I got it! Is one of them the customer you told Jocelyn to go find?"

Oops. I tried looking neutral.

Hands on hips, Kelsey sneered at me. "I've heard that police officers like donuts. Is that the customer you want Jocelyn to run to? A cop?"

My ankles and feet were getting used to the chilly river water. "I don't know who's up there." It was true. I didn't know who the people staring at Landsdowner were. They could be tourists, but I hoped they were Hooligan and Samantha. Trying not to let my tentative relief show on my face, I asked a question of my own. "Why were you following Philip Landsdowner earlier today?"

"I wasn't following *him,* not at first, anyway. Mama Freeze told me you were asking about a bag of donuts and planning to come out to the campground to look for your parents, so I told Mama Freeze I wasn't feeling well. I left work and came to the campground and drove around until I saw your car. Maybe you thought you hid it, but you didn't, not completely. Then I saw you on a trail and followed you."

"Why?"

"Because you were too interested in who might have picked up a certain bag of donuts. I lost track of you on that trail, but I found Philip and followed him in case he would lead me to you. Only, he was mistakenly going after Jocelyn and ended up stuck on a rock. I tried to get him to come back and help me search for you, but then I lucked out and saw you. By then, you had seen me in my red hoodie. I shouldn't have worn that to work today, and I should have taken it off before I followed you up that trail, but I was in a hurry. I should have thrown that hoodie out sooner, on the night of the Fourth."

Looking baffled wasn't difficult. Again, I asked, "Why?"

"You said you saw me leaving the fireworks. You could have seen me in that hoodie that night." Now almost completely waterlogged, the hoodie had partially sunk. The eddy held it against a stone, though, preventing the river from carrying it downstream. The end of one sleeve waved feebly in the current.

I said, "I saw you that night, but I didn't see a hoodie, and even if I did, I don't understand what it has to do with . . ." I gestured at the water all around me. "Anything."

"Maybe this will help." Again, she flung herself at me. Her body-checking stunts were becoming tiresome.

Still clutching my backpack, I stumbled backward into

deeper water. It pulled at the knees of my jeans and felt almost freezing on my lower legs.

This time, Kelsey's plan backfired. She lost her grip on the slippery stones and fell face-first into the river. She was closer to shore than I was, but farther downstream.

Jocelyn threw her jacket onto the bank and waded in.

Kelsey's arms and legs splashed. Her face surfaced. She gasped, "I can't swim!"

I shouted, "You don't have to. You can touch bottom. *Put your feet down!*" Trying to rescue Kelsey was also becoming tiresome. I yelled at Jocelyn, "Don't go near her!"

I glanced up the river. Moments ago, trees on the bank had prevented me from seeing Landsdowner, but now that I was out in the river, he was in plain view. He was still sitting on that boulder. It was closer than I'd realized.

He was pointing his camera down the river, toward us.

I might have known.

Following my shouted instructions, Kelsey managed to get her feet underneath her, but although she was closer to the bank than I was, she'd found a hole and was in water up to her hips. The current forced her to hop sideways.

I shouted at her, "Wade back to shore!"

"So you can ruin everything else?" she yelled back. "All my life, Taylor got everything. The best grades. The boy I wanted. Head cheerleader. Awards. And then she was going to be promoted at Freeze and boss me around. For once, I hadn't tried to compete. I didn't enter the Fabulous Fourth royalty competition. For once, I didn't lose to her. No one was going to suspect me of hurting her. They were going to suspect Gabrielle, who also spent all of her life losing to Taylor and who was livid at coming in only second and had to settle for duchess instead of queen. Then you asked about that bag of donuts I found in Freeze and I knew I had to find some way of stopping you from telling the police what you think I did with those donuts. Plus, Mama Freeze said you were planning to come out to the falls, where you could be seriously hurt in all sorts of apparent accidents."

Mentally translating "seriously hurt" as "killed," I argued, "The campground isn't all that dangerous."

"How was I supposed to know that? And besides, you did come up near the falls, just as I hoped." The water was too deep for Kelsey to move quickly, but instead of heading toward shore, she was sort of bouncing toward me. She must have noticed that the water was shallower where I was. "You ruined everything, Emily Westhill," she hollered, "and you're going to pay!" She glanced toward Jocelyn waiting watchfully in the shallows near the shore. "You, too."

With Kelsey no longer in my way, I could have waded out of the river. However, I needed to stop her attacks on Jocelyn and me, and I had a better chance of subduing her in the water where, despite its chilly temperature, I felt at home. Obviously, Kelsey didn't. On land, we might be more evenly matched.

Jocelyn waded in deeper.

"Go back," I told her.

"I can swim." Jocelyn was probably a better swimmer than I was. Besides, she wasn't holding a backpack in one hand and trying to keep it above water.

I thought Jocelyn was coming closer in case she needed to rescue me.

I was wrong. She turned and hurled herself at Kelsey.

Chapter 36

✺

"No!" I screamed, striding through the water in slow motion toward Kelsey and Jocelyn.

At first, I couldn't tell whether Kelsey was deliberately trying to harm Jocelyn or if she was merely grabbing at Jocelyn to save herself.

Kelsey managed to put her feet down and stand in the water. She clutched a fistful of Jocelyn's hair and forced Jocelyn's head under.

Jocelyn struggled. Kelsey gave me a smugly triumphant look. "You're next."

I was not only next. By then, I was next *to* Kelsey and her latest intended victim.

Although I was certain that Jocelyn had the strength and agility to overcome Kelsey, I wasn't about to wait to find out if I was right. Holding my backpack by one strap, I swung it at Kelsey's head.

It connected. Yelping, Kelsey let go of Jocelyn.

I tossed the backpack into shallower waters closer to shore, grabbed Jocelyn's shoulders, and pulled her to her feet.

She wiped hair out of her face. "Thanks."

I hadn't knocked Kelsey out, but I had knocked her over, and she was apparently too frantic to remember to put her feet down and her head up.

Jocelyn and I each grasped one of Kelsey's upper arms and

yanked her to her feet. Kelsey tried to get away from us, but we weren't about to let her. We waded with her toward dry land.

Suddenly the shore became a whole lot safer, at least for Jocelyn and me.

Samantha and Hooligan plunged down from the upriver section of Noisy Cawing Crow Trail. At the same time, Misty, Scott, and Brent swooped down the embankment from the other direction.

Apparently ready to join the fray in the water, Samantha and Scott tore off their shoes.

They didn't need to. Jocelyn and I brought Kelsey, stumbling over stones, entangling her feet in the hoodie she'd discarded, and trying to pull away from us, to the bank.

"I heard you shouting about preventing Emily from telling the cops about that bag of donuts," Hooligan told her sternly. "You're under arrest."

Kelsey demanded, "Says who?" I didn't blame her for being skeptical. None of the three officers were in uniform, and Hooligan looked more than usually boyish with his reddish hair sticking up and his T-shirt untucked over jeans.

Brent, however, was still dressed for work in khakis, a white shirt, and a black blazer. He reached into his jacket, just happening to flash his shoulder holster, and pulled out a badge. "I do. You might remember me from our previous discussions. I'm Detective Brent Fyne, Fallingbrook Police Department. I heard what you said, too, and not only about donuts. And I saw you push Jocelyn's head under the water. These two off-duty officers are taking you to the station." He nodded at Misty, who looked forbidding despite the loose bug-repellant shirt she wore over skinny jeans and the pictures of happily grinning cats on her sneakers.

She and Hooligan gripped Kelsey's arms. "We'll take her now," Misty gently told Jocelyn and me.

I gratefully relinquished the arm I'd been holding.

With a slightly diabolical twitch of a grin, Brent pulled

black plastic strips from a pocket. "Thanks to the messages you left me, Em, I brought some of these." Holding Kelsey's hands behind her back, he cinched a zip tie around her wrists, and then he told Hooligan and Misty to take her to the trail on the bank above us and wait for him there. "Since you two aren't on duty, I'll call for backup officers." He pulled out his phone.

No longer having to concern myself with Kelsey, I turned around and waded into the river.

Samantha screeched, "What are you doing, Emily? Come back!"

"I, um, *dropped* my backpack." The coins, credit cards, and ID in my wallet would probably survive, and the bills could be dried. The flashlight and first-aid kit might need replacing. The donuts wouldn't be in great shape, but that had probably been true for at least the past half hour.

The next thing I knew, Scott and Samantha were up to their ankles, pant legs and all, in the river with me and Scott had one supportive hand under my elbow. I toed around near where I'd left my backpack and then inched my way downriver. Luckily, the current hadn't tumbled my backpack far.

Smiling in triumph, I brought it up dripping, and the three of us waded toward the embankment. I asked Scott and Samantha, "Why did you two get wet?"

"Might as well join the party," Samantha said. "Why should you have all the fun?" I wondered what would have happened to the tints of blue and turquoise in her hair if she'd accidentally dunked her head.

"And there's more fun," I said, pointing to the riverbank.

Brent pocketed his phone. "What?"

He was on the bank with Jocelyn near the hoodie, which was now mostly out of the water. Kelsey must have kicked it away from her feet.

I pointed at it. "Kelsey was wearing that red hoodie earlier this evening. After she realized that I might have seen her in it, she hid it behind that rotten log up there. Later I found it and tried to give it to her, but she batted it into the river." I couldn't help a slight grin sort of like Brent's when he'd shown us the zip ties. "And then she stumbled over it when we brought her out of the river."

With his phone, Brent took flash pictures of the hoodie. I told him about Kelsey crouching behind the juniper, and he took photos of that spot, too. He pulled another zip tie out of his pocket, dragged the hoodie all the way out of the water, and secured it to the trunk of a smaller juniper. He took out his phone again and said into it, "Tell the backup officers to make sure they bring an evidence bag up the trail. Big enough for an adult-sized sweatshirt."

Finally, with Brent's hand resting lightly on the middle of my back, we climbed up the bank behind Jocelyn, now carrying her damp jacket. She was drenched, and I wasn't much drier. "Are you two okay?" Brent asked us.

"Just wet," I said. Dangling from one hand, my backpack was dripping. I was not about to put it on.

Jocelyn agreed with a smile in her voice, "I like swimming."

Frowning, Brent eyed my face. "I'm going to see that this person gets locked inside the cruiser I left in the parking lot, but I'm going to need statements from you and Jocelyn about what went on up here. No rush, but can you meet me in the parking lot?"

Jocelyn and I both said we would.

Samantha sat on the ground and started putting on her shoes. "What about the guy on the rock?" she asked Brent.

Chapter 37

"What guy on what rock?" Brent asked. "Philip Landsdowner?"

Samantha and I explained.

Scott slipped his feet into his shoes. "I'll call swift-water rescue." Luckily, his phone must not have gotten wet. I heard him tell his team to start preparing for a rescue above Fallingbrook Falls. He also told them he'd confirm in a few minutes whether he actually needed them.

Brent gave Jocelyn an apologetic look and said to me, "You and I guessed a few days ago that Landsdowner could be stalking you and your assistant. When you called me earlier this evening, you said he was following her."

"He was. And from what she told me tonight, he has definitely been stalking her."

Glancing at me occasionally as if for support, Jocelyn told Brent about Landsdowner watching her when she worked at Freeze and then peering at her house through his camera and its telephoto lens.

Brent became so stern that his face could have been made of rock.

Jocelyn added, "I've been hiding in my parents' trailer down in the campground, but he found me today."

I asked Brent if Landsdowner was living at the campground.

Brent paused, but must have decided he wouldn't be telling us anything he shouldn't. "He gave us the address of a condo on Packers Road."

I said, "I suspect he knew about Jocelyn's parents' place here at least as long ago as Monday, when I saw him driving around the campground." Kelsey was on the trail near us. Misty and Hooligan, each of them holding her with both hands, had turned her away from us. I lowered my voice, anyway. "Thanks to Kelsey, probably, who has apparently been trying to win her way into Landsdowner's heart by telling him whatever she knows about Jocelyn."

Brent spoke loudly enough for Misty to hear. "Misty, I'll take over for you so you can keep an eye on Philip Landsdowner, who might be up the river on a rock. In case I don't intercept the backup officers first, tell them to cuff Landsdowner and bring him into headquarters. I want to talk to him."

"Okay!" Misty didn't let go of Kelsey.

Beside us, Scott said, "I'll stay with Misty."

"I'll keep an eye on the guy on the rock, too," Samantha said, "in case he needs medical care, and I'll stick around until the on-duty EMTs who accompany Scott's rescue team get here. I'll also keep an eye on Jocelyn and Emily until we can get them somewhere warm and dry."

"I'm okay," I said. "It's July eleventh. It's warm." My teeth betrayed me by chattering.

"Me, too." Jocelyn didn't sound like she was shivering at all.

Samantha countered, "It's northern Wisconsin. And that water is *cold*."

Scott asked Brent, "Will it be okay with you if the five of us—Misty, Samantha, Emily, Jocelyn, and I—stay together until the backup you requested arrives?"

"Perfect," Brent answered. Handing Misty something, he took Kelsey's arm. He and Hooligan started down Noisy Cawing Crow Trail with Kelsey.

Grinning, holding up a fistful of Brent's zip ties, Misty bopped over to us in her cat-printed sneakers. "Where's this rock Landsdowner's on, if he's still there?"

Samantha pointed up the river. "Around the bend."

We all started in that direction.

Misty asked, "What is Philip Landsdowner doing out in the river on a rock? You left me a message that you were following him, Emily. What did you do? Heave him onto a rock and leave him there?"

I smiled. Jocelyn giggled.

Samantha explained, "He claims he was trying to get a photo and slipped." A hint of a smile edged into her voice. "He wants someone to rescue his camera, and then he thinks he can make it out by himself."

"I'll rescue his camera," I muttered. "Before he deletes photos that *prove* he was stalking Jocelyn."

It was still light enough out on the river to see Landsdowner hunched on the boulder. He was no longer holding his camera up to his eye. He was using his hands to brace himself, like he was afraid of falling off the rock and into the water.

Scott called his swift-water rescue team and confirmed that he needed them. He disconnected, folded his arms over his chest, and told us, "If anyone goes out on those stepping-stones or into that water before my team arrives, it will be me. I have swift-water training."

"Which," Misty countered, "requires the rest of your swift-water rescue team and some sturdy ropes. Plus wet suits, flotation devices, pulleys, hooks, and I'm not sure what all. Maybe an inflatable raft."

Far from being put off by Misty's brand of humor, Scott laughed down at her in a way that should have set Misty's heart racing. In a healthy way.

Misty added, "No one, not even your swift-water rescue team, can go in after him until the police backup Brent called arrives. Landsdowner might be armed."

I couldn't help snickering. "He's clinging so desperately to his rock that it wouldn't matter if he had twelve bazookas, two cannons, five spears, and a bow and arrow. He needs both hands to hold on to that rock."

"Good," Misty said. "He can stay that way."

Shouting at Landsdowner, Scott introduced himself as the fire chief. "Stay where you are! Rescuers are on their way!"

Landsdowner nodded and continued sitting morosely on his rock.

I set my sopping backpack down on the trail, took out my flashlight, and tried turning it on. Maybe it would work after it dried.

Jocelyn positioned herself behind the rest of us, where Landsdowner was less likely to see her, much less stare at her.

I asked her, "Do your parents know where you are?"

"Not specifically."

I turned to the others. "Can one of you lend Jocelyn your phone? She left hers at home and mine's a little damp."

Jocelyn shook her head. "They don't expect me back yet and won't be worried. And they almost never answer their phones."

I couldn't help sighing. "They sound as bad as my folks."

Jocelyn glanced up toward the indigo sky. "Worse, probably." A dimple showed beside her mouth. "Though I guess I shouldn't complain about them after leaving my phone at home."

I admitted, "And I didn't exactly take good care of mine."

Misty looked at us, shook her head in mock exasperation, and grumbled, "If Landsdowner falls in before your swift-water rescue team arrives, Scott, he can get himself out."

Scott grinned at her. "If he falls in, I'll probably have to grab you to keep you from attempting to rescue him."

Misty made a scoffing noise and turned away, probably to hide a blush that we wouldn't be able to see in the deepening dusk underneath the trees. She and Scott were off duty. If she wanted to, she could wade into the river for the fun of being grabbed by Scott. . . .

I reminded myself that we were still in a serious situation in which my matchmaking fantasies had no place. However, first responders were notorious for the slightly warped sense of humor that helped them cope, and I was used to and rather fond of their humor. And maybe I had adopted some of it, myself.

Misty asked me what had happened since I'd left the message for her. I explained, using our long-ago code words. Samantha told us that she was the one who streamlined the arrow. Misty had recognized the donut arrow when she was climbing the trail with Scott and Brent. She was horrified by Jocelyn's and my adventures on steep cliffs and behind the falls, but she didn't scold. "Good thing we got all that practice out here when we were kids."

Samantha and I agreed.

Jocelyn told us that she'd also spent a lot of time scrambling up and down rocks and behind the falls.

Scott looked down at me and shook his head as if to clear it. "Skinned knees, popcorn, noisy cawing crows, donut arrows, and shower curtain grottoes?"

"State secrets," Misty said.

I grinned up at him. "Misty, Samantha, and I used to play detective up here in these woods, all summer, every summer until we had summer jobs, but we still hung around here a lot before we went off to college. We had secret signals and our own names for the trails and for the cave behind the falls."

Scott shook his head, but his smile widened. "I wish I'd paid more attention to you three in high school."

"You were two years ahead of us," I reminded him. "Too sophisticated."

"I had my head in my books."

"That's not something to regret," I said. "Right, Jocelyn?"

"I guess."

Misty winked at Samantha and me. "Looks like we'll have to rename everything up here."

Without cracking a smile, Samantha asked, "Did we have a name for the boulder where that guy is sitting?"

"We do now," I retorted. "Stalker's Rock."

Teasing each other and keeping track of Stalker's Rock, the five of us stood close together for warmth. It was fully dark when Hooligan arrived with two uniformed police officers wearing heavy vests and carrying their usual load of equipment. All three men had, I was glad to see, working flashlights. They shined them across the water to Stalker's Rock. Landsdowner was still sitting there.

Aiming his light near his own feet so it wouldn't be in anyone's eyes, Hooligan told Misty, "You and I have been assigned to accompany Emily and Jocelyn down the trail to the parking lot."

Scott and Samantha decided to stay near Stalker's Rock with the two uniformed officers until the rescue team and the EMTs arrived. After offering to drive Samantha home later if Hooligan couldn't, Scott turned to Misty and told her, "Go back to town with one of your friends if I'm up here too long."

She smiled up at him. "I'll wait."

"Take my keys, then." He put them into her outstretched hand.

Wide-eyed, I teased Misty, "*You* rode in a vehicle that someone else was driving?"

"Only if he's a fire chief," she answered, "and can drive those big shiny red trucks."

"Misty let me drive a cruiser once," Hooligan said.

I remembered the time. "She wasn't in uniform or on duty, and you were."

Samantha's smile was a very happy one. That evening was when she and Hooligan had met each other for the first time. The attraction had been obvious. I smiled, too, just thinking about it.

Leaving Scott, Samantha, and the two uniformed officers behind to watch Landsdowner, the rest of us started down the trail. I really didn't want to wear that cold, wet backpack, but I wanted to keep my hands free to catch myself against trees or rocks if I tripped, so I put the backpack on. We traveled slowly, since Hooligan was the only one with a working flashlight and he made certain that Misty, Jocelyn, and I saw the obstacles. Dampness seeped from my backpack into my sweater and shirt. I tried not to shiver.

We hadn't gone very far when Brent and Rex, each with his own powerful light, met us.

Chapter 38

Brent's eyes sought mine. "How are you doing?"

"We're fine," I said. "Right, Jocelyn?"

"Yes. Thank you for believing me about that man stalking me."

"I have no difficulty believing that," Rex said. "He has a lot of explaining to do."

Hooligan and Misty asked Brent if he minded if they returned to the group waiting for the swift-water rescue team.

Brent thanked them for what they'd done that evening. "Take the rest of your off-duty night off," he teased.

The smile on my face was huge. Hooligan and Misty probably wanted to be near the action when Landsdowner was rescued and taken away, but they probably also wanted to return to their dates that evening—Hooligan with Samantha and Misty with Scott.

Misty gave Brent his zip ties. Hooligan shined his light on the trail upriver, and he and Misty followed its beam away from us.

Brent and his flashlight led Rex, Jocelyn, and me down Noisy Cawing Crow Trail. While we were still far enough from the roaring falls to hear each other, I told the two detectives about the things they should see near the falls that would help them understand what we were going to tell them when we gave our statements. Near the top of the falls, Rex and Brent took flash pictures when I pointed at the donut arrow, the railing I'd flipped over, and the ledge partway down the cliff.

We started down again and had to step aside to let EMTs wearing large backpacks hurry uphill past us. Farther down, we stepped aside again for the swift-water rescue team. Shining flashlights, wearing and lugging a huge amount of equipment, they were obviously taking their time and moving cautiously.

At the bottom of the hill, the boxy bright red search and rescue vehicle dominated the parking lot. Next to it was an ambulance. I also saw a couple of other fire department trucks, one marked police cruiser, two unmarked cruisers, and Scott's and Hooligan's SUVs.

No one was in any of the police cars at the moment.

I asked Brent, "Where's Kelsey?"

"A pair of officers are driving her to headquarters."

The two unmarked cruisers were facing in opposite directions so the drivers could open their windows and talk to each other. They could also, if they needed to, watch each other's backs.

Rex escorted me to the passenger seat of one of the unmarked cruisers.

I hesitated. "My backpack was in the river. It's kind of drippy."

"That doesn't matter. Put it on the floor."

I sat in the passenger seat and set my backpack beside my feet.

Brent put Jocelyn in the front seat of the other cruiser. Both cruisers' windows were closed.

Rex slid into the driver's seat of his cruiser, turned the interior lights on, and asked if I was okay.

I said I was.

"You're wet." He started the engine and cranked up the heater. "Tell me if that's too much hot air." Did I see a twinkle in his eyes? Not sure I trusted his apparent kindness, I was glad that Jocelyn was with Brent. I knew for certain that my longtime friend would treat my young assistant compassionately and sensitively.

I asked Rex, "Are we going to police headquarters?"

"I'll take your statement here, unless you'd prefer the comfort of our interview room."

"My car's over in the campground, so this works better for me. But if you want to go interview Kelsey, I can talk to you another time."

"Kelsey isn't going anywhere tonight, and we'd like Jocelyn's and your descriptions of the evening's events while they're fresh in your mind." He paused for a second and then added emphatically, "*And* before we interrogate Kelsey."

As I'd thought before, my story sounded, at least to me, too bizarre to be true. Almost entirely expressionless, Rex wrote it down. I reminded myself that he had taken whatever he'd heard from Brent seriously enough to come all the way out here. He asked lots of questions and had me go over the story several times.

With no lighting source other than the insides of the two unmarked cruisers and the three-quarter moon high in the sky, the parking lot was almost totally dark. The car's windows were closed and its engine was running, but I could hear the falls.

Flashlights shining ahead of them, the two uniformed police officers we'd left up near Stalker's Rock came off the trail and into the parking lot with Philip Landsdowner between them. Landsdowner was still wearing the strap around his neck holding the long-lensed camera, and his hands were cuffed behind his back. Below his knees, his jeans looked darker, as if they were wet.

One of the officers carried a paper evidence bag, sealed, with something bulging at the bottom. Water dripped from the bag. Misty and Hooligan must have directed him to Kelsey's hoodie.

Rex turned on his cruiser's spotlight, aimed it at Landsdowner, excused himself, and slipped out of the cruiser. Brent got out of his cruiser a split second after Rex closed his door.

Jocelyn looked at me, tilted her head, and raised an eyebrow.

Rex hadn't told me to stay in the cruiser.

I pointed at the officers and Landsdowner, made a *let's go* gesture, opened the door of Rex's cruiser, and eased out.

Not wanting to call attention to ourselves, neither of us closed the doors of our cruisers, and Jocelyn avoided walking between the spotlight and the men in the parking lot by going around the back of the cruiser I'd been in. The interior lights in the cruisers had been on when we left the cars. They stayed on. Together, Jocelyn and I tiptoed closer and halted in the darkness several feet behind Brent and Rex. I made certain that we weren't between Rex's cruiser's dash cam and Landsdowner.

If any of the officers heard us above the rush of falling water, they chose to ignore us. If they looked toward us, they would have seen little besides the glare of Rex's spotlight.

That spotlight was probably blinding Landsdowner when he turned his head toward the two detectives between him and us. He whined, "I had nothing to do with that murder. I did not light the firework."

"Who did?" Brent asked him.

"I don't know."

Rex folded his arms across his chest. "Earlier, you told us you did know. You said it was the woman from Deputy Donut. You provided us with a picture of her near the deceased. She was carrying a stack of donuts with a fuse sticking out the top of it."

Landsdowner shuffled his feet. "It looked like her. The woman was wearing a red hoodie. She bent over this stack of donuts on the ground, which was weird, but I didn't take her picture at that moment, and I didn't actually see anyone light anything. Later I saw Jocelyn's boss in a red thing, and she'd been splattered with jelly-filled donuts. She had to have been near when the firework exploded. It was easy to figure out that she blew up her own donuts and killed that woman."

"That photo was faked, wasn't it." Brent did not make it into a question.

Landsdowner muttered, "I . . . um—"

Rex interrupted him. "It's a simple question. Was that photo faked? Yes or no. Just answer the question. You're chin deep in trouble already. Lying will only make it worse for you."

Landsdowner said, "I sort of put two photos together."

Brent asked him, "Were you trying to hide the fact that *you* actually planted and lit that firework?"

Landsdowner was obviously becoming unnerved. Raising his voice, he claimed, "I had nothing to do with it!" The two uniformed officers holding him by the arms didn't move. They just stood there gripping his arms and staring straight ahead. Like Landsdowner, they probably didn't want to look toward Rex's spotlight.

Rex demanded, "Were you trying to protect someone, Landsdowner?"

Landsdowner probably didn't know that Kelsey had been arrested. From his boulder, he could not have seen the river-bank where Brent had handcuffed her with plastic ties and he could not have seen Brent and Hooligan taking her away. Scott, Misty, Hooligan, and Samantha would have stayed quiet about the arrest. If Landsdowner's rescuers and the two uniformed police officers knew about it, they must have been discreet, too.

Landsdowner shifted his shoulders and neck like anyone might after a heavy camera had been on a strap around his neck for hours while he was too busy clinging to a rock to adjust the strap or redistribute the camera's weight. "I told you, I don't know who lit that thing. I didn't see it happen. Just this woman in a red hoodie who was near it before it exploded."

"If you didn't know who lit it, why did you tell us it was the woman from Deputy Donut?" I'd never before heard Brent sound so exasperated.

"I told you. I thought it was her."

"Thought," Brent repeated. "You *thought* it was the woman from Deputy Donut, so you composed a picture to make it look like it was her."

"I was only trying to help," Landsdowner said.

Rex made a rude noise.

"Okay." Landsdowner sounded hoarse. "I needed to discredit her."

Barely restraining myself from erupting with questions or noises even ruder than Rex's, I stayed in the background and let the detectives do the interrogating. Jocelyn moved closer to me.

"Why would you need or even *want* to discredit the woman from Deputy Donut?" Rex asked Landsdowner.

"Because she's Jocelyn's boss and I've loved Jocelyn ever since she first started winning competitions and being on the news." Landsdowner's tone made it clear that he thought his reasoning was not only obvious but also completely sensible.

I glanced at Jocelyn in sympathy.

She was coping in her own fashion. Grasping her throat in both hands and sticking out her tongue, she pretended to be choking. She was silent, though, and none of the five men seemed to notice her clowning.

Rex made a show of scratching his head. "I don't understand what that has to do with discrediting Jocelyn's boss. Perhaps you can explain it to me."

"Jocelyn used to work at Freeze. A clerk there, Kelsey, thought that *she* had a chance with me. To get my attention, she told me everything she knew about Jocelyn."

Rex prodded, "Like what?"

"Where her gymnastic competitions were, so I could take pictures, that sort of thing. I wanted Jocelyn to notice me and fall for me like I fell for her."

Beside me, Jocelyn shuddered.

Brent asked Landsdowner, "Did Kelsey also tell you where Jocelyn lived and where her parents had their trailer?"

"She might have. I don't remember." Landsdowner was so oily that it was a wonder he didn't ooze out of the hands of the two officers holding him and melt into a puddle in the gravel parking lot.

Rex asked, "And did she tell you where Jocelyn's new job was?"

"I suppose."

Rex reminded him, "Remember what I told you about lying."

"Okay, yeah, Kelsey must have told me all that stuff."

Rex asked, "Did you say you saw the woman from Deputy Donut toss a paper bag into a trash can near the 1950 Ford with the donut on top?"

"I thought it was her. I caught a glimpse of this short woman in jeans and a red top. She was wearing a backpack, and I was sure it was Jocelyn's boss, and that I'd also seen her bending over the firework before it was lit."

"You just told us you weren't nearby," Brent stated.

"Not *when* it was lit," Landsdowner answered. "Before."

Rex scratched his head again. "And I'm still confused about why you kept photographing the woman from Deputy Donut on the Fourth of July, beginning early in the morning in her shop, long before the fireworks display, and why you published pictures of her that made her look bad."

"That's obvious, isn't it?" Landsdowner demanded. "First, I just took pictures of Jocelyn's boss looking disagreeable. Then someone was killed that night when Jocelyn's boss was nearby and I saw how I could completely discredit her. If Jocelyn's boss went to jail for murder, her donut shop would have to close." He raised his chin. "And now I have photographic evidence that Jocelyn's boss attempted murder." He lowered his head. "Take my camera and look at the pictures I took earlier this evening of three women in the river. Jocelyn's boss tried to drown both Jocelyn and Kelsey." Actually, Kelsey had been trying to drown Jocelyn and had told me I was next, but even though the camera was fitted with a long lens, I wasn't sure that any pictures Landsdowner had taken would show exactly what had happened.

"Let me get this straight," Brent said. "You're voluntarily lending us your camera and any memory cards in it so we can look at the pictures you took?"

There was a slight pause, and then Landsdowner answered with a little less confidence, "Yes. The pictures will prove that Jocelyn's boss attempted to drown Jocelyn and Kelsey. If these two dudes hadn't handcuffed me, I could give it to you. Take it. Or take these handcuffs off."

Brent gently lifted the strap and guided it over Landsdowner's bowed head. Pictures in that camera might not show Kelsey forcing Jocelyn's head underneath the water and probably would show me clobbering Kelsey with my backpack. I might end up in a little trouble for that, but I was fairly sure that my self-defense argument would hold up in court, if it came to that.

I really hoped that camera held evidence of Landsdowner stalking Jocelyn. Photos of her house, for instance, and had he taken pictures of her in the campground and as he followed her up Skinned Knee Trail?

Holding the camera carefully, Brent asked, "Why do you want the donut shop where Jocelyn works to close?"

Landsdowner raised his head and stated clearly, as if the two detectives questioning him were inattentive toddlers, "Jocelyn would be out of a job. I could support her. She would turn to me."

That was apparently too much for Jocelyn. "Never!" she shouted. Several backflips took her to the opposite side of the moonlit parking lot.

Chapter 39

Probably worried that Jocelyn might hurt herself in the dark or that Landsdowner might escape his captors and run after her, Brent took off toward the woods across the parking lot. He was sprinting, not doing backflips like Jocelyn had. "Jocelyn! Come back!"

"Okay!" Hearing the release of pent-up anxiety in the exultant way she sang that one word, I couldn't help smiling.

Rex told the two uniformed officers, "Take him in. I'll be in later to question him further."

As one of the uniformed officers guided Landsdowner to sit in the back of the marked cruiser, Landsdowner shouted, "I didn't kill that woman!"

Without responding, the officer closed the cruiser door. The other officer shut the dripping evidence bag into the trunk, and then both policemen tucked themselves into the front seat. The cruiser pulled out of the parking lot and turned toward town.

Brent accompanied Jocelyn to Rex and me. Brent and Jocelyn were both smiling. Jocelyn asked, "He's not going to bother me anymore, is he?"

Rex answered, "Not if we have anything to say about it." He winked at me. "That guy should be happy we didn't leave him on his rock all night and then question him there in the morning *before* we rescued him." I grinned at this latest example of cop humor.

Brent told Rex, "I'm taking Jocelyn to her parents' trailer." He turned to me. "When you left messages for me earlier, you said your car was in the campground. Is it still there?"

"It should be."

"I'll take you to it."

"Okay." I could have walked along one of the trails through the woods to my car, but I'd explored those woods enough for one night. Thanks to the heater in Rex's cruiser, I was nearly dry. I grabbed my backpack from his cruiser. It wasn't anywhere near dry.

Rex told Brent, "Meet me at your office after you get these two women safely to their destinations. We'll discuss how we're going to approach our suspected murderer and our adventurous stalker."

Saying that he planned to drop Jocelyn off first, Brent let her sit in the front passenger seat of his cruiser. The back was cramped. I was glad that I wasn't taller and we didn't have far to go.

As Brent drove us through the parking lot on our way out, I saw lights coming down Noisy Cawing Crow Trail. The swift-water rescue team and the EMTs must have taken plenty of time to gather all of their equipment in darkness lit mainly by lights they'd carried up there, and then they'd have needed to negotiate the trail carefully in the dark. My two best friends and their dates would have stayed behind to help, and now they were probably letting the rescue team and EMTs go first. Misty and Samantha might take time to show Scott and Hooligan where we had played and explored during our preteen and early-teen summers.

Jocelyn directed Brent to her parents' trailer, which was shiny, obviously new, and about the size of a school bus. Brent asked me, "Mind staying in the back a few minutes longer, Em? Then I'll let you out so you can ride in front."

"I'm fine." I knew not to try to unlock the back door of a cruiser, even an unmarked one, from inside.

Brent walked with Jocelyn all the way to the door of her parents' trailer and stayed there until lights went on, the door opened, and a man and a woman embraced Jocelyn and pulled her inside.

Brent ushered me to the cruiser's front seat. He buckled himself into the driver's seat. "You were in serious danger." His comment sounded completely non-judgmental.

"It was lucky that Samantha, Misty, and I had climbed around those cliffs and behind the falls when we were kids. And Jocelyn did, too. She's a good person to have on your side."

"She said you are, too."

"Luck," I said again.

By the light of the dash and reflected from his headlights, he studied my face for long and uncomfortable seconds. Finally, he pulled out of the driveway beside Jocelyn's parents' trailer.

He stopped beside the weedy campsite where I'd left my car. Keeping his engine and heater running, he shut off his headlights, and then he turned toward me and rubbed a hand through his short light brown hair. "Do you mind going over it again?" he asked.

"Don't you need to get back to the office?"

"Rex has a lot to do before I get there. And a night in a cell won't hurt Kelsey or Landsdowner. Kelsey, at least, might as well get used to it."

I told the entire story again. Every time I mentioned one of the code names that Misty, Samantha, and I had given to trails and the cave behind the falls, he grinned. When I finished, I thanked him for showing up at the falls. "How did you know you should come?"

"Misty phoned and said she thought you might be in trouble. Considering that you'd left me messages that you were following Landsdowner, I drove here at full speed and met Misty in the falls parking lot. She had a better idea than I did of where you might be. She came with Scott, by the way. Your matchmaking seems to be working."

I held both thumbs up. "Yes!"

"What is it about women and matchmaking?"

"You're the detective. Figure it out."

"Ha. I'm glad that's not in my job description. You can go now. I'll follow you home."

"The danger's over," I reminded him.

"I might have to apologize to Dep for keeping you out late."

"Good idea. She'll blame you, not me." That wasn't very likely. "Do you mind if I drive the long way through the campground so I can check my parents' site again?"

"Drive wherever you like, but I'm warning you. I'll be right behind you."

I threw him a mischievous grin. "Do you have a full tank of gas?"

"I probably have more than you do."

He got out, walked around, and opened the door for me. One hand on my elbow, he accompanied me through the long grass to my car. Usually, my car unlocked when I came near it with the key fob. This time, nothing happened.

"My key fob got wet," I muttered. I pulled the fob out of my pocket and tried to free the manual key, which could unlock and start the car. Releasing the manual key from the fob wasn't easy in the dark, however, and fearing that I'd lose the small key in the weeds was probably making everything more difficult.

Brent asked, "Do you have a spare fob?"

"At home."

"How about, rather than fussing with the manual key in the dark, I'll take you home and bring you back tomorrow in daylight after you're done at Deputy Donut?"

That sounded easier for me, but maybe not for him. "Won't you have to work?"

"Thanks to you, we've got this case nearly tied up, and I'll be free tomorrow evening. I'm way overdue for time off."

"Okay, I accept." I was almost too tired to drive, anyway.

Brent drove us past my parents' campsite. Their RV wasn't there. He took the shortest route back to Fallingbrook. On the way, I told him about my years of avoiding County Road G. "It's silly, I guess."

"Not if that's how you feel most comfortable." He reached over and squeezed my hand. "Are you going to avoid Fallingbrook Falls and all of the trails that you, Misty, and Samantha named from now on?"

"I hadn't thought about it. Probably not, especially if I go back there soon, in daylight."

He let go of my hand. "I have a deal for you. Can you go back there with me tomorrow after you close Deputy Donut? And show me everything you told us about tonight? I need to see them in daylight as part of the investigation." He turned his head and flashed me a grin before returning his attention to the road. "Besides, now that you've told me your formerly secret names for trails, I want to see them."

"Sure. So much for you taking the evening off."

"I'll have the evening off after we do all that."

It was late when Brent pulled into my driveway. He came with me to the front door. While I was fishing my totally non-electronic house key out of my pocket, he called, "Dep?"

"Mew." The plaintive cry from beyond the door reminded us that although Dep had plenty of food, water, toys, and fresh kitty litter, she'd been abandoned since about six. I opened the door, plunked the backpack down, and scooped her into my arms.

Brent scratched her under the chin and told her that it was his fault she'd been alone for such a long time. She jumped down and headed toward the kitchen. Maybe she was blaming both of us.

Brent asked me, "Do you trust me with your phone, key fob, and any other electronics that might have gotten wet? I know a retired forensics guy who fixes things like that."

"Of course I trust you." I gave him a fierce glare and then took the backpack into the kitchen. Brent followed me. I set my backpack on the granite island and pulled out my first-aid kit.

Brent did a double take. "No wonder you nearly knocked Kelsey out with your backpack."

"Actually, it was the donuts." The wet paper bag tore. Soggy donuts spilled out onto the granite. "Kelsey went to the fireworks armed with donuts. I went to Fallingbrook Falls armed with donuts."

"Those things are lethal. Maybe you and Tom should reconsider owning a donut and coffee shop."

"Nuh-uh. You're not going to convince me to go back to working at 911."

"I've mostly given up on that."

"And I'm not going into policing, either."

"You'd be good, but I know you don't want to, so I've mostly given up on that, too."

He helped me flatten the bills from my wallet on the counter and spread out everything else that might be salvageable. I put the phone and key fob in a plastic bag and gave it to him.

Dep must have gotten over her little snit. She came along when I accompanied Brent to the front door. I picked her up.

She gazed at Brent. "Meow."

Brent grinned at her. "I couldn't have said it better myself."

"What?" I asked. "Are you both telling me not to forget the dead bolt?"

"You got it. I'll pick you up here at six tomorrow night, Em, unless something happens, okay?"

"Sure."

"Take care, you two."

It was, apparently, a knuckle-rub night. Brent gave Dep hers first, and then he gave me a light one.

I stood there mutely staring at the top buttons of his shirt and holding my warm and purring cat.

Brent let himself out.

Chapter 40

✼

"Meow," Dep said.

"Sorry he couldn't stay longer," I told her. "Lots happened tonight, and I wish I had someone to discuss it with."

"Mew?"

I rubbed my face against her warm, furry neck. "Yes, I can talk to you." Telling her more about the evening than she probably wanted to hear, I took her upstairs to the laundry cupboard in the hallway outside my bedroom, threw my damp things into the washing machine, and then showered and went to bed. Dep curled up near my feet.

I was still rehashing the evening—mentally, since I didn't want to awaken Dep—when the washer stopped. I got out of bed and moved the wet laundry to the dryer. When I crawled underneath the covers again, Dep jumped off the bed. She was capable of walking silently. Instead, she thumped. I might as well have continued regaling her with the evening's events.

Punching my pillow and listening to the hardware on my backpack clatter in the dryer, I told myself that in the morning, assuming that neither Jocelyn nor I slept in, I would have someone to talk to about our frightening experiences on and near the trails of Fallingbrook Falls. And later I could discuss it all with Brent while I led him up and down those same trails.

The next thing I knew, my alarm woke me out of a deep sleep. It turned out that I didn't have to worry about Jocelyn making it to work on time after our late night. She came in shortly after Tom and I did. She apologized for missing two days of work without warning us ahead of time.

"We're just glad you're okay," I told her.

The morning was busier than usual with people wanting to chat about Kelsey's arrest. They had to talk to one another, though, because Jocelyn's and my memories were still too biting for us to discuss them with customers. Maybe we never would. As far as I knew, no one mentioned Philip Landsdowner, which was just as well. It was fine for Jocelyn to be famous for her gymnastic skills, but not fine for her to be known as the victim of a stalker.

Jocelyn and I didn't mind telling Tom about the night before. Whenever we had a spare moment, we filled him in. His empathy made me, at least, feel better. Tom was obviously upset about the danger we'd been in. "I'm glad it worked out," he said, "but I wish I'd been there."

The Knitpickers sat at their usual table and teased the retired men, but no one pulled out newspapers or displayed photos of me glaring at anyone. I didn't think that Philip Landsdowner would be submitting more of those to the paper soon, if ever.

Ian came in and handed me another coupon. "Thank you for being on my side."

"I believed you. I was sure the police would figure out who was actually guilty, and they did." I didn't tell Ian that I'd had a hand in helping catch Taylor's murderer. Ian ordered a peach jelly–filled donut and the day's special coffee, a light, fruity roast from Honduras.

Midway through the afternoon, when Misty and Hooligan were enjoying their break on the patio, my mother phoned. "We're back! Can you bring your friends to a bonfire tonight? There was a sale on marshmallows at the supermarket."

I laughed. "Welcome back. I'll see who can come."

"Everyone you know, please. These marshmallows are threatening to take over the RV." My mother liked to exaggerate. "I know you're not a night person, so we'll start the bonfire before sunset, at eight thirty."

"Can I bring anything?"

"All winter, I thought about that ice cream you got last summer at that new place where they make their own."

"Freeze. Okay, I'll bring some."

"Not for the whole crowd tonight, just for Dad and me. Our freezer is packed." I didn't have time before she ended the call to ask how much space she had.

Out on the patio, Misty and Hooligan were standing up, about to leave. I ran outside and invited them to the bonfire. They both said they'd come and they'd bring Samantha and Scott.

Inside, I asked Tom if he and Cindy could join us at my parents' marshmallow roast.

"I don't see why not," he said, "but I'll check to see if anything has come up for tonight since I last talked to Cindy." He always pronounced Cindy's name with love in his voice. Alec had been the same when he said my name.

I turned to Jocelyn. "How about you and your parents?"

"I don't think so. I skipped gymnastics the past couple of evenings, so I have to go tonight, and after that, I'm taking Detective Clobar on a tour of where we went last night." She had a very impish grin. "I'm not taking him across the stepping-stones or into what you call Shower Curtain Grotto."

"I'm going to the falls with Brent Fyne after work. I won't take him down any slippery slopes or behind the falls, either."

"He's nice. Is he your boyfriend?"

Tom went very still. He wasn't looking directly at me, but I could tell he wanted to hear my reply.

I shook my head vigorously. "He was my husband's— Tom's son's—best friend."

"He's a good man," Tom started.

"I know, a *Fyne* man," I finished for him.

"Have I made that joke before?" The innocence he put into the question was so fake that Jocelyn and I laughed.

After we closed for the evening, I told Dep I'd be back for her soon. "You can play in your office a little while longer."

Almost running, I hurried to Freeze.

Mama Freeze was at the counter. "Did you hear what happened?" She didn't give me a chance to reply. "Kelsey was arrested! For killing Taylor! There are going to be charges for murder and attempted murder, though how they can charge her for attempted murder when she was *successful* at it I'll never know."

I didn't tell Mama Freeze that although the actual murder had been on the Fourth of July, the attempts had been much more recent. I also didn't tell her that the intended victims had been Jocelyn and me. That information would probably come out during Kelsey's trial, but for now I was happy to remain anonymous. And maybe Kelsey would plead guilty and there would be no trial. I could hope.

Mama Freeze went on, "You know, I'm not all that surprised. I never did trust that Kelsey. There was something sly about her. Taylor was the best employee here, ever, and Kelsey never seemed to recognize that fact or try harder to be like Taylor. But there you go! Jealousy can do strange things to people. What can I get you?"

"A pint of dulce de leche and a pint of fudge ripple." I hoped my parents could cram two pints into their freezer.

After I paid for the ice cream, I raced back to Deputy Donut and put Dep's halter and leash on her. She wasn't keen on walking quickly, and I was afraid that the ice cream would melt or Brent would get to our house before we did. Neither of those things happened. I put the ice cream into my own freezer and then ran upstairs.

We'd be sitting on the ground at my parents' campfire. I changed into dark gray pants, a long-sleeved pink shirt, socks, and a dry pair of sneakers.

As I was tucking my spare key fob into a pocket, the doorbell rang.

Chapter 41

✬

Dep helped me let Brent in. His light brown hair was damp as if he'd just taken a shower. He was dressed suitably for an evening in the woods—black pants and a casual gray jacket, which he wore over a white dress shirt. And probably over a shoulder holster. He was even prepared for exploring rocky trails, with hiking boots on his feet. He handed me a box about the size of a cake box but sturdier. "We have time to eat and then tour the falls before it's too dark to see."

The box contained a hot meal, more than enough for two people. There were generous portions of the beautifully seasoned sauerkraut known as *kapusta,* garlicky kielbasa, and potato-cheddar pierogies topped with caramelized onions and dollops of sour cream. We ate at the kitchen island. I told him about my parents' invitation.

"Marshmallows," he repeated with a slightly dangerous grin. "When I was a kid, I was the best marshmallow toaster on our block."

"Being the best marshmallow toaster at one of Dad's bonfires could be a challenge," I warned him. "Dad likes *big* fires."

"I'm up for it." Cutting off another slice of kielbasa, Brent told me, "My friend is certain he can get your fob and phone working again."

"Does he like donuts?"

"Who doesn't?"

"He's going to receive a lot of them."

Brent also told me that the investigators had received the results of the fingerprint testing on the smaller Deputy Donut bag, the one that had been found in a trash can near my car and that had contained at least one blue sugar star as well as a slightly melted birthday candle. I knew they could soak paper in a chemical called ninhydrin to cause fingerprints to show up in a pretty shade of purple. "There were prints from lots of people," he told me, "including you and Tom. Kelsey's fingerprints were over other people's, but no one else's fingerprints covered any part of Kelsey's."

"Plus, three police officers—Hooligan, Misty, and you—heard at least part of her telling me why she killed Taylor and that she'd followed me to Fallingbrook Falls because I'd been asking about that bag of donuts and she was afraid I would report her."

"We've got a good case, largely thanks to you and Jocelyn."

I flapped my hand at him. "You would have figured it out on your own, if only from those fingerprints. Her attacks on Jocelyn and me didn't help her look innocent, though."

"They certainly didn't. She had prepared that skyrocket ahead of time with plans to use it to try to kill Taylor during the fireworks when an extra explosion might not be noticeable. Then, that afternoon, she found the bag of your donuts in Freeze and came up with a method that would disguise her firework and also cause us to focus on who might have had access to those donuts."

"That backfired," I said, "pun intended."

He groaned. "It did, again thanks to you for finding out where those donuts ended up."

"*You* should think of opening a donut shop," I teased. "Working there and talking to people, you'd learn a lot about what's going on in town."

"Right. I should open a donut shop and you should become a police officer."

"Or we both should stick to what we love doing."

"Touché."

"Together, we put people in jail who deserve to be there."

Naturally, that comment prompted a reminder that even if I had a theory about a crime, I should not act on it except to tell him or other police officers. He added, "Kelsey should be going to jail for a long time. When Landsdowner was sitting on that boulder in the river and taking pictures of you three in the water, he'd set up his camera the way he does, I mean the way he *did,* during gymnastics and other sports events. He set the camera to snap pictures continuously, as fast as it could. It's not a video, but that rapid-fire sequence clearly shows Kelsey pushing Jocelyn's head under the water. And you helping Jocelyn out of the water."

"She'd have gotten out by herself. Do they show me attacking Kelsey with my backpack?"

His smile became diabolical. "There might have been some cheering in the office when we saw you do that. No one's going to charge you with anything. You were trying to save your own life and Jocelyn's, too. Plus, you helped apprehend a murderer. I know, 'innocent until proven guilty.' An *alleged* murderer."

"What's going to happen to Landsdowner?"

"We let him go for now. We'll review his images, including some he took through the windows of Jocelyn's home, and he might find himself in jail. He definitely will if he disobeys orders to stay away from her and from gymnastic events."

Knowing that there would be marshmallows, perfectly roasted or maybe merely waved through flames, we skipped dessert. I also decided not to take the ice cream along on this trip, since Brent and I were planning to tour the trails around the falls before going to my folks' campsite. I would invite my parents over for dinner the next night, and if they had room in their freezer, they could take the two pints of ice cream home with them afterward. If not, the three of us could start on them here. Or I could buy them some more another time. I was glad that Mama Freeze hadn't turned out to be a killer. Or Felicia, either. I didn't want either of their shops to close.

Brent had brought his own vehicle, a sports car with a reputation for being even faster than mine. His was black and could have passed for an unmarked cruiser.

He drove through my neighborhood and then made a turn toward County Road G, the scenic route that passed the river valley that hadn't always lived up to its calm appearance, the road that still sometimes gave me nightmares.

"Do you mind?" he asked.

"No." I wouldn't be alone. "I'll be okay."

He parked at the top of the dirt track that led down into the valley. "Do you want to get out?" he asked.

"I guess I should."

"Want company?"

"Yes, please."

I opened the door and climbed out of the low seat. Hugging myself, I leaned back against Brent's car and gazed down into the valley. The sun wouldn't set for over an hour and was high enough to glint off the river. In that valley, the water was flat again after the tumult of the falls several miles away. The sky, the river, the fields, and the woods all looked completely peaceful.

His feet crunching on the gravel shoulder of the road, Brent walked around the car to stand beside me. We stayed a few minutes longer, not speaking, until I turned toward him. He was wearing sunglasses. I could barely see his eyes. "Thank you," I said.

We got back into the car and didn't talk until we were almost at the entrance to the campground. "Let's start at your car," he said, "where you first saw Landsdowner following Jocelyn."

He parked beside the uninhabited trailer and we got out. I

made certain that my spare fob unlocked and relocked my car, and then I pointed across the narrow road. "I saw them between those birch trees over there, near this end of Skinned Knee Trail." Brent took photos and wrote in his notebook.

I led him up Skinned Knee and showed him where I had again spotted Landsdowner. "He was up there, ahead of me. I went back down to the trail that Misty, Samantha, and I named Popcorn."

Brent took more photos, wrote in his notebook, and asked, "Show me?"

I took him up Popcorn to where I'd ducked between hemlocks to make calls. "Kelsey said she'd been following me, but she must not have seen me duck back down to Popcorn. She must have continued up Skinned Knee while I was here leaving a message for Misty and talking to Samantha."

"Even though you didn't go farther up Skinned Knee last night, do you mind if we go back and have a look at that trail, since Landsdowner and Kelsey were on it? We can circle back this way, can't we?"

"Sure."

We returned to Skinned Knee and hiked up it until it ended at Noisy Cawing Crow. Stalker's Rock was in front of us, with no stalker sitting on it. We could see some of Jocelyn's stepping-stones in the swiftly flowing river, and I pointed out the approximate place where I'd seen Kelsey push her hood back while she was calling to Landsdowner and trying to get him to come back to shore.

Brent and I started down Noisy Cawing Crow and then stopped for more photos where Jocelyn and I had tackled Kelsey and where we'd heard Kelsey's shouted reasons for wanting to eliminate her rival, Taylor.

We hiked down Noisy Cawing Crow Trail to the top of the falls. The water roared, so I merely pointed at the flat rock. All traces of the donut I'd left on it were gone except for a line of ants harvesting the last drops of grape jelly.

Where the Fallingbrook River slipped over a rock lip and plunged into the gorge below, I mimed flipping over the railing and pointed down at the slimy ledge and the narrow pathway leading into Shower Curtain Grotto.

Brent stood for a long time, just gazing down at that ledge, at the rocks and turbulent water below it, and at the almost invisible narrow gap behind the curtain of water, and then he transferred his gaze to me. He'd removed his sunglasses when we left his car, but his eyes were unreadable, and I had to look away until he went back to detective mode, taking pictures and writing in his notebook. Finally, he pocketed his phone and notebook, touched my shoulder, and gestured toward Popcorn Trail.

I led the way. Helping each other over rocks and around stumps, we barely talked. We got into our own cars. Close to my parents' site, vehicles were lined up along the side of the dirt road. I parked behind Scott's SUV, and Brent pulled in behind me.

I'd gotten my curls from both of my parents and my height, or lack of it, from my mother. Tall, white-haired, and so thin that his jeans bagged at the knees, my father was poking a log into a huge campfire. His light blue eyes brightened. He dropped the log, ran around to our side of the fire, and hugged me. Because of Alec, my father knew Brent. He shook Brent's hand. I explained that Brent and I had been going over something at the falls that was related to one of Brent's cases.

My mother followed Scott and Misty out of the RV. They were each carrying several bags of marshmallows.

Squealing, my mother ran to us. She looked adorable in an ankle-length tiered skirt and frilly top in a matching floral print. Her silver curls, partially tamed by a stretchy headband, would be long enough to excite Felicia and Felicia's wildly snapping scissors when my mother finally let Felicia cut her hair. My mother gave Brent and me hugs that were, considering her size, startlingly ferocious. She was so short that I would have felt tall if I hadn't been next to Brent.

Tom and Cindy, both in cargo pants and jackets, had brought lawn chairs. Samantha had tinted her hair brilliant scarlet during the almost twenty-four hours since I'd last seen her. She was teasing Tom and Cindy about being too civilized to sit on the ground. Cindy jumped up and gave me a big hug. Tom shook Brent's hand.

Seemingly unable to stop smiling, Hooligan handed out some of my parents' many toasting forks.

It turned out that Brent was the only one of us who could perfectly tan a marshmallow without leaving it stone cold or covering it with bitter black ash. I sat beside him and helped him devour them.

When everyone had eaten more than enough marshmallows, my mother brought out her banjo and my father tuned his guitar. The chattering around the fire subsided.

"You probably wonder what took us so long to get back to Fallingbrook," my mother said. "We had adventures! There was this perfectly beautiful longhaired ragdoll kitten who decided to live with us in our RV. The trouble was, we didn't notice her right away."

My father took up the story. "That was in Georgia. We turned around and drove for several hours, back to the campground where we'd been the night before. We asked everyone if they'd lost a kitten, but no one had. We went to the vet in the town closest to that campground, and the tiny little thing was already microchipped!"

My mother was eager to continue the story. "She was from Iowa, so we went back to the campground and asked around. The people at the campground office knew that an RV from Iowa had left the campground earlier on the day we left. The campground people told us where the Iowa people had said they were heading next. We followed them, but when we got there the next day, they'd already left. Same thing with the next campground and the next. Strangely, they always told the campground management where they were going and they gave the first campground a phone number, but they never answered their phone or returned our calls."

My father told us, "We weren't about to drive to Iowa and dump the kitten off at the vet who originally microchipped her. We were sure we were just about to catch up with her owners, so we kept following them."

My mother again took over the storytelling. "We went to parts of the country we'd never seen before. It was wonderful! It was also quite a chase, zigzagging all over the South and the Midwest. Twenty-five days and umpteen states later, we reunited the kitten with her owners. They were ecstatic."

I asked, "Why didn't they return your calls?"

Shaking his head, my father answered, "They were very apologetic about that. They forgot to take their phone on their trip." I smiled. My parents weren't much better. They remembered their phone, but kept it turned off except when they wanted to make calls, which they hardly ever did.

My parents launched into the first of many songs in their repertoire, and we all sang along whenever we knew the words. Sitting beside Brent, I enjoyed listening to his rich bass voice. As an added plus, he stayed in tune.

The enormous fire died down and the evening became chillier. Samantha and Hooligan, neither of them wearing a sweater or jacket, snuggled together. Scott and Misty leaned against each other's shoulders.

Misty was watching me as if reminding me of what she'd said several days before. *Try not to hurt Brent.*

I remembered the way he'd gazed down at the water frothing beneath the algae-covered ledge, where one slip of my feet could have sent me to my death, and the way he'd gazed at me after pondering that dangerous cliff. His eyes hadn't been, as I'd told myself then, entirely unreadable. I'd merely refused to admit to myself that I'd seen pain in them along with a strength of affection that I'd been pretending didn't exist.

I thought about the times Brent had given me quick hugs or knuckle-rubs, of the way we laughed together. Of the way Dep always seemed to want him to come over and then, when he did, to stay close to her. And to me.

Dep was a very intelligent and perceptive cat.

Shivering, I scooted over until Brent's and my arms touched.

He lifted that arm, put it around my shoulders, and pulled me close.

A branch broke in the fire. Beyond the sparks shooting skyward, Tom winked at me. Cindy gave me a gentle smile. I imagined her saying, *We'll all be okay. Life will go on.*

My heart hammered and my breathing went all wonky. I couldn't sing.

Brent stopped singing, also.

As if making up for the silence from Brent and me, my parents sang and played even more loudly than before.

Recipes

Lorne's Quick Winter Dessert

Try this first if you're not sure about the combined flavors of maple and cheddar.

Place cubes of Wisconsin cheddar in small dessert bowls. Drizzle maple syrup over the cheese. Eat with a spoon. After you taste that, you'll probably want to make Maple Cheddar-Filled Donuts, even though the flavor of the cheese in the donuts is much more subtle.

Maple Cheddar-Filled Donuts

1 cup less 3 tablespoons warm water
¼ cup unsalted butter, softened
2 tablespoons active dry yeast (yes, this is a lot!)
¾ cup maple syrup
3½ cups all-purpose or bread flour
½ teaspoon salt
1 egg or 2 egg whites, room temperature
Wisconsin cheddar, sharpness according to taste (medium is
    yummy and buttery)
If frying your donuts: vegetable oil with a smoke point of
    400° or higher (or follow your deep fryer's instruction
    manual)
Maple butter or maple glaze (recipe is on p. 280)
Coarse salt, maple sugar, maple flakes, or crisp crumbles of
    bacon for topping (optional)

In your mixer bowl fitted with a dough hook, combine the warm water, butter, yeast, and maple syrup. Let stand for 15 minutes.

Add 2 cups of the flour, the salt, and the egg to the yeast mixture. Stir with the dough hook. Add the remaining flour ½ cup at a time and knead with the dough hook. If the dough is too sticky, add ¼ cup of flour and knead with the dough hook. If the dough is still too sticky, carefully add more flour 1 teaspoon at a time. Continue kneading with the dough hook until the dough cleans the sides of the bowl, is satiny, doesn't stick to your fingers, and doesn't keep its shape when pinched. It should still feel slightly sticky. Too much flour will make the donuts tough.

Divide in half and refrigerate one half.

For each half, roll the dough to about ¼ inch thick between two sheets of parchment paper.

Remove the top sheet of parchment paper and cut rounds from the dough with a round cookie cutter.

Press a small chunk of Wisconsin cheddar, about 1 inch by 1 inch by ¼ inch, or the equivalent amount if the cheese is too crumbly to cut, for rounds that are 2 inches in diameter, smaller if you used a smaller cookie cutter, into the center of half of the rounds.

Working with one donut at a time and using your fingers, rub water around the edge surrounding the cheese, place a plain round on top, and pinch the edges together.

Allow to rest for 10 minutes.

Fry the filled donuts at 375°, turning when golden, about 30 seconds per side. Lift from the oil and allow to drain.

OR bake on cookie sheet lined with parchment paper or a silicone baking sheet in a 375° oven for about 10 minutes until the tops are golden.

When cool, glaze the tops with purchased maple butter or make your own maple glaze (see p. 280). If you like, sprinkle coarse salt, maple sugar, maple flakes, or crisp crumbles of bacon on top.

Maple Glaze

½ cup maple syrup
Confectioners' sugar

Stir confectioners' sugar by teaspoonfuls into maple syrup until glaze reaches desired consistency for spreading.

Jelly-Filled Donuts

1 cup plus 2 tablespoons warm water
¼ cup unsalted butter, softened
2 tablespoons active dry yeast (yes, this is a lot!)
1 cup sugar
3½ cups all-purpose or bread flour
½ teaspoon salt
1 egg or 2 egg whites, room temperature
If frying your donuts: vegetable oil with a smoke point of
    400° or higher (or follow your deep fryer's instruction
    manual)
Jelly in flavors of your choice
Confectioners' sugar (optional)

In your mixer bowl fitted with a dough hook, combine the warm water, butter, yeast, and sugar. Let stand for 15 minutes.

Add 2 cups of the flour, the salt, and the egg to the yeast mixture. Stir with the dough hook. Add the remaining flour ½ cup at a time and knead with the dough hook. If the dough is too sticky, add ¼ cup of flour and knead with the dough hook. If the dough is still too sticky, carefully add more flour 1 teaspoon at a time. Continue kneading with the dough hook until the dough cleans the sides of the bowl, is satiny, doesn't stick to your fingers, and doesn't keep its shape when pinched. It should still feel slightly sticky. Too much flour will make the donuts tough.

Divide in half and refrigerate one half.

For each half, roll the dough to about ½ inch thick between two sheets of parchment paper.

Remove the top sheet of parchment paper and cut rounds from the dough with a round cookie cutter.

Allow to rest for 10 minutes.

Fry the donuts at 375°, turning when golden, about 30 seconds per side. Lift from the oil and allow to drain.

OR bake on cookie sheet lined with parchment paper or a silicone baking sheet in a 400° oven for about 10 minutes until the tops are golden.

When cool, use a paring knife or skewer to make a small hole in one side of each donut and create a small cavity inside. Then use a piping bag fitted with a small tip, a turkey baster, or a pastry syringe to fill the cavity with the jelly of your choice. Note: Jams or thick spreads will clog the nozzle. If desired, sift confectioners' sugar over the tops.

Party Fun—Fill Your Own Donuts

Feeling brave? Let party guests fill their own donuts! Fry the donuts ahead of time and remove the hot oil from the vicinity. (This is crucial for children's parties.) Set out a variety of jellies. Let each guest inject whichever flavor (or combination) they like into their donut or donuts.

Connect with Us

Visit us online at
KensingtonBooks.com
to read more from your favorite authors, see books
by series, view reading group guides, and more.

Join us on social media

for sneak peeks, chances to win books and prize packs,
and to share your thoughts with other readers.

facebook.com/kensingtonpublishing
twitter.com/kensingtonbooks

Tell us what you think!

To share your thoughts, submit a review,
or sign up for our eNewsletters, please visit:
KensingtonBooks.com/TellUs.